BEACON STREET GIRLS

This book belongs to:

VERITAS AMICITIA GAUDIUM
truth friendship fun!

BEACON STREET GIRLS

Be sure to read all of our books:

The Great Scavenger Hunt

BY
ANNIE BRYANT

ALADDIN MIX

NEW YORK LONDON TORONTO SYDNEY

Special thanks to the National Park Service residential enviornmental education
(NEED) program at Cape Cod National Seashore.

ALADDIN MIX
An imprint of Simon & Schuster Children's Publishing Division
1230 Avenue of the Americas, New York, NY 10020
Copyright © 2009 by B*tween Productions, Inc.,
Home of the Beacon Street Girls.
Beacon Street Girls, KGirl, B*tween Productions, B*Street, and the characters Maeve,
Avery, Charlotte, Isabel, Katani, Marty, Nick, Anna, Joline, and
Happy Lucky Thingy are registered trademarks and/or copyrights of B*tween Productions, Inc.
Designed by Dina Barsky
Manufactured in the United States of America
First Aladdin MIX edition May 2009
2 4 6 8 10 9 7 5 3 1
Library of Congress Control Number 2008940516
ISBN: 978-1-4169-6442-1

Who's Who

BSG

Katani Summers
a.k.a. Kgirl . . . Katani has a strong fashion sense and business savvy. She is stylish, loyal & cool.

Avery Madden
Avery is passionate about all sports and animal rights. She is energetic, optimistic & outspoken.

Charlotte Ramsey
A self-acknowledged "klutz" and an aspiring writer, Charlotte is all too familiar with being the new kid in town. She is intelligent, worldly & curious.

Isabel Martinez
Her ambition is to be an artist. She was the last to join the Beacon Street Girls. She is artistic, sensitive & kind.

Maeve Kaplan-Taylor
Maeve wants to be a movie star. Bubbly and upbeat, she wears her heart on her sleeve. She is entertaining, friendly & fun.

Ms. Razzberry Pink
The stylishly pink proprietor of the "Think Pink" boutique is chic, gracious & charming.

Marty
The adopted best dog friend of the Beacon Street Girls is feisty, cuddly & suave.

Happy Lucky Thingy and alter ego **Mad Nasty Thingy**
Marty's favorite chew toy, it is known to reveal its alter ego when shaken too roughly. He is most often happy.

more on beaconstreetgirls.com

Part One
Cape Cod Dreaming

1

Mad Adventure Anyone?

Charlotte was having a difficult time focusing in Ms. O'Reilly's first period social studies class. She had to keep pretending there was a big red sign in front of her blinking PAY ATTENTION! This was unusual for her, because social studies involved one of her favorite topics— the adventures of famous people in history. Charlotte figured whoever had thought of teaching such a thing should get a prize or something.

But how on earth was she supposed to pay attention to Ms. O'Reilly when her mind was on a different kind of adventure: the surprise adventure that she and Nick and Chelsea had been planning for weeks. The adventure she was supposed to announce to the class in five minutes!

Charlotte heard Ms. O'Reilly introducing an important research project—the type of thing that would have normally set Charlotte's mind whirring in anticipation—an oral report on a historical figure who was a Massachusetts native. "I don't want this to be just another research paper," Ms. O'Reilly explained. "I want you to pick a person who means something to you and write about how he or she has left a mark on history."

Charlotte wasn't quite sure who to pick. She loved to write, so perhaps someone like Louisa May Alcott or Henry David Thoreau. Thoreau was one of the first environmentalists in the country and wrote about the beauty of nature at Walden Pond—one of Charlotte's favorite places to go swimming with the Beacon Street Girls. And *An Old-Fashioned Girl* by Louisa May Alcott was one of her favorite books.

Or maybe she'd pick Benjamin Franklin. He was born in Boston but then ran off to Philadelphia, where he became a statesman, inventor, publisher, and signer of the Declaration of Independence. He also thought the national bird should be a turkey! *That's such a hoot . . . or gobble,* she thought, chuckling. Charlotte really hoped they'd see some wild turkeys on the adventure she had planned. The big, goofy-looking birds traveled in flocks and acted like they weren't afraid of anything . . . even coyotes!

Charlotte glanced over at Maeve, who seemed transfixed by something on her computer screen. Charlotte strained to see, and then had to bite her lip to keep from laughing out loud. The sparkly redhead had typed her name followed by a selection of names from the Hollywood yellow pages—Maeve Kaplan-Taylor Blackstone, Maeve Plume, Mrs. Ontario Plume . . . Blackstone and Plume were the biggest names in movies right now, with their award-winning series of pirate movies.

Charlotte turned around, expecting Avery to be staring longingly out the window at a group of eighth graders playing kickball outside. But to Charlotte's surprise, Avery's hand was madly waving in the air and she was pleading, "Ooh! Ooh! Ms. O'Reilly! Right here!"

Ms. O'Reilly smiled. "Yes, Avery."

"Can I do Tom Brady?"

Isabel, sitting at the desk next to Charlotte, gave her a sly grin and mouthed, *Big surprise!* Avery was the total sports nut of the BSG.

Ms. O'Reilly looked pained. "Well, the assignment is to do *historical* figures from Massachusetts. . . . I'm just not sure the Patriot's star quarterback is exactly—"

Quick-as-a-whip Avery smartly replied, "Well Tom Brady *will* go down in *sports* history as being the quarterback responsible for two Patriot Super Bowl victories. He's history in the making. Am I right, people?" Dillon Johnson and some of the boys gave Avery approving cheers and high fives.

"I'll tell you what, Avery. If you can come up with some more compelling arguments, then we will see," Ms. O'Reilly offered. "Does anyone else have any suggestions?"

Of course Betsy Fitzgerald's hand shot into the air. Charlotte and Isabel had to stare ahead to keep from rolling their eyes at each other. Betsy was famous at Abigail Adams Junior High . . . and not in the way Tom Brady was famous. Betsy had a knack for sounding like a complete know-it-all every time she opened her mouth in class.

While Charlotte and Isabel both liked Betsy, she was a little hard to take sometimes.

"I think Paul Revere would be an *exemplary* figure to do a report on, Ms. O'Reilly," Betsy said in her superconfident voice. "My father is a historical reenactor who plays Paul Revere. Did you know that if it weren't for Paul Revere, there might not even be an America? In fact, Paul Revere was famous in his own time for his silver work *before* his midnight ride. And did you know—"

"Thank you, Betsy," Ms. O'Reilly interjected. "It sounds like you will have ample material for your report."

Charlotte noticed a few kids smirking. *Poor Betsy*, Charlotte thought with a sigh. She just couldn't help herself. Her older brother went to Harvard and Betsy lived in fear of not getting in there too. The fact that she was only in seventh grade didn't appear to slow down Betsy's drive at all.

Not wanting to be outdone by Betsy, Danny Pellegrino, also a major fact-chaser, stretched his hand up.

"I have a figure that is just as historical but not as well known as Paul Revere," he proudly announced. "Ms. O'Reilly, you might not have heard of Black Sam Bellamy, but he was a famous pirate whose ship, the *Whydah*, was discovered off the coast of Cape Cod."

Charlotte almost gasped. Danny was actually trying to one-up the teacher!

"Thank you, Danny. And yes, I am familiar with Sam Bellamy. And I think he would be a great figure to research," Ms. O'Reilly agreed patiently.

"Yes, Henry?"

Henry Yurt, aka the Yurtmeister, was class president *and* class clown rolled into a short ball of wit and fuzzy hair. All the Beacon Street Girls, even serious Katani, enjoyed the Yurt's antics. Charlotte was eager to hear what historical figure Henry wanted to choose—probably someone like Bozo the Clown.

Henry coughed loudly and importantly before asking in a serious voice, "Might I do JFK, Ms. O'Reilly?"

Charlotte almost fell off her chair. *Henry Yurt, serious?* Even Ms. O'Reilly looked surprised. But she smiled broadly. "Why, yes, Henry. President Kennedy would be an excellent person to research. What made you think of him?"

Yurt sat up as tall as he possibly could, leaned forward on his desk, clasped his hands, and explained. "Well, isn't it obvious? JFK and I are both superpopular presidents!"

Everyone in the class, including Ms. O'Reilly and Betsy Fitzgerald, burst out laughing as Henry stood up at his desk and waved just like a president would. "Thanks for your support," he said, grinning.

The only one in the class who didn't crack a smile was Anna McMasters, Queen of Mean #1, who used to be Henry's main crush. Anna was still mad at Henry because he dumped her for Betsy Fitzgerald, who dumped *him* a week after the Valentine's Day dance because she felt the Yurtmeister wasn't dedicated enough to his studies. Betsy said she was afraid Henry might distract her from hers.

"A tragic romance destined for the history books," Yurt had moaned to Charlotte when it happened.

When the laughter died down, Anna tossed her sunshine-colored hair over her shoulder and primly raised her hand.

Ms. O'Reilly, who was still dabbing her eyes, managed to say, "Yes, Anna?"

"I call Ben Affleck," Anna stated. "He's from Cambridge, Massachusetts, he's made Oscar-nominated movies set in Massachusetts, *and* I got to meet him at Kiki's house once." She sounded extremely proud of herself.

"Try to focus on historical figures, please, Anna," Ms. O'Reilly instructed, as she raised her eyebrows at Avery, who had burst out laughing.

A movie star? Avery mouthed to Charlotte, who was not about to tell Avery that she didn't think a sports figure was much better. Meanwhile, Maeve was scanning her list of movie star last names, trying to remember if any of *them* were from Massachusetts, too.

As Anna began to object that Ben Affleck *was* historical, Charlotte felt something being crushed into her left hand. It was a note from Isabel. Charlotte, using her best secrecy skills, silently unfolded the note under her desk.

AHHH! How can U stand it? Isn't the big announcement 2day?

Charlotte flipped the scrap of paper over and wrote back:

Yes! Any second now! I just hope everyone likes the idea and signs up. So so nervous . . .

Iz ripped off another piece of paper, scribbled something, and sent it to Charlotte.

Chill! Nick Montoya will get the guys to come and you and Chelsea will get the girls. I think this will be the most fun in the history of 7th grade! Maybe I'll even write my research paper on you. ☺ Ha!

Charlotte gave her friend a grateful smile. Isabel was such a sweetheart—she had a real knack for making her friends feel better, no matter how awful the situation. Charlotte was so happy to be a part of the Beacon Street Girls. Since she had joined forces with Maeve, Avery, Katani, and Isabel back in the beginning of 7th grade, life had been a blast—and when it wasn't, they were always there for each other, through thick and thin, as her dad always said.

"Charlotte, is there something you'd care to share with the class?" Ms. O'Reilly's voice boomed. "Please come to the front of the room."

Charlotte felt her stomach do a somersault. It was bad enough that she'd been caught passing notes, but now she was going to be humiliated by having to share the note with the whole class. She probably should have been used to public humiliation by now considering that she was the class klutz. But she wasn't. In her mind, embarrassment was embarrassment no matter how many times it happened.

Face flushed, Charlotte reluctantly made her way to the front of the room. With the speed of a hermit crab slowly shrugging out of its shell, she unfolded the crumpled note.

"Ummm . . ." she began to read. Then Charlotte noticed the doorknob turning.

"If it isn't the cocaptain of the Outdoor Adventure Club herself!" Mr. Moore, their goofy science teacher, announced as he strode into the room. If she hadn't been so nervous, Charlotte would have laughed at his tie. It was printed with tiny cows bouncing over his bright purple shirt. "As club advisor, I couldn't be late for the big announcement! Please, Charlotte . . . proceed."

Charlotte gulped back a sigh of relief. Total humiliation was out, but she *still* had to talk in front of the class—one of her top ten "I hate to do" things. However, she gave Mr. Moore a grateful smile. He had helped her, Nick Montoya, and Chelsea Briggs organize the super surprise adventure, so it was really nice to have his support.

Suddenly, Charlotte realized she was missing the most important part of her presentation! Isabel caught her panicked look and passed the rolled-up poster beside Charlotte's desk up to the front of the room. Charlotte, Nick, and Chelsea had slaved over that poster.

Unlike Maeve, the actress extraordinaire of the BSG, Charlotte was distinctly uncomfortable in the spotlight. *Why did I let Nick and Chelsea talk me into presenting this?* She groaned inwardly as her hands began to tremble. Nick would have been a much better spokesperson.

As Mr. Moore helped her pin the poster up to the front of the room, Charlotte felt her heartbeat slowing down at the sound of her classmates' *cool*s and *wow*s. And she hadn't even explained anything yet!

When she saw Katani and Isabel nodding encouragingly, Maeve giving her two thumbs up, and Avery looking like she was about to jump out of her seat and start cheering, her shaky confidence returned.

"A treasure map! Nice!" murmured Dillon.

Once again, Charlotte took a deep breath and began her prepared speech. Unfortunately, just as she opened her mouth, she hiccupped . . . loudly . . . very loudly.

"Nice one, Char." Yurt clapped as the class began to snicker. Charlotte wanted to slink out of the room. Instead, she looked over at the one person who might rescue her. Maeve sat tall at her desk, and then leaned forward in a bowing motion. Charlotte understood immediately. Maeve always said, "Join the laugh! It puts the audience on your side even if you've messed up."

So Charlotte, mimicking her friend, grinned, bowed, and started over again. Thankfully this time . . . no hiccup.

"Next weekend the Outdoor Adventure Club will have its first official field trip. The club leaders—myself, Nick, and Chelsea—have organized a scavenger hunt."

She paused for applause, but the class was still waiting to hear more. *Have I just bombed?* Worried, Charlotte added in a rush, "It's on Cape Cod, there will be three teams, and the winners will receive an incredible prize!"

"Cape Cod?" Dillon called out. "I love the Cape!"

"What's the prize?" shouted Henry.

"Um . . . the prize?" Charlotte glanced nervously at Mr. Moore. The prize part was something she'd just made up on the spot to get people excited. The truth was she had no idea what the prize would be. For Charlotte, just going on the adventure was prize enough.

"It's a surprise, Henry," Mr. Moore answered quickly. "To be announced at the prize ceremony." Charlotte would have to thank the cow man later for coming to her rescue.

"You forgot the best part!" Avery blurted, then clasped her hands over her mouth, remembering that this was supposed to be Charlotte's big announcement—not hers.

"Oh, yeah!" Charlotte said, remembering. She couldn't believe she'd forgotten. "The trip is a *two-day* hunt. Which means we'll be spending an overnight someplace cool . . . by the beach!"

There it was—finally the cheers and clapping she'd been hoping for. Of course people would be excited about a big beachside overnight on the Cape.

Spending a night somewhere other than in your normal, old, safe bed is so thrilling, thought Charlotte. And she loved everything about Cape Cod—the beautiful sandy beaches, salt water taffy, sailing, and digging for clams. Before she and her dad moved to Tanzania, then Australia and Paris, they had spent several precious weeks on the Cape.

Kids were talking so loudly they could just barely hear the bell for last period ringing. Charlotte felt as though she were walking on air as she packed up her bag. Judging from the class's response, it looked like the scavenger hunt was going to be a huge success.

"Dude! Where do we sign up?" Dillon shouted across the room.

"We must approach the captain of adventure!" Henry Yurt held out his arms like a game show host as he trotted up to Charlotte. "Team Yurtmeister is ready to win the jackpot!"

Charlotte pulled out the sheet. "The trip is on a first-come-first-serve basis. You have to bring back a signed permission slip and photo release form by Wednesday! We are taking only three cars down, driven by teacher chaperones, so space is limited," she warned.

That announcement set off a mad scramble as kids tried to be the first to get their name on the list.

"Photo release forms?" Dillon asked. "Why do we need those?"

"Mr. Moore is going to film some of the trip for an AAJH Outdoor Adventure Club website," Charlotte explained.

"I'm helping with the site," Chelsea added. "We're going to put some of the team photos up too."

"Oooh, imagine if we were photographed by a TV station!" Maeve beamed at the thought of fifteen minutes of fame.

"You never know!" Charlotte smiled.

"Do we pick our own teams?" Riley Lee asked as he signed his name.

"No, Mr. Moore is organizing them."

"Should we bring history books?" Betsy Fitzgerald asked, just as Danny bumped in front of her. "Who is fact-checking the clues?" he interrupted. "I could provide valuable assistance there."

Avery was about to tell Danny to get real, but Katani grabbed her arm and shook her head. "He can't help himself," she whispered.

Charlotte did her best to answer all the questions and was relieved when Joline and Anna haughtily marched out of the room *without* making any comments *or* signing up. Nature and the Queens of Mean were not a good mix.

Besides, since the QOM paid way more attention to their eye makeup than they did to getting their homework in on time, they probably couldn't go on the trip. Mr. Moore said that the trip was kind of a reward for turning in all your assignments. Charlotte knew Joline, for sure, was not up-to-date. "Schoolwork is *so* not my thing," she'd proudly told Charlotte once.

As kids continued jostling around the desk, Charlotte noticed Kiki Underwood sprint into the room. *Uh-oh,* she thought. The QOM might be out of the picture, but Kiki was a totally different kind of royalty.

"Mr. Moore!" Kiki simpered sweetly. "Oh, thank goodness I caught up with you. Listen, it's about that detention you gave me this morning. . . ."

2

All Boggled Up

If Anna and Joline were the Queens of Mean, then Kiki Underwood was the EMPRESS. Kiki didn't just whisper mean things about you—she blurted them out loud . . . to your face . . . in front of people!

The BSG tried to make a point of not focusing on other people's troubles. As Maeve often said, "you never know when the thunder and lightning are going to come crashing down on you!" But Katani, who couldn't tolerate Kiki Underwood, was more than a little curious about what the Empress might have done to deserve a detention.

"No excuses, Miss Underwood," Mr. Moore said sternly. "I know it was you who drew that mustache on my Lydia. There were several very reliable witnesses who came forward."

Mr. Moore's obsession with cows was weird and kind of cute at the same time, Charlotte thought. When Kiki had drawn a thick black mustache on Mr. Moore's poster of a brown cow (whom he'd named Lydia) last week, she must have messed with the wrong farm animal.

"Please, Mr. Moore! I'll do anything. I'll even sign up for whatever volunteer thingy all those people are doing. What are we . . . feeding the homeless? Saving puppies? Helping old people? I'm in, I swear. I'm sorry about your cow picture, um, Lydia? . . . It was just a teeny tiny joke," she simpered.

"Joke?" whispered Katani to Charlotte. "She forgot to add 'mean' before 'joke.'"

Mr. Moore was firm. "As touching and heartfelt as your offer is, Kiki, what those people are signing up for is a privilege, not a punishment. It happens to be an overnight scavenger hunt adventure on Cape Cod."

"Perfect!" cried Kiki. "My family has a house on the Cape. How about if instead of detention I host a huge barbecue blowout for the trip! There will be food and entertainment! It will be killer. Don't you think that in the end a party for everyone would be better than me wasting a whole afternoon in detention? It would show my . . . my . . . team spirit!"

Mr. Moore paused for thought. "Well, Kiki, that's very generous of you. But you'd have to be an active participant in the activity, and the rules state that you can't come unless you have turned in all your assignments."

"That's no problem," sang Kiki. "All my stuff is in. Duh. Why do you think I need to get out of detention? I'd have nothing to do there."

"This isn't exactly your usual crowd, Kiki," Katani couldn't help pointing out.

"That's not very nice, Katani. I like everyone in the class." Kiki pouted, pretending to be deeply hurt.

Katani could not believe what a good actress Kiki was. She would have to tell Maeve about Kiki's potential. . . . She would make such a good witch!

"Well, I'll give it a tentative yes," Mr. Moore acquiesced. "The scavenger hunt is open to all interested students who have completed their work. If you're willing to stay after and help me stuff envelopes with letters home about the trip, I can let you off detention. As for the barbecue . . . talk to your parents tonight and get their written approval."

Kiki skipped out of the room with a superior-than-thou glance at the BSG.

"I can't believe it!" Charlotte shook her head. "Kiki Underwood is coming on our first Adventure Club outing."

Avery made a face. "The Empress of Mean coming on our trip really frosts my cookies."

Isabel, who had fallen victim to Kiki's stunts more than once, actually looked ill. "And I was so looking forward to this . . . ," she muttered mournfully.

Maeve decided she'd better step in fast. "Chin up, you guys! First of all, Char, this is the Adventure Club's trip, not Kiki's. Second of all, a party in a Cape Cod summer house—and you know Kiki's place is probably amazing— is going to be fabbity fab *fabulous*! You all have to stop being such, such . . . Negative Nancys . . . Sorry Susans . . . Debbie

Downers . . . Moany Monas . . . Whiny Wilmas . . ."

"'Kay, Maeve, we get the point." Charlotte giggled.

"Boring Berthas . . ."

"Maeve, enough!" Katani pleaded.

"Oh, before I forget," Charlotte interrupted, "Mr. Moore only agreed to this trip provided that we had three older kids to chaperone. Nick's sister, Fabiana, is coming and so is Chelsea's brother, Ben."

"Ben Briggs is coming?" Maeve gasped. "No way! He's on the high school football team and is—no joke—a total dreamboat."

Charlotte, Avery, Katani, and Isabel groaned in unison. Trust Maeve to turn an outdoor adventure into a romance novel.

"The point is," Charlotte continued, "Avery thought Scott could come. . . ."

"And he could! Up until yesterday," Avery explained. "Then he found out this famous chef, Terrence Tortellini or something, was coming to do a special demonstration for his cooking class that weekend and he canceled."

Avery's brother was a total foodie. Nothing would stand in his way if he had the opportunity to work with a famous chef.

"Right," Charlotte nodded. "So I was wondering, Isabel, if you could ask Elena Maria—or Katani, is Patrice busy?"

"Elena Maria is going to that cooking thing too. I already asked her last night," Isabel offered. "Sorry, I meant to tell you before class."

Charlotte turned to Katani. Seeing Katani's blank face, she began to beg in her best fake English accent, "As a poor only child without an older sister to volunteer, I would be eternally grateful if your dear sister, Patrice, would consider accompanying us on this rollicking great scavenger hunt to beautiful Cape Cod."

"Why, Charlotte Ramsey," Maeve exclaimed. "That sounded so tragic! You should try out for the school musical with me. You could play Cordelia Weatherbee. . . ."

Katani, feeling the pressure that this whole trip came down to her asking Patrice, tried her best to look positive. But she was worried. Her sister Patrice could be so difficult when it came to things you could win, like sports and . . . scavenger hunts.

Not wanting to disappoint Charlotte, however, Katani replied in an upbeat tone, "I'll check."

"Awesome!" Avery cried, clapping Katani on her back. "Patrice rocks!"

The girls waved good-bye. Charlotte and Isabel were off to a newspaper meeting, Maeve was practicing for the spring musical tryouts, and Avery had soccer practice.

Only Katani had her afternoon free . . . well, not exactly free. It was a Kelley day. Though Katani's autistic sister, Kelley, was older than Katani by a year, Katani often felt like the older one. While her older sister was nearly a genius at remembering random things—like details of events or TV commercials, when it came to certain social stuff it was like Kelley just didn't get it at all.

Katani loved her sister more than anything, but

sometimes Kelley's autism was hard for her to handle. Like today, when Katani had way more important issues to think about . . . for example, the Adventure Club trip and her having to ask Patrice to chaperone.

Katani kept thinking on her walk home from school that there were two major problems with Charlotte's plan. The first, and biggest, was that Katani herself really didn't want to go on the trip. She just wasn't the outdoorsy type like her sister. The second problem was Patrice herself. She could be so bossy and loved to win. *More like,* has *to win,* Katani thought, sighing.

I like winning too; who doesn't? But, really, she preferred indoor activities: math, science, sewing—things that required a steady table and nice, cool air conditioning. Biking for miles in unattractive clothes with her superathletic sister really wasn't her thing. *Of course, if we were on horseback, that would be a different story.* Katani loved everything to do with horses, especially riding them. Riding was something that Patrice didn't know how to do. In fact, Patrice was afraid of horses. *But Patrice isn't afraid of biking,* Katani thought.

Unfortunately, Katani also realized, there was no way out of this trip. Charlotte, one of her best friends in the world, had organized it, and all the BSG were going. She had to go too. But now she was supposed to ask her sister Patrice to not only come but *supervise!* This was a disaster in the making. Katani could feel it in her bones.

When she reached her house, Katani dragged her feet up her front stairs like they were attached to blocks of concrete. Once inside, she was surprised to see that Patrice and Kelley were sitting at the kitchen table playing a game.

"Moat," Kelley said with a wide grin.

"Aw!" Patrice shook her head. "Hey, Katani, want to get in on the next round? We're playing Boggle and Kelley is beating me big-time."

Kelley bit her bottom lip and seemed nearly giddy with excitement. "I learned Boggle today in school," she revealed. "I was the best in my whole class. Boggle boggle boggle boggle. Who's got the Boggle?"

There was one thing that all the Summers girls had in common: They were all competitive about something,

Katani shook her head. "Nah, I got a lot of homework to start. I thought you were just going to walk Kelley home and go off to practice," she said as she cautiously took a seat at the kitchen table and grabbed a celery boat stuffed with peanut butter and raisins.

"Patrice and I made them," boasted Kelley. "It's ants on a bog! Bog-boggle-bug!" Kelley hooted at her little joke. She loved to play with words. The problem was that sometimes Kelley would go on and on rhyming and making weird word connections for days.

Patrice laughed with Kelley, and then confessed, "I'm loving spending time at home now that basketball season is over. It's kind of boring to practice when the season is over, so I told them I had to Kelley-sit today. Besides, spending time with Kelley is da bomb!" She and Kelley slapped each other five.

"That's great!" Katani said, trying her best to be supportive, but deep down inside she felt a little jealous of Kelley's sudden infatuation with Patrice. Katani was used to being Kelley's favorite and she wasn't crazy about this new little twist.

"Now my only problem is figuring what I'm supposed to do on the weekends without games or practice. Two full days in a row . . . I'm gonna have to learn how to sew or something," mused Patrice with a slight twinkle in her eye.

That did it. Sewing was Katani's thing—there was no way she was going to compete with her sister at the one activity she loved most. "Hey, I might have something for you to do," Katani began.

"Really? What?"

Katani bit her lip. "Well . . . next weekend there's this outdoor exploration trip to Cape Cod. It's an overnight-slash-scavenger-hunt type of thing. There are three teams and each team needs one older kid to chaperone. Ben Briggs and Fabiana Montoya are doing it. I know it must sound kind of babyish—"

"No! It sounds like a blast. I know Ben and Fabiana really well. What, do you guys need, like, one more chaperone or something?"

"Yeah, I mean, only if you're not too busy," Katani mumbled, secretly hoping that Patrice would say no.

"Busy! I'm wide open. Oh, Katani! This will be great! I can finally use all my camping stuff I got when I did that Outward Bound trip last summer. Seriously, I've got a compass, rope, water bottle, sleeping bag, lantern. Whoever gets to have me as their chaperone is gonna hit the jackpot, sister!"

Katani gulped. Patrice was already gearing up to win. Katani wanted to win as well, but heading into the great outdoors with her supercharged sister . . . she might as well give up before she started.

But she also knew better than to let Patrice see her defeated. "So you're in, then!" she feigned enthusiasm. "Awesome! I'll call Charlotte and let her know."

"What about me?" asked Kelley in a panicked voice. "I want to be in too!"

"Oh, Kelley, I don't think it's possible," said Patrice gently. The Summers girls knew better than to get Kelley's hopes up, and there was just no way she could go along. Kelley had a knack for getting lost wherever they went. An outdoor excursion on the Cape with Kelley would spell disaster with a capital *D*. "This trip is just for seventh graders and high school people."

Kelley's jaw dropped. "That's not fair, Patrice. You're mean. Meany, mean, mean . . . a meany boggle bug." She stood up in a huff and stomped out of the kitchen.

"Come on, Katani. Let's get outta here!" Kelley shouted over her shoulder.

"Guess I'd better try to calm her down," Katani muttered and jogged off behind her. Just like that, order had been restored. Katani was Kelley's favorite sister again. It was a small victory, but a victory nonetheless.

3 people here

montoya33
shutterbug12
skywriter

montoya33: do we have another high school chaperone yet??? Mr. Moore called. He's trying to reorganize the groups again. . . .

shutterbug12: ben asked his gf but shes busy. this is kinda last minute, huh?

skywriter: don't worry, guys!!! Katani came through for us!

shutterbug12: which sister is coming?

skywriter: Patrice. The basketball superstar.

montoya33: rock on!

shutterbug12: I wish Mr. Moore would let us pick the groups

skywriter: hes really into the whole surprise thing. He told me he and his wife are driving down to the Cape after school tomorrow to put little flags next to all the stops on the scavenger hunt!

montoya33: I saw all the clues stacked in separate envelopes on his desk

Later that evening, just before bed, Charlotte saw that she had an e-mail. *That's weird*, she thought as she saw it came from Mrs. Summers's computer.

To: Charlotte
From: Mrs. Summers
Subject: Scavenger Hunt

Dear Charlotte,
I think it's very mean that I can't
come to the scavenger hunt.

Your friend,
Kelley Summers

Charlotte wrote back immediately.

To: Mrs. Summers
From: Charlotte
Subject: Re: Scavenger Hunt

Dear Kelley,
I promise we will have another
scavenger hunt that you can come
on . . . real soon!

Your friend,
Charlotte Ramsey

CHAPTER
3

The Ice Cream Bandit
Strikes Again

The week dragged on so slowly for Charlotte that she wondered if it would be possible to invent some way to fast-forward time. *How great would it be to skip over the annoying parts and press play for the fun ones?* She wondered what that would be like for each of the BSG. Avery would probably fast-forward everything that wasn't soccer and recess, Maeve would pause her every moment in the spotlight, and Katani would skip all the way to her dream future as CEO of Kgirl Enterprises. Isabel would probably be the only BSG who might decide to play everything at normal speed — she wouldn't want to miss anything beautiful or interesting that came her way.

When Saturday morning finally arrived, Charlotte leaped out of bed and ran to the window. She was pleased to see that her patience had been rewarded — it was a breathtakingly gorgeous day outside. The kind of day that just screamed, *Hey, let's go to the beach!* And Charlotte, knowing that was exactly the plan, twirled around her room, feeling like she might just float away with excitement.

"Time to get ready, Charlotte," her father called up to her.

"Be down soon, Dad!" Charlotte pulled out her journal from her bottom desk drawer and slipped her lucky jean jacket over her shoulders. Charlotte's journal was where she kept all her deepest thoughts and secrets, and the jean jacket was her most prized possession. It used to belong to her mother, who had died when Charlotte was little. She missed her mother dreadfully some days, but wearing the jacket, especially when she was writing, made Charlotte feel comfy and inspired. Her most creative thoughts came out when she wore that jacket.

She wrapped the jacket tightly around her shoulders, opened her journal, and began.

Charlotte's Journal

Saturday is finally here! Nick Montoya's parents took us to the Cape a few weeks ago to help brainstorm ideas, and somehow we came up with this scavenger hunt and actually turned it into a real live school field trip that IS HAPPENING TODAY!

I can't wait to go adventuring and I am so excited that we are heading to one of my favorite places to go around here. . . . Cape Cod. When you open the window going over the Sagamore Bridge and smell the fresh sea air you understand. It's like you've traveled to a different world where time is slower and you feel like you are living in a lovely postcard. And the big extra-special bonus is that I'm going to the Cape with all my friends . . . and Nick Montoya!

Go us! I think the trip will be amazing, but I'm a little nervous. Typical me. But still, I can't help it.

What happens if the trip is a disaster? Everyone will blame me, because I organized it. Kiki Underwood is coming AND hosting a party at her house. I hope the Empress of Mean doesn't have something terrible up her sleeve. I'm sorry, but I just don't trust her.

Also, what if I'm not on a team with any of the BSG or Nick?? It's been a while since our dreamy Valentine's Day Dance kiss . . . my first and only kiss. I wonder if I will remember that kiss for my entire life?

Well, that's the story, dear journal. Stay tuned to hear about our fabulous adventures to come. And with the BSG, you KNOW there will be!

"Knock knock," said Charlotte's father, rapping lightly at her open door. Charlotte turned as she heard the mournful yipping of the official BSG mascot, Marty, who was smart enough to know when Charlotte was going to be leaving him, even if only for an overnight. "Are you all packed and ready to roll?" asked Mr. Ramsey, poking his head into her room.

Marty leaped into her room and right into Charlotte's

arms, covering her with little dog kisses. Charlotte nodded, and rubbed the little dude's belly. "I was packed on Thursday night. And, Dad?" Charlotte put on a pair of sunglasses and said in a low voice, "I was *born* ready."

"That's my global girl . . . ready to travel at the drop of a hat." Mr. Ramsey chuckled and picked up Charlotte's backpack to carry downstairs. "I really wish I was going with you kids. Too bad I have this conference in Chicago."

"I know. But you'll have fun in Chicago. You love those professor brainiac writing conventions."

"Oh, yes. We professors do adore our brainiac conventions. I'm thinking of running for treasurer of the brainiacs," Mr. Ramsey joked as he loaded up the car. "Say bye, Marty! You be good for Miss Pierce!" Marty howled a tragic good-bye bark as Ms. Pierce waved his paw. Charlotte blew him kisses from the car. The little dude would be just fine with the Ramsey's kindly landlady and downstairs neighbor taking care of him for the weekend.

"I am a little sad that I'm not going along," her father said on the ride over.

"Next time, Dad," Charlotte promised. "I'll fill you in on everything when we get back!"

But the truth was Charlotte felt a little relieved and excited that they didn't have any parents chaperoning the trip. As much as she loved her travel writer father, Charlotte was looking forward to having a friends-only trip to the Cape. It made her feel so very grown up.

When she and her father arrived at Abigail Adams Junior High, the first thing Charlotte noticed was the mayhem. The parking lot was an absolute zoo of kids, cars, and worried parents trying to figure out who was in charge. Charlotte's stomach did a little flutter. Who *was* responsible here?

"Are you sure you want me to leave you in this circus?" asked Mr. Ramsey. Charlotte almost giggled at her father's face—he looked more nervous than she felt!

"I'll be fine, Dad. If it wasn't complete craziness it wouldn't be a BSG adventure, right?"

As Charlotte hugged her father good-bye, she looked around for a familiar face.

Katani and Patrice marched over, looking especially cranky. "Some little boy in an army suit just spilled ice cream on my foot and ran away. Honestly, what kind of parent gives their kid ice cream at eight a.m. on a Saturday?" bemoaned Patrice. "And why are there little kids running around, anyway . . . and where is everyone?"

"We're not morning people," Katani grumbled in explanation to Charlotte, who looked a little uncomfortable at Patrice's outburst.

"All I know is that we'd better get this game on," Patrice declared. "'Cause our team is going to be one lean, mean, scavenger-hunting machine!"

"Yoo-hoo! Ladies!" Maeve Kaplan-Taylor skipped over. She was decked out in a pair of seashell pink shorts, a white-and-blue-striped sailor shirt, and matching starfish earrings and necklace. "You girls like my look? I call it Seagirl or Maeve on the Seashore. . . . I haven't settled on an exact name yet."

Charlotte shook her head. She couldn't believe that she

had a best girlfriend who actually named her looks, but she adored Maeve for being the kind of girl who did.

"BTW, have you guys seen my dad and my brother?" asked Maeve. "Sam has been on the warpath with his new squirt gun. I *told* them they could leave, but . . ."

"*En garde!*" piped a little boy wearing full army garb who suddenly jumped out from behind a Volkswagen, brandishing a squirt gun in one hand and a dripping half-eaten ice-cream cone in the other. "Take that!" And before the girls had a moment to run, they were all super soaked. "Ha ha! The ice-cream bandit strikes again!" Sam shouted in triumph and disappeared into the crowd leaving a trail of ice-cream puddles in his wake.

"Well, that solves *that* mystery!" Patrice remarked, shaking her sticky right foot.

"Your little brother, Maeve . . . is completely wild!" Katani moaned, wringing water out of her hand-beaded T-shirt.

"Sam's not the only one here in a costume," whispered Isabel, who'd just walked up from behind to join the group. "Check it out. . . ."

Betsy Fitzgerald was waltzing over with a grown man in tow who looked like he'd just stepped out of the Revolutionary War.

"Are they serious?" Maeve's eyes widened. The man was wearing britches and carrying a musket!

"Hey, be nice—that's Betsy's father," Charlotte said, reminding her friends of Betsy's little speech in class the week before.

"Why didn't anyone tell me that this was where Nerd-opalooza was meeting?" Kiki Underwood sauntered over from a gleaming red convertible, speaking loud enough to evoke giggles from a few people around her.

Avery scowled. She did not find Kiki funny at all and she hated it when Kiki made fun of other kids.

Charlotte, for her part, was relieved that Betsy was so busy showing off her costumed father to Mr. Moore and spouting out facts about Paul Revere that she completely missed Kiki's remark.

"Hey, Char, I've been looking everywhere for you."

Charlotte started when she heard the familiar voice. She couldn't help feeling slightly off-kilter every time she saw Nick Montoya. Sure, it went away after a few minutes and then they were totally cool. Because Nick was just like her buddy . . . a buddy with deep, chocolate eyes and the most adorable little wave in his hair . . . *STOP!* Charlotte firmly ordered herself. *This is Nick Montoya, and we planned this trip. Get a grip. Hey, that rhymed. . . .*

"Nicholas, there you are. Fashionably late as usual." Maeve kissed the air near Nick's head. Nick looked at Maeve like a UFO might have just unloaded a half gorilla– half space creature hybrid onto the city of Brookline.

"Hi, Maeve. Um, Charlotte . . . we need to get going and no one is doing anything about it. . . ." Nick gestured at the busy parking lot. In one corner Mr. Moore and his wife were talking to Henry Yurt's father, a professor at MIT, about the positive effects of organic feed on cows. Ms. O'Reilly was rummaging around in the back of a minivan, and Dillon Johnson and Avery were flinging a Frisbee back and forth.

"Well, I found one chaperone who wants to make her team into a—" Charlotte began.

"Lean, mean, scavenger-hunting machine," finished Patrice, folding her arms smartly. "So who's with me?"

"Ummm . . . ," Nick started, glancing at Charlotte.

"I'll get the team assignments," she promised, and trotted over to Ms. O'Reilly, who had just pulled a canvas tote bag full of envelopes out of her van.

Charlotte handed out one bundle each for Patrice, Fabiana Montoya, and Ben Briggs, who had just arrived with his sister, Chelsea, toting all the team cameras. Patrice held up a manila envelope labeled TEAM SALTY CODS and cleared her throat. "All right, shorties. Let me show you how the big kids play! Listen up, everybody! If you are any of the following people, please report to my office IMMEDIATELY!"

Patrice opened the envelope in her hand very dramatically, like she was announcing an Academy Award. Maeve clasped her hands together accordingly. "My team, the Salty Cods, are . . . Dillon Johnson, Riley Lee, Charlotte Ramsey, and my very own little sis, Katani Summers!"

Charlotte felt a sudden stab of disappointment. Nick wasn't on her team? In a way it made sense; Mr. Moore had put Katani with her sister, so maybe Nick was with his sister. Or maybe the teachers thought there should be one trip organizer on each team.

"I'm Dillon," shouted a voice from the Frisbee game,

"and no one told me where your office was. . . ."

"RIGHT HERE—you ready to roll?" Patrice cheered. Katani wanted to hide. Patrice sounded like a drill sergeant and their trip hadn't even started! And wouldn't you know it? All the other chaperones started to follow Patrice's lead.

Ben Briggs of the Beach Barnacles, in a milder voice than Patrice's, gathered his brigade—Avery Madden, Henry Yurt, Chelsea Briggs, and (*gag*) Kiki Underwood—with a direct "Barnacles, over here, now!" Fabiana Montoya's team, the Cranberry Boggers, was composed of the remaining students: Betsy Fitzgerald, Maeve Kaplan-Taylor, Danny Pellegrino, Isabel Martinez, and Nick Montoya.

Maeve was elated to be on Nick's older sister's team. With her long, silky brown hair and colorful flowy shirts, Fabiana reminded Maeve of a pretty flower child of the sixties. She was always smiling and friendly, and an amazing actress. Exactly the kind of sister Maeve would have wished for if she had one of her own. And of course Isabel was a doll—always easy to get along with.

If only Riley were on the team, too! Maeve sighed. They could talk music; maybe even sing some songs together. Maeve glanced at Nick shuffling his feet beside his big sister and suddenly had a fabulous idea. She put on her sunglasses and imagined she was a secret agent on a mission to Malibu. She was sure Nick would go through with her plan.

"Okay, kids, I am impressed!" declared Mr. Moore. "You've done a very effective job organizing yourselves after all." He smiled as Chelsea, the other trip organizer, took a picture of him in his black and white cow sweat-shirt. Charlotte glanced at Nick with raised eyebrows, wondering if the grown-ups had left them alone on purpose. Maybe this do-it-yourself trip that they'd organized had a do-it-yourself theme. But Nick was busy talking to Maeve about something. Charlotte figured it was up to her to take charge.

"The team captains have sealed envelopes with all the clues and detailed maps of our search area!" Charlotte announced. The teams moved in closer. "They also have copies of your parents' signed permission slips and emergency contact info. When we arrive at the Cape, the teachers will drop us off at the start point—Nickerson State Park—and meet up with us when it's time for dinner."

"Excellent work, Charlotte!" Ms. O'Reilly piped up. "We expect you kids to obey your high school chaperones and do everything they say."

Avery rubbed her hands together. She couldn't wait to start. Then she noticed Kiki filing her nails and looking totally bored. But without Anna and Joline around, nobody seemed to care one bit what Kiki thought about anything.

"Woo-hoo!" whispered Avery to herself.

"One last thing before you board your pirate ships, er, I mean automobiles, driven by your most beloved teachers," Mr. Moore added. (This time Avery couldn't help laughing a little. Mr. Moore was just *too corny*.) "I am presenting each team with one student-appointed Talkie Trekker. Any volunteers?"

Suddenly Avery wasn't laughing anymore. Her arm shot up into the air. Walkie-talkies were one of her absolute favorite things in the world. When she was little, she'd even made some walkie-talkies the old-fashioned way by connecting two cans to a string. Mr. Moore, appreciating her enthusiasm for the job, granted her the bright yellow, brand-new device.

Meanwhile, Betsy and Danny Pellegrino were arguing over their team's walkie-talkie. Finally Danny suggested they play rock, paper, scissors, and he immediately creamed her scissors with rock. "No fair. You know it's always best two out of three!" Betsy protested.

"Fine. Two out of three." Danny then pummeled her again by covering her rock with paper. While he was doing a little victory dance, Betsy smiled brightly. "Danny, that was just so *chivalrous* to offer me the privilege," she said as she accepted the portable high-tech trophy from Mr. Moore.

Danny opened his mouth, then closed it, obviously completely confused about what just happened.

"And what about the Salty Cods?" asked Mr. Moore.

"Ooh! I'll do it!" cried Dillon. But it was as though Mr. Moore couldn't even hear him.

"What about you, Katani? I think you'd be a marvelous Talkie Trekker. Don't you?"

Katani almost balked. "Me? But Mr. Moore . . . I'm not very outdoorsy."

Mr. Moore placed the walkie-talkie in her hand and explained, "But it's not about being outdoorsy, Katani. It's about being responsible. Now come, Salty Cods! You are with me. To the Cowmobile," he cried.

🐚 Henry Yurt = Not a Clue

From the outside, Mr. Moore's white van seemed innocent and ordinary enough. But inside, it was a *whole* other story. Mr. Moore and his wife had gone to town with cow decorations. The seats all had cow-print covers—the black and white Vermont cow-print that was oh-so-hot right now. The air freshener was "barn grass," the horn on the wheel went "moooooo," and there was a little cow bobblehead doll in a lei and hula skirt jiggling beneath the windshield.

As Charlotte and Katani mooed out the wide windows to Avery, Isabel, and Maeve, Charlotte worried for a moment that maybe they were being hauled off to a dairy farm in another galaxy far, far away. "If I come back from this trip mooing . . . I'm blaming you!" Katani whispered, pointing at Charlotte.

"Ready, set . . ." Mr. Moore hit the horn and a low "mooooo" sound filled the van.

"Wait! Where's Riley?" Patrice held up her Salty Cods team list and looked from face to face.

Just then, the sliding door opened, and Nick popped his head in. "Hi, Mr. Moore, Patrice, Charlotte, everyone . . . I'm on your team now, guys!"

Charlotte felt her cheeks go pink. "Did you . . . switch with Riley?" she asked, thinking to herself *That is so sweet!*

Nick nodded. "Uh-huh. Let's go, Salty Cods!"

Mr. Moore honked the horn again, and started up the

engine. "Well, I never said you *couldn't* switch . . . so I'll let it slide. We need to get mooo-ving!"

Nick looked at Charlotte and they dropped their heads to keep from bursting out laughing at the cow man's directions. Katani moved over so Nick could slide into the center seat next to them, and the Cowmobile was off. All the Salty Cods knew that traveling with Mr. Moore would be a mooo-arvelous adventure in itself.

"Now listen up, troops!" Patrice turned around from the front seat, and tore open an envelope labeled MISSION. She unfolded the paper and read in the same take-charge voice she'd used in the parking lot:

Greetings Brave Scavenger Hunters of Abigail Adams Junior High School,

Your mission, should you choose to accept it, is simple. You must find the 6 "treasures" specified in the clues. For each treasure you find and photograph, you will receive 3 points. The team that reaches the finish line first will receive 10 points. The team to reach the finish line second will receive 5 points. The team who reaches the finish line last gets 0 points. I know it is sad, but as the age-old saying goes, "The early bird catches the worm!"

But never fear! If any of you turns out to be Pokey McSlowpokes, there is always the bonus point list:

fox

surfboard

sandpiper

street named after an animal

scallop shell

pirate-themed anything

sailboat

tide pool

sand dune

park ranger

If you spot any of these items and take a picture of it, you will be rewarded 1 point for each item photographed.

Happy scavenger hunting!

Patrice glanced back at her team and pulled down her sunglasses from her nose to look ultraserious. "Um, guys, we're coming in first, uuuh-huh!"

Nick high-fived Charlotte, Katani, and Dillon. Katani wasn't feeling so gung ho about the whole thing, however. This was supposed to be a fun, relaxing weekend with her friends . . . after all, they were only bike riding and figuring out a few clues. But her sister really expected them to beat the other teams. *What if,* Katani thought nervously, *I slow my team down?* What if Patrice wouldn't want to wait for her little sister to catch up? Katani stared out the window wishing that there had been some way for her to back out of this trip.

"Are you ready for the first cloooooo?" Mr. Moore asked in his ultra cow voice.

"Oh, yeah!" Nick exclaimed. His enthusiasm granted him the privilege of being the first clue reader.

One is big, the other small, and neither a
precipice at all. Near these places, in the dirt,
get ready for a yurt alert.

"Yurt alert? Henry?" Charlotte shook her head. "That can't be right. . . . I'm sure I've heard that word somewhere else before. . . ."

4

The Cranberry Sing-along

Outside the Cranberry Boggers' van, driven by Ms. O'Reilly, Isabel, who had been Danny Pellegrinoed once before, gave Maeve's shirt a tug. "I *cannot* sit next to Danny on the ride. I just can't! Remember . . . the famous Danny "the stalker" Pellegrino Museum Incident?"

Did Maeve ever! Poor Isabel had been stuck in the same group as Danny when the seventh-grade class visited the Museum of Fine Arts. Danny P. had glommed on to her like orange powder to a Cheese Doodle, and followed her around the whole trip trying to impress her with his (annoying) knowledge of art. Danny was lucky Isabel was a kind girl. Otherwise he might have found himself locked in a sarcophagus with a mummy!

"Okay, crawl in the back, FAST! I'll be right behind you." Maeve hurried Isabel into the back seat and, true to her word, squeezed in next to her. "Hey, look! It's Riley!"

She grinned and waved to the lead singer of their grade's only cool band, the Mustard Monkeys. It looked like her plan had been totally successful! Charlotte and Nick were together, as they were always meant to be, and Maeve got to sit next to the cutest musician in the seventh grade. "Riley, there's an empty seat back here!" she called.

"Isn't Riley on Charlotte's—" Isabel started, but stopped when she saw Maeve's triumphant face. Fabiana hadn't noticed the team member swap—she was up front digging through her huge canvas art bag and piling CDs on the dashboard.

"Seat belts?" Ms. O'Reilly checked. Danny hurriedly buckled himself in next to Betsy in the middle seat, and Fabiana Montoya popped in the first of her awesome CDs as the van pulled out of the parking lot. "Every chapter of your life should have the perfect soundtrack," Fabiana explained.

"Ooh, put on the Royal Brothers! They are sooo charming!" Maeve squealed.

Fabiana shook her head, jangling her dangly earrings, "I've got something even better . . . *West Side Story*!"

As Fabiana sang along to the beautiful songs, Maeve remembered watching her perform in the high school musical. *Maybe Fabiana could give me some singing tips this weekend!* Maeve hoped as she opened her mouth to join in on the chorus. To her surprise, even Ms. O'Reilly was singing!

"Betsy, I saw your dad back there in the parking lot. That was a pretty nifty costume! I wish my dad was a historical reenactor!" Danny confessed over a break in the music as they merged onto Route 95.

A very serious Betsy turned to face Danny.

"You know," she explained, "it's very hard to be a reenactor. First, you must be a talented actor, then you have to know tons of important facts about the Revolutionary War. In high school, I'm going to try out for the part of Betsy Ross. I mean, of course she sewed the first American Flag, but she was also a member of the Fighting Quakers during the Revolutionary War, and, best of all, she has my name!"

Betsy was practically glowing, but Isabel's eyes began to close as her head drooped. She hoped this trip to Cape Cod wasn't going to be one long Betsy Fitzgerald fact fest!

"Betsy is a very strong woman's name, you know. . . ." Betsy continued.

"Iz," Maeve whispered to Isabel, "check it out. Danny is basically drooling. You, girlfriend, could be off the hook!" Isabel opened her eyes, suddenly grateful that Danny seemed dazzled by Betsy's command of Revolutionary War facts. Maybe Danny would forget all about her on this trip. She crossed her fingers for luck.

Before Betsy could continue listing all the famous Betsys in history, Ms. O'Reilly gave Fabiana the envelope so she could read the instructions and first clue aloud. "'One is big, the other small, and neither a precipice at all. Near these places, in the dirt, get ready for a yurt alert.'"

"Well, we know neither is a precipice at all," Maeve pointed out. "That's very good. Considering I have no idea was a precipice EVEN IS!"

"Ahem, if I may?" Betsy cleared her throat. "Precipice, noun, a very steep or overhanging place, example, cliff or ledge.'"

"It can also mean a dangerous situation," added Danny.

Isabel elbowed Maeve, who was struggling to keep down a serious case of eye rolling. "Maybe we should look at the map and see if there are any, um, not-clifflike places around Cape Cod?" Maeve suggested.

"Ooh, great call, Maeve. I have the map right here in my art bag," Fabiana informed her. She bent over and starting digging through the enormous canvas tote. "Hmm . . . it should be right . . . that's weird. It's in here . . . wait . . . no . . . um, hold on guys, give me one minute." After five minutes had passed, the realization began to sink in for the Cranberry Boggers that Fabiana had no map.

"Oh, wow, I don't know what happened," she murmured. "I thought I tucked it right into the side of my bag."

"Well, what are we supposed to do now?" an anxious Betsy demanded. "Ms. O'Reilly, you can't expect us to be able to compete without a map. It's just not fair!"

"Yeah," piped Danny. "We'll never find anything! This totally stinks."

"You all are very intelligent young people," said a

nonchalant Ms. O'Reilly. "I'm sure you'll be able to figure something out."

"I'm sure we won't," Danny groaned. "I hate losing."

"Me too," seconded Betsy. "It's almost worse than getting a B."

"It's like—it's like—like . . ." Danny's face melted into a grimace. "Like getting a B *minus*." He and Betsy shuddered in sync. Fabiana looked embarrassed and defeated at once, but she just kept burrowing farther into her tote searching in vain for that map.

Maeve could feel her own heart melting. Poor Fabiana! Maeve knew all too well what it was it was like to lose something important. She couldn't even count the number of times she would remember putting her homework into her backpack only to arrive at school, go to class, and at the vital moment find that her homework had disappeared. It was so frustrating, not to mention humiliating.

"You two need to chill out!" Maeve ordered. "There are, like, a gazillion maps of Cape Cod around. My dad has tons that he bought at gas stations. If we all chipped in, like, fifty cents, couldn't we just get another?"

Betsy folded her arms. "Don't look at me. I'm trying to save up for medical camp this summer."

Maeve had never heard of medical camp, and didn't really want to know more. "Well, here is fifty cents from me," she volunteered.

"And me," added Isabel.

Fabiana turned and gave the girls a grateful smile. "Tell you what. Since I was supposed to be responsible,

I'll contribute two dollars, which should do the trick. I'd give more, but I want to save a little so I can get my mom this Cape Cod cookbook that she's been wanting." No one could argue with that.

"I'll pull off at the next rest stop," Ms. O'Reilly promised. "And you can pick up a new map."

Maeve thought Danny and Betsy were being impossible as they ignored the whole conversation and instead decided to play a game of Cape Cod trivia. Those two Cranberry Boggers had a case of bad sportsmanship in the worst way, and they hadn't even gotten out of the car. Maeve almost said so, but a little voice told her to just sit back and let Betsy and Danny play "know-it-all" for a while. Maybe things would get better once they knew where they were going.

A Cowmobile Full of Codfish

"So if this clue doesn't mean find Henry Yurt, what does it mean?" asked Dillon from the back seat of the Cowmobile. They were all poring over the superdetailed, laminated, color-coded map Patrice had brought in a special compartment in her businesslike messenger bag.

"I think it would help if we had an exact definition of 'precipice,'" Patrice pointed out. "Unfortunately, that is one crazy intense vocab word and it's way too advanced for anyone in this car . . . except Mr. Moore, obviously," she hinted.

"That's not entirely true," Charlotte replied mischievously. "At least, I might have an idea. Doesn't a precipice mean, like, a cliff or something?" She caught Mr. Moore's eyes twinkling in the rearview mirror.

"Nice job, Char!" Nick congratulated her.

"Now what? We just have to find something that's *not* a cliff? Well, that narrows it down." Dillon chuckled.

"That's it!" Nick shouted, making everyone in the car jump. "Sorry, I mean, that's it," he repeated, only this time much more softly. He pointed at the map. "Check it out—those two ponds in Nickerson State Park. They're called 'Big Cliff' and 'Little Cliff.' Those have got to be our *not precipices*, right? Boy, are we lucky to have such a great map."

"Nick, you got it!" Charlotte cheered and leaned over to give him a hug, and squeezed his shoulder instead.

Nick turned a little red and responded shyly, "Well, I couldn't have done it if you hadn't known the definition of precipice." The two shared a sweet look.

When Katani caught Dillon goofing at the sight of Charlotte and Nick's mutual admiration, she mouthed, *MYOB!* Dillon immediately stopped drawing hearts on the back of Nick's seat with his finger.

The Barnacles Cross the Bridge

"You're in Cape Cod and I'm not riiiiiiiiight NOW!" cried Avery the moment the front tires of Mrs. Moore's station wagon hit the Sagamore Bridge, propelling Mrs. Moore and Ben Briggs into Cape Cod a millisecond before the rest of the passengers. The Sagamore was a big suspension bridge which crossed over the canal and brought them onto the Cape. "Woo-hoo!" Avery and Henry Yurt rolled down their windows and stuck out their heads like two Labrador puppies to get a whiff of the salty sea air.

"I think we should try to figure out that clue," Chelsea mentioned softly to Avery and Yurt. Unfortunately they were too busy howling out the window to answer. "Can't we just try to enjoy some peace and quiet until we get there?" Kiki griped.

"Yeah, besides we already have the first clue right in this car. . . . It's me!" Yurt cheered.

"I doubt that Mr. Moore would make it *that* easy," Chelsea mumbled.

"Chelsea's right, kids. My husband is a very, very complex and intelligent man. He has . . . many layers," Mrs. Moore mused. "Like a sweet vidalia onion. Why, look— there he is!"

As they drove along at a steady fifty-five miles an hour, a car full of Salty Cods passed by—all of them waving and making faces.

"Sooo mature!" Kiki remarked sarcastically.

Avery and Yurt looked at each other and immediately contorted their faces into freakiness with pulled-out mouths and pulled-down eyelids. She noticed that even Mr. Moore was participating in the festivities. "Look at Mr. Moore's silly face!" Mrs. Moore waved. "Isn't this fun, already?"

"What am I doing here!" Kiki groaned, sinking down in her seat.

"Relax, Ms. Cool. Have a good time. . . . You'll live

longer," Yurt whispered to an astonished Kiki. No one at school ever talked to her like that.

Avery thought Mrs. Moore was a very nice lady with her pretty blond curls and cat-eyed glasses. And she thought it totally hilarious that cow-loving, bald little Mr. Moore was like a movie star to his adoring wife.

"Hey, Ben," Avery asked. "Since we might already know the first clue, could we just go biking as soon as we get there?" She had been going to the Cape with her mom every summer, and she and her brothers always raced along the Rail Trail. Avery was thrilled she'd get a chance to practice her bike racing this year before the big event!

"We don't know if we've figured out the first clue!" protested Chelsea. "What if we're wrong? I think we need to take out the map and focus."

Ben Briggs turned around. "Yo, relax, Chels. There'll be plenty of time for that once we get there. This trip is supposed to be fun, ya know."

Chelsea, who thought her older brother, Ben, was pretty much the coolest kid ever, instantly felt terrible. Did he think she was being a huge dork?

"Isn't the point of this trip *supposed* to be the scavenger hunt?" she asked. But no one heard her over Henry Yurt and Avery's loud cheering.

Let the Hunt Begin!
The vehicles all pulled up to Nickerson State Park at the same time. Mr. Moore filmed from the front seat of his van as the Salty Cods jumped out of the Cowmobile with their

The Great Scavenger Hunt

Salty Cods
Leader: Patrice Summers
Dillon Johnson
Nick Montoya
Charlotte Ramsey
Katani Summers
Driver/Chaperone: Mr. Moore

Beach Barnacles
Leader: Ben Briggs
Avery Madden
Chelsea Briggs
Henry Yurt
Kiki Underwood
Driver/Chaperone: Mrs. Moore

Cranberry Boggers
Leader: Fabiana Montoya
Maeve Kaplan-Taylor
Isabel Martinez
Betsy Fitzgerald
Danny Pellegrino
Riley Lee
Driver/Chaperone: Ms. O'Reilly

backpacks on like it was a well-practiced military maneuver. "Come on, Cods, I mean it. Move, move, MOVE!" barked Patrice.

The Cranberry Boggers and the Beach Barnacles watched in disbelief as Patrice traced a few places on her map to her group and they raced off into the park, clearly on a mission for victory.

"Remember," Mr. Moore bellowed after them, turning off his video camera. "Keep your walkie-talkie on at all times, and meet us at Kiki's house for the barbecue at five sharp! Your leaders have the directions."

The only one on the Salty Cods team who wasn't huffing and puffing out of the parking lot was Katani. She wanted to be as excited and enthusiastic as the rest of her fellow fishes, but her sister Patrice's *we-can-win* attitude was beginning to grate on her nerves. *How come all the other kids are following her and doing exactly what she says?* Katani took her sweet time making her way to the NON-precipices. It was sort of gratifying, she thought, that Patrice had to slow down so she could catch up.

Back in the parking lot, Mrs. Moore waved good-bye to the Beach Barnacles while Ms. O'Reilly made sure all the Cranberry Boggers had full water bottles and well-adjusted helmet straps.

"Remember, Fabiana," Ms. O'Reilly reminded Nick's sister. "You have your team's permission slips and photo release forms in the envelope with all the clues! So be careful not to misplace it," she said with a twinkle in her eye.

"I'll guard it with my life!" Fabiana promised.

As she tugged her helmet tighter, Isabel noticed that Betsy looked miserable. She figured it was the sight of Avery Madden cheering on her team as they disappeared from sight down the bike path while the Salty Cods were already long gone and probably miles ahead of everyone else.

"We Cranberry Boggers need some of that gung ho spirit!" Betsy complained. "We just got here and we're already in last place!"

"Cheer up!" Fabiana grinned, flipping her brand-new map around 180 degrees for the third time. "This isn't a race, really."

"Yeah, but it's a *hunt*," Danny said from right behind Betsy's shoulder. "That's almost the same thing."

"I don't know if this map is really kid-friendly enough," Maeve remarked.

"The *old* map had all the names of landmarks in big, bold letters," Fabiana sighed. "I guess this one is more for a car driver. Sorry, guys," she said as she looked up at her team's downcast expressions.

"Hey, maybe we could just skip ahead to the second clue," Betsy suggested.

The group glanced at each other as if they were all thinking, *Typical Betsy, always trying to skip ahead to come in first.*

"Think about it," Betsy continued. "If we stay in this park all day looking for precipices we'll miss out on the other clues! We can always come back once we figure it out."

"It's actually not a bad idea," Fabiana contributed.

"Not a bad idea at all. Let's read clue number two!" Danny shouted. Maeve, being very perceptive in the ways of boys, secretly took note of how enthusiastic Danny was to help Betsy. She wondered if Betsy could pull her head out of the clues and maps long enough to notice too.

Fabiana produced another envelope and handed it to Betsy to do the honors. Maeve supposed Betsy was the only other person in the group who genuinely enjoyed having all eyes on her as much as Maeve did.

From the Orleans circle round, toward a
coastal town you're bound. There is much for
you in store at the harbor's rocky shore.

Betsy opened her mouth to comment, but before she had the chance to announce her opinion, Danny shouted, "The rotary! The Orleans Rotary . . . it's right here on the map."

Betsy leaned over to Maeve and whispered, "Should we clue poor Danny in that no one likes a know-it-all?"

Maeve—for the first time in a long time—was speechless. Betsy's cluelessness about her own know-it-all attitude was shocking. *Doesn't Betsy know who she is?* Maeve wondered.

"Hey, according to the map, the Orleans Rotary is four miles away," Fabiana informed them. The collective groan from the team was loud enough to disturb a flock of sparrows that flew off in a rush.

"Well, let's go!" Isabel urged, and with that, they climbed on their bikes and finally left the parking lot—dead last.

CHAPTER
5

Bigger Fish to Fry

At Cliff Pond and Little Cliff Pond, the Salty Cods had bigger fish to fry. "I need more information about this Henry Yurt kid," Patrice demanded. "Who is he? What does he do? Did he leave something here?"

Charlotte was certain that she'd given Patrice her best journalist-quality report about Henry Yurt, but it didn't make a difference. They'd ridden their bikes around the pond three times and absolutely nothing had jumped out at them as particularly "Yurty."

"Whoa! Check out those mad weird tents over there in the clearing!" Dillon called the group over to examine a clearing that had been filled with mustard-colored structures set up in a circle. There were bikes leaning up against one of them, and the voices of campers discussing plans for the day echoed from inside another.

Suddenly, Charlotte burst out laughing. "Guys, those tents are called *yurts*."

"I thought Yurt was just Henry's last name," Dillon said.

"Yurts are also what the Mongolian nomads called their homes. They are like huge tents that can easily be set up and taken down. The Mongolians were *nomadic,* which means that they liked to move around from place to place," Charlotte explained. "I guess this campground set some up as, like, a tourist attraction."

"'One is big, the other small, and neither a precipice at all. Near these places, in the dirt, get ready for a yurt alert!'" Patrice read the first clue aloud again.

"Hey, *check it out!* There's a flag in the middle!" Dillon cried as he ran over and plucked the red flag from the ground. In the middle of the flag someone had stamped the letters AAJH—Abigail Adams Junior High.

"Cods, it looks like we just got ourselves three points!" Patrice announced proudly. "Let's take a picture and move on down the road," she said with a little *Wizard of Oz* shuffle for emphasis.

Charlotte took out her digital camera and captured the yurts in the clearing. As the group examined the snapshot on the screen, Katani noticed a little orange blur in the woods out of the corner of her eye. "Hey, isn't that a—"

"FOX!" Nick finished, pointing at the tiny fiery flash taking off into the woods.

Patrice began running. "Come on, guys, what are you waiting for? That fox was part of the bonus point list."

Charlotte, Dillon, and Nick took off after her. Katani was left standing alone to watch the bikes. "Hey, guys, a fox is only worth one point, and isn't the goal of this thing to be the first team to finish?" she cried after them. "Besides," she added, "it's not safe to chase wild animals." But there was no one there to listen to her warning.

Barnacle Wishes

For creatures famous for their ability to stay put on a rock or seashell for their whole lives, the Beach Barnacles were definitely *not* living up to their name. As soon as Avery climbed on her bicycle, she was off like a rocket.

She couldn't understand what all the other teams were making such a big deal about with the maps and the clues. The scavenger hunt had to be super easy if the first clue was Henry Yurt! In her opinion, the most important, no-brainer reason to have a weekend trip to Cape Cod was to go biking.

As she pedaled her feet at warp speed, churning through the gears of the bike, Avery felt like she might actually lift off the pavement and fly into the air. Now *that* was a great idea . . . flying bicycles . . . just like in *E.T the Extraterrestrial*! Why hadn't anyone invented one of those puppies yet?

"C'mon, slowpokes!" Avery taunted. "Last one to the beach is a rotten snail. Get it?" She consulted Henry Yurt, who was the only person on the team riding next to her.

"On top of it, Ms. Barnacle," he retorted and adjusted the setting on his, like, 120-speed bike as he raced by her. Henry and his dad were avid bikers and could be seen all over Brookline with their matching father-and-son frizzball hair poking out of their bike helmets. Just as Henry was really taking off, who went whizzing by him and Avery but Mrs. Moore—on a cow-painted bicycle no less.

"Woo-hoo! See you at the barbecue tonight!" she teased as she passed the two bewildered students, leaving them in a cloud of dust. Avery and the Yurtmeister heaved and huffed to go faster. Not wanting to look like the loser of the group, Kiki stepped up her game and quickly caught up to the other two.

"Whoa, looks like I'm going to have to break a sweat after all," Ben Briggs remarked. Ben was the type of kid people called "big-boned" who really *was* big-boned. There was nothing tiny about Ben Briggs. In fact, Ben was one of the strongest underclassmen on the high school varsity football team. When he kicked his bike into high gear, he was soon at the head of the group.

The only one who didn't feel like going quite so fast was Chelsea. Actually, it wasn't so much that she didn't feel like it. . . . It was just that no matter how hard she pushed down on those pedals, it just didn't seem to make her bike go as fast as her teammates'.

By the time she finally caught up to the group, Chelsea's heart was beating like a drum solo. A year ago she might have felt bad that she was last, but now her attitude was, *I'm in the game and that's what counts!* She gave herself an imaginary pat on the back for keeping up.

Still, she suggested to her brother, "Hey, Ben . . . maybe we could slow down a bit. I've passed, like, three things on the bonus point list already. Don't you think it would be a good idea to stop and take a few pictures?" Chelsea gulped.

"Chels, are you crazy? If we slow down now, we'll lose our lead. And that's the one edge we have in this competition!" Avery argued.

"Avery's got a point, kid," Ben agreed. "Just hang in there. It won't be much longer." *Betrayed by my own flesh and blood!* Chelsea couldn't believe it. After what seemed like an eternity, the bike path finally merged with civilization— and there was the adorable little town of Orleans.

"So are we still looking for a yurt alert or not?" a frustrated Kiki asked. She had a valid point. In Chelsea's opinion it was a genius point. The group had biked for miles and they had no idea if they were even headed in the right direction or what they were looking for.

"Hey, dude, I'm aaall the Yurt alert you'll ever need," sang Henry Yurt. He got off his bike and did a weird little Yurt dance around Kiki, who stared at him with a horrified expression on her face. The group cracked up at the antics of their class president and Kiki's reaction to him.

"Let's check out the second clue," suggested Chelsea. "Maybe we'll get somewhere with that one."

Ben nodded. "Good idea, Chels," he conceded, patting her on the back and handing the next envelope over. "You do the honors," he said and bowed to his sister. Chelsea wanted to bonk him over the head. *Ben is so goofy sometimes*, she thought as she opened up the envelope and began to read. "From the Orleans circle round, toward a coastal town you're bound. There is much for you in store at the harbor's rocky shore."

Avery's face lit up. "Hey, you guys! Do you have any idea what this means? Orleans circle . . . coastal town . . . this clue is talking about Nauset Beach in Orleans, and we're practically already there! I love that beach!"

"Are you sure the clue is talking about Nauset Beach, though? Is that the only beach in Orleans?" Chelsea asked.

"Who cares about the other beaches?" Kiki said dismissively. "Nauset Beach is the only cool one. Besides, I know an awesome shortcut. This way we won't have to go through the rotary."

Avery shrugged. "I'm in. Hey, maybe it'll put us in the lead."

Avery and Kiki were off immediately in the direction of Nauset Beach, and the group followed right behind. Chelsea, who had spent a good amount of her life being on the shier side, knew a thing or two about leaders from observing them in action. People tended to do exactly what the leader said or did without even thinking about whether or not the plan made any sense at all. It could be very frustrating.

As she followed her team zipping down the bike path to a destination that might have nothing to do with their scavenger hunt, Chelsea was pretty sure that the Beach Barnacles weren't thinking about the scavenger hunt at all.

Dandelion Dreams

When the Cranberry Boggers finally reached the famous Orleans Rotary mentioned in clue #2, the whole team burst out in cheers. "We have to be doing something right!" Betsy chirped to Danny Pellegrino.

"I agree!" he announced, but then he grabbed his stomach and complained, "I'm starving! When's lunch?"

"It's only ten thirty!" Betsy balked.

Danny shrugged. "I'm too hungry. I need high octane fuel to ride. . . . Give me a cheese . . . burger!

"Eat an apple and a piece of cheese. We have to figure out this clue first!" Betsy commanded as she pedaled over to Fabiana who was guarding the second clue with new resolve. "Look at that sign for Rock Harbor," Betsy directed. "Didn't the clue say something about the harbor's rocky shore? I vote we go that way."

"I vote we take a snack break," Danny piped in again as he popped a cheese chunk in his mouth.

Riley gave him a thumbs-up and agreed, "I'm with you, dude!"

"He's kidding," Betsy persisted. "They're both kidding. What do you think, Isabel?"

Isabel, who wasn't a big fan of being put on the spot, murmured, "I guess that beach sounds like a good idea." Plus, it was really hard to resist Betsy's intimidating attitude.

Maeve, who loved being put on the spot and was disappointed that Betsy *hadn't* consulted her, declared in loud voice, "Well, come on, then! Boggers unite! Fabiana, lead the way! NEVER GIVE UP! NEVER SURRENDER!"

Maeve loved being a cheerleader. It was definitely in her future to be on the squad when she got to high school.

If she could just get Betsy to loosen up a bit and realize Maeve and Isabel were on her side, they might actually stand a chance to win this.

"Yeah, Maeve! Let's go, Boggers!" Riley echoed in a deep singsong voice. As the group took off down the path, he stuck close to Maeve. "I'm really glad Nick switched groups with me," he confided. "Cranberry Boggers is a much cooler name than Salty Cods! I mean, who would want to be a smelly fish?"

"I totally agree!" Maeve's heart thumped in her chest at the way Riley's hair flew back as he pedaled his bike. "I'm glad, um, Nick had the idea to switch groups too. I mean," she whispered conspiratorially, "we performers need to stick together." Then she flashed him her A+ movie-star smile. She was very pleased to see Riley's cheeks flush and his front tire wobble as he turned away.

Halfway to the beach, Isabel hit the brakes on her bike. Betsy had to swerve to stop herself from flying off the path and into a thorny wild rosebush. "You guys, look!" Isabel said in a hushed voice. "I think that bird over there might be a sandpiper. Isn't that one of the items on our bonus list?"

"Excellent, Isabel!" Fabiana cheered, but just as the words escaped her lips, the bird skipped off into the bushes.

"Oh, shoot," an embarrassed Fabiana muttered. "Did I do that?"

"Don't worry about it," Maeve assured her. "Pipers are all over the Cape, and I've seen my brother track 'em a billion times. I'm practically a professional."

Betsy groaned. "A professional piper tracker? Is that

even a real thing? Besides, pipers only hang out on the *beach*, not in the *woods. . . ."

But no one was paying any attention to her. Betsy looked horrified as Isabel, Danny, and Maeve turned their bikes down a little dirt path and took off after the little bird with the Speedy Gonzales stick legs.

Not even Fabiana, the authority figure in the group, felt like barking any sense into the runaway Boggers. Their fearless leader took her Red Sox hat out of her bag, plopped it on her head backward, giggled, and announced, "When in Rome." Then she zoomed off behind the kids, leaving Betsy stunned on the bike path.

"Am I the only sane one here?" she wondered out loud. When no one answered, Betsy reluctantly pushed her bike into the brush.

After fifteen minutes of wandering about, one thing was for sure—that silly little sandpiper was long gone—and *nobody gave a hoot*. Fabiana and Isabel were constructing dandelion crowns, and Maeve, Riley, and Danny were involved in a hard-core game of leapfrog.

"Hey, Betsy, we need another frog!" Maeve called.

Betsy primly shook her head, rattling her long braids. "All that grass is probably *full* of deer ticks! They're really dangerous this time of year and they carry Lyme disease. Those tiny black bugs latch on to your skin, like mosquitoes, only ticks stay there for three to five days! When I was seven I read an article all about it."

Isabel inspected her dandelion crown with horror. *Ticks? Am I putting bugs in my hair?*

"And Lyme disease is super serious. It starts like a fever, but if it gets into your nervous system—"

"Betsy!" Danny interrupted. "You know that as long as we're really careful to check for ticks after, we'll be fine." He sounded like somebody's dad.

"What about those blackberry prickers? You're getting covered with scars playing this ridiculous game!"

Riley glanced at his leg, which was covered in tiny white scratches. "These aren't scars," he noted. "They're battle wounds!" He raised his arm in a cheer.

Maeve gave Riley her brightest smile. "I love a guy who can think positive," she said. Isabel thought Riley looked like he had just been sprinkled with fairy dust.

Fabiana flitted over with a yellow bouquet in her hands that she tenderly bestowed onto Betsy's matted braids. "That supposed sandpiper is long gone," Betsy complained feebly. "Don't you think we should try to find Rock Harbor?"

"Betsy," Fabiana soothed. "Sometimes life isn't about the destination. . . . It's about the journey."

Betsy sighed, "Well, I already know my journey. My journey is to win this hunt and no one here seems to be interested in that!"

Just then her plan was interrupted by the sound of Danny's voice from behind, hollering, "INCOMING!"

Maeve watched, giggling, as Danny Pellegrino whizzed through the air like a flying squirrel, straight at Betsy. She dropped to the ground and curled up, turtle-style, just in time for Danny to bounce off her back and into the air.

"Your turn, Betsy!" Maeve huffed. "Keep the chain going."

"I am not a human trampoline!" Betsy protested.

The group froze for a minute, anticipating that Betsy was going to yell at Danny for leapfrogging her without permission, but instead the oddest thing happened.

Betsy began running, jumped into the air, and pounced on Maeve, then Danny, then Riley, and finished by making a running leap for Isabel who curled up and instantly joined in the game.

As Betsy played she kept one hand securely on the dandelion crown that Fabiana had made for her. Before long, every person had completely forgotten about the sandpiper, the bike path, *and* the scavenger hunt, and they were all lying on their backs in the grass.

All of a sudden Fabiana's stomach began to growl. First it was just a little grumble, and then it grew into a big rumble. Everyone was silent until Fabiana bellowed, "Feed me!" There were cheers all around when Danny Pellegrino took out a package of Oreo cookies, which he and Maeve claimed were the most delicious not-homemade cookies that money could buy.

As they snacked and chugged on their water bottles, the girls took turns inspecting each other's legs and ankles for tiny black ticks. Betsy instructed the boys to do the same. Thankfully, all the Boggers found were twigs, leaves, and specks of dirt. The Boggers were officially tick free.

"Maybe we should head on to Rock Harbor," Betsy suggested. Maeve was surprised to hear a little hesitation in her voice. *I think Betsy was actually having fun procrastinating!* Maeve suddenly felt proud of her group for bringing out the fun side of Betsy Fitzgerald—a side that until today, no one at Abigail Adams Junior High had ever seen.

"Um, guys," Danny started, poised on his bicycle, "do any of you remember which way we came from?"

"Yeah, we definitely came from that way." Betsy pointed to the left.

Fabiana tilted her head. "Not to interfere, kids, but I'm pretty sure we came from that way," she countered, pointing towards the right.

"How sure?" asked Isabel.

"Uh . . . pretty sure . . ." Fabiana raised an eyebrow and held up the yellow wreath in her hand. "Dandelion crown?" she offered one to Maeve.

"Are we lost?" Maeve replied, bending over to examine her reflection in the mirror of her bike. "On the bright side, this flower crown thingy looks faaabulous on me!"

As Fabiana took out the map and puzzled over a solid green splotch near the bike trail to Rock Harbor beach, Isabel held her breath and the boys kicked at the grass.

Betsy looked nauseous. "We definitely came *this* way," she insisted, turning her bike around and pushing it into the weeds.

"Shouldn't we wait for Fabiana to figure out where we are?" Maeve called out,

"That map won't help at all!" Betsy turned around and put one hand on her hip. "I happen to have a very keen sense of direction."

"I think Betsy's right." Danny chipped in. "That tree over there looks familiar."

"Come on," Riley urged Maeve. "We've got a scavenger hunt to win!"

But as they rode farther and farther into the woods, Maeve began to wonder, *Are we ever going to find that bike path?* Isabel looked anxious, and Fabiana concerned. Still, Betsy pushed on, an eager Danny right behind her.

6

The Rock Harbor Patrice Show

Katani pedaled furiously with the rest of the Salty Cods out of Nickerson Park to the Orleans Rotary. She felt herself being pushed, and it wasn't from biking so hard. It was her patience—her patience with Patrice in her role as super coach to the Salty Cods to be exact—that was pushing her to the edge.

"C'mon, guys, is that all you got? Let's pump it!" Patrice cried, "We are the team to beat! Ooh yeah yeah, ooh yeah yeah . . ." Patrice began to mimic Sugar-N-Spice's old-school hit. It took every ounce of strength Katani had to keep up with her excited teammates.

Nick and Dillon were working the pedals like they were in the Tour de France and Lance Armstrong, the greatest speed biker in the world, was coming up fast. They were also chanting, "PUMP IT! PUMP IT! WE ARE THE TEAM TO BEAT."

I can't believe they're actually enjoying this! Katani looked around. *Even Charlotte looks like she is having the time of her life!* Katani stared at her as she pedaled like the energizer bunny. All the Cods were biking so fast there was no time to appreciate the beautiful bike path and views of the ocean.

I was right from the beginning. I shouldn't have come on this ridiculous scavenger/survivor trip, Katani thought. Surely she wasn't the only one who found Patrice's triathlon mentality aggravating. Katani was pretty sure she'd heard Dillon grumbling to Nick that he couldn't believe they'd wandered around the park for a half an hour and didn't even find that "stupid fox." But as they pedaled, the guys were acting like Patrice was the best trip leader ever.

By the time they reached the Orleans Rotary, however, the only one who still seemed to be exerting energy was Patrice. As Katani rolled up, she saw that Dillon's and Nick's faces were bright red, and there was so much sweat on Charlotte's face she looked like she had just stepped out of the shower. Katani could feel her own hair turning into a giant fuzzball.

"All right, then!" Patrice clapped her hands. "Shake it out, group, shake it out. Let's take a quick breather and then push it to Orleans Beach."

Katani pulled at her frizzy ponytail. "I don't know, Patrice," she objected. "The clue says something about the harbor's rocky shore. I think we should check out Rock Harbor."

"I kinda think Katani might be right," seconded Nick.

"Sorry . . ." he mumbled when he saw the disappointment on Patrice's face.

"Yeah, me three," Dillon echoed his friend.

Charlotte's eyes danced between the Summers sisters. As a very observant only child, she knew better than to interfere when there might be a sibling disagreement.

Katani couldn't even celebrate the boys siding with her against her sister because Patrice looked so stricken, like her whole team had let her down. Katani didn't want Patrice to think she was trying to instigate a revolt. She just wanted her sister to SLOW DOWN.

Suddenly, Patrice smiled. "That's cool." Then she asked in a super mellow voice, "You guys ever been to Orleans Beach before?"

Nick and Dillon and Charlotte looked at one another sheepishly and shook their heads no.

"Oh, really? So then maybe you don't know what it looks like. . . . Do you?" Patrice asked innocently.

"Uh, no, but if the clue says rocky shore . . ." a suddenly unsure Nick tried to defend the team's choice.

"No, it's totally cool," Patrice replied, her smile growing wider, into—in Katani's expert opinion—a smile that meant: *I know something that you don't.*

"I just thought you guys were too smart to fall for the oldest trick in the book. Why would the clue just tell you exactly where to go? Haven't you heard the expression 'if something sounds too good to be true then it probably is'?"

Dillon smacked his head and turned to Nick and

nodded. "Ohhh, dude. I forgot about that one!"

Charlotte and Nick looked at each other like they were a pair of kindergarteners who'd just spelled cat with a *k*.

"Patrice has that effect on people," Katani mumbled under her breath. Charlotte chewed on her lip.

Patrice stood in front of her team with her arms folded. "Well, I happen to know for a fact that Orleans Beach has a very rocky section."

Nick shrugged. "Cool. I mean . . . whatever. What do you think Char . . . Katani?"

Charlotte looked at Katani with a tentative expression that read *What am I supposed to do now?* Char said quietly, "Well, I guess we better follow the leader."

Katani opened her mouth to object, but Patrice spoke too quickly. "Sweetness! Let's go, team!" She hopped on her bike and began to zip away. Charlotte, Nick, and Dillon leaped on their bikes and zoomed after her with seemingly renewed energy.

Katani followed right after them but soon discovered that her gearshift was stuck in low gear, making it almost impossible to pedal with any speed. As the Salty Cods sped up, Katani cried out, "Patrice, STOP! My gears . . ."

Patrice looked over her shoulder and, seeing her sister struggling with her bike, circled back to her. "Kgirl, would you take a chill pill?" But then her volume dropped and she added, "You can do this, little sis. Just hang on. It looks like there's a gas station ahead."

"Okay." Katani sniffed. She felt better that her sister at

least recognized that she wasn't trying to be a poor sport or anything.

But then Patrice ruined the moment by adding, "Just don't be a crybaby."

"You big . . ." Katani pedaled faster, unable to think of anything to quash her annoying big sister.

"Big *what*?" teased Patrice with a wicked twinkle in her eye.

"Big . . ." Katani could feel the anger bubbling up inside of her like hot magma, and she bit her tongue to stop the mean words from spewing out. "You know what? Never mind. You know what you're being and I'm not going to say it because you would just tell Mom later and get me in trouble." Katani concluded, "SO THERE!"

"Oh, *that* was mature," scoffed Patrice.

"Just shut—" Katani began.

"Shut what?"

Katani put her head down and pedaled like there was no tomorrow.

"No, tell me. I'm sure Nick, Charlotte, and Dillon are curious. Right, guys?" Patrice turned to the rest of the Cods who had pulled up in front of the gas station.

Charlotte wished Mr. Moore were around to put a stop to the sister insanity. Though she was usually way jealous of her friends with siblings, today was *not* one of those times.

The funny thing was that Patrice didn't seem to be bothered at all by her tiff with her sister. Charlotte wondered if she was just being an oversensitive only child.

Nick and Dillon seemed okay, and now that Patrice was helping Katani walk her bike to the garage mechanic, Katani seemed fine too. Charlotte sighed. She would never understand the whole sibling thing.

Suddenly, she had a great idea and ran over to Patrice.

"Hey, Patrice, maybe we should talk to some locals and see which place is rockier," Charlotte suggested.

Patrice looked at Charlotte like she'd just invented the cure for the hiccups. "Why, Charlotte Ramsey, no wonder they say you're so smart," she complimented her.

Charlotte beamed. "Thanks . . ."

As Patrice walked into the gas station convenience store to ask about where the rockiest shore was, Katani asked, "Charlotte, are you siding with Patrice over me?" Katani heard her voice crack and prayed that tears would not follow.

"No way, Katani, I would never do that! But I do think that you and Patrice are getting on each other's nerves and it's not all that fun for the rest of us," Charlotte confessed.

"Yeah, me too!" Nick said. "You two need to calm down."

"*I* need to calm down?" Katani balked. "But she's the one—"

"I'm hungry," Dillon interrupted, turning to Charlotte and Nick. "You guys want to eat lunch down at Rock Harbor? That looks like a sandwich shop right over there by the beach," he said, pointing. "We can get some cold drinks."

Charlotte felt a wave of relief wash over her. "That sounds like the most brilliant plan of the day!" Charlotte pronounced.

"Wordage," Nick agreed.

"We'll meet you at the shore!" Charlotte called out as the three of them took off on their bikes, leaving Katani and Patrice, who had just walked up, confused. The sisters watched as Charlotte, Nick, and Dillon laughed their way down to the harbor.

"The locals say *both* beaches are rocky. I doubt we'll find anything down there, but whatever." Patrice shrugged at Katani and hopped on her bike. Katani followed, testing her newly adjusted gears. They seemed to work just fine now, but somehow, it didn't make her feel any better.

Finally Patrice muttered, "Are you gonna sulk all day?"

Katani ignored her sister.

"Oh, I get it. You're doing the whole silent-treatment thaaang. That is *so* cute!"

Katani was not doing the silent treatment thing, she was doing the ignoring thing. As Patrice blathered on and on about absolutely nothing, Katani did her best to pretend she was totally alone. She knew Patrice was trying to be friendly, but Katani needed time to chill out before she could deal with her sister and her win-at-all-costs attitude.

As they rode down toward the beach, Katani noticed that Charlotte and Dillon were shouting on the boulders ahead—shouting and jumping up and down. She felt a rush of panic in her throat hoping that no one was hurt. In spite of her annoyance with her sister, she stole a glance at Patrice, whose eyes also were also filled with worry.

"Where's Nick?" asked Patrice. She hopped off her bike and ran, her long legs moving at the super speed she usually reserved for sprinting on the track field. Katani followed quickly behind her.

When they reached the top of the stony hill Charlotte jogged over and gave her hand a friendly squeeze. "We found it! Clue number two!" Charlotte beamed triumphantly and read the clue again for everybody. "'From the Orleans circle round, toward a coastal town you're bound. There is much for you in store at the harbor's rocky shore.'"

"It *is* Rock Harbor," Patrice said. "Which means . . ."

"I was right," Katani couldn't help smiling.

"Good job, Sis," Patrice admitted. "Sometimes I let the power go to my head a bit," she joked.

"Ya think?" Katani shook her head.

Charlotte leaned in and added to Katani in a whisper, "Family trait?"

Katani grinned sheepishly. "Yeah, yeah, I know. Sorry I snapped at you before."

Charlotte shook her head and gave her friend a forgiving smile. "Water under the bridge. The Salty Cods are on fire! I vote we charge ahead and try to get some bonus items while we're on this beach."

"Agreed!" cheered Nick and Dillon.

"On one condition," Katani added. "Please, can everyone not *ever* say 'pump it' again?"

"No problem," the rest of the group shouted cheerfully.

She placed her arm in the center of their circle. "Everybody in!" she ordered, and the rest of the Salty Cods followed. "1 . . . 2 . . . 3 . . . WIN!" they yelled.

Katani's face brightened. She loved winning way more than fighting with Patrice, and that word coming from her friends' mouths sounded like the most glorious thing she'd heard all day.

"I'm starving!" Dillon suddenly announced. "Who's ready for some grub?"

Actually, *that* was the most glorious thing Katani had heard all day.

What Bog Are We In?

Normally, Maeve wouldn't have minded being lost in the woods. Pretending that she was a lost princess waiting for a fabulous prince driving an all-terrain vehicle to her would be sooo fun. In fact, "let's pretend" was #1 on Maeve's list of favorite things to do. There was that time just a month before when she and Sam got lost in the grocery store and pretended they were space aliens from Planet Pickle-sausage who could survive only on the human super power fuel foods of chicken sausage and dill pickles.

Of course, that little fantasy had only lasted for ten minutes, until their mother found them and demanded that they replace the six jars of pickles and four packages of sausages that they were toting around with them. The problem was that this time, in these woods, the person in charge was also lost!

And Betsy's insistence that they were heading in the right direction when they were so obviously not was making Maeve too nervous to get her fantasy groove on. Instead, she chewed on her finger as she watched Fabiana trying to keep her cool.

Unfortunately, Fabiana kept scrunching her eyebrows together and checking her cell phone every two seconds — which was a dead giveaway that they were totally lost. Even Betsy finally stopped talking and looked at Fabiana, who said feebly, "Maybe we should turn around."

What if we never find our way back to society again? Maeve wondered. Maybe they would have to learn how to make houses out of leaves and tree branches, eat berries and squirrel meat, and start their own society. Maeve shuddered to think of the awfulness of it all.

When the Boggers had been wandering around the woods for more than an hour, Maeve had to tell herself to stop thinking that any moment a space ship would land and they would all be taken off to another planet where people had big huge bug eyes and collected human beings to keep in hamster cages. Her one consolation was that at least Riley would be with her, and they could hold hands and sing their troubles away.

"Isabel," she whispered. "Doesn't it seem weird that in a place as tiny as Cape Cod we can't find any signs of intelligent life around?"

"I was just thinking the same thing," said Isabel as she clutched her friend's hand. "I mean, what if we've like stumbled through one of those portals into another time period, you know, like those kids in *A Wrinkle in Time*?"

Suddenly, out of nowhere, a voice boomed in the distance, "Arg, avast me buckos!"

Everyone froze—just like in the statue game. Riley looked like he was drumming. Betsy had her arms crossed like a stern first-grade teacher, and Fabiana looked very perplexed, with her head cocked to one side.

Maeve would have giggled if a horrified Isabel, her brown eyes wide with fear, hadn't said in a trembly voice, "What was that?" *Poor Izzy.* Maeve knew her friend hated anything scary. She reached over, grabbed her hand, and squeezed it gently.

"It sounded like pirates—real ones," said Danny in a high-pitched voice.

Betsy nodded. "In pirate lingo that sentence translates to: 'Who goes there, mates?' He sounds angry."

Riley and Maeve looked at Betsy, who turned to look at Fabiana, who for some strange reason didn't seem nervous at all. *Is that a good sign,* Maeve wondered, *or has Fabiana already been taken over by the alien pirates?*

Finally, Riley asked "Where *are* we?"

Betsy's face turned white. "The path should be right ahead. . . ."

"Betsy!" Maeve exclaimed. "There is no path. The bug-eyed aliens are going to come join forces with the pirates, and the prince will never make it out of the swamp. . . . Oh," she wailed, grabbing her hair, "why, why didn't we follow that map?"

"Are you okay, Maeve?" Riley looked worried.

For once, Betsy had nothing to say. She just hung her head, and shoved a couple of twigs around with her foot.

Fabiana ran ahead and turned around. "Please tell me someone else can see that."

Isabel crept up to join her and gasped. "It's a . . . a . . . *village*! And is that a—"

"Pirate ship?" Fabiana finished and exhaled deeply. "Yes! Thank goodness. I thought I was losing my mind."

"Thank goodness?" Isabel squawked. "No, no, no, *not* thank goodness. A pirate ship is a bad, bad, very bad thing."

Maeve agreed and began to feel a little dizzy. Before them, in the clearing, was a village full of pirates and women in shabby gowns, carrying buckets of water. There was even a cow walking down the street.

"They look like real people," Danny said matter-of-factly.

"And that's where they live," Isabel whispered, pointing to the tiny little thatched houses and huge, colorful Native American tepees surrounding an enormous, very old-looking pirate ship. Men in raggedy britches were hoisting sails and shouting "Arrgh!" and "Shiver me timbers!" at each other, and the women, looking angry and feisty, were carrying trays of silver mugs overflowing with frothy liquid.

So this isn't just my imagination, Maeve thought. They really had stumbled into another century, maybe even another dimension. *Could we actually be in Neverland?*

"Oh, no," groaned Isabel. "That man over there just saw me. Should we run?"

Fabiana touched Maeve and Isabel on the shoulder and motioned for the Cranberry Boggers to stand still and be quiet. Just as Maeve was wondering if Fabiana would be able to protect them, she heard a voice yell, "CUT!"

7

Real Pirates Don't Wear Makeup

With mouths agape, the Cranberry Boggers watched as the villagers stopped what they were doing and began acting normal. The pirates stopped talking like pirates, and, from out of nowhere, regular-looking people appeared, handing them coffee and water bottles.

"Oh, wow!" Riley exclaimed. "It's a real movie set." He turned to Maeve and grinned. "We have just landed on Planet Pirate Movie!"

Duh! How could I, with all my professional actor experience, have missed something so obvious? Maeve thought, looking up at the bright lights and wires hanging from the trees and the gigantic cameras lurking behind the houses.

Me and my imagination . . . , she scolded herself as she clasped her hands together in delight. After all, a movie set was way more fun than a lost princess trying to battle aliens while time traveling to some weird galaxy.

All of a sudden Maeve heard footsteps, but before she could turn around, a shadow fell over Isabel. Maeve had never before seen her friend jump so high!

"Who's there?" Izzy yelped, and, feeling shaken, turned to see a scowling woman wearing moon-shaped sunglasses and a backward baseball cap.

"Where have you kids been? Call time was over an hour ago." She glanced at her watch and sighed. "Oh, well. I'm Bethany, the costume director. Come with me. Hair and makeup are waiting."

"I think there's been some mistake," a calm and in-charge Betsy began to explain. "We aren't with the movie. We're just on a field trip and we got a little lost in these woods." Maeve knew that honesty was the best policy, but would it have killed Betsy to keep quiet just this one time?

The woman in sunglasses frowned. "Bummer. Ozmond is going to flip! How am I ever going to find replacements for extras at the last minute?" she sighed and walked away, slapping her hands against her legs in frustration.

Maeve's heart was thumping. "Wait!" she called out.

Bethany frowned and peered over the top of her glasses. "Look, I'm very busy here, in case you haven't noticed."

"We could be your extras," Maeve blurted.

Bethany turned around. "Hmm . . . you are the right age. . . . We needed more boys, but with the right costumes . . . We'll just need to get you some release forms," Bethany said, as her expression changed from *My life is quite possibly over* to *Things are definitely looking up*.

"Maeve, have you forgotten? We have clues to solve and we should be getting back to the bike path. . . ." Betsy scolded. "Besides, who's going to sign our release forms?"

"*Dude!*" Fabiana whispered to Betsy. "This is a once-in-a-lifetime opportunity!"

Betsy looked skeptical. "But—"

"We can take a break for a little while to *be in a movie!*" Fabiana assured her. Then she chimed to Bethany, "We'd be happy to fill in. In fact, I have signed photo and film-release forms right here!"

Bethany scanned the papers and nodded briskly. "Great! Everything seems to be in order."

Fabiana to the rescue, thought a grateful Maeve.

"After losing that map, I made extra sure to keep track of the envelope with all the papers," Fabiana whispered to Maeve. "Lucky for us I did!"

Fabiana, who had played a starring role in the high school musical *West Side Story*, looked as eager as Maeve to be part of a real live movie. The other Cranberry Boggers' heads bobbed up and down enthusiastically. Being in a movie was something to tell their friends and family. The scavenger hunt was completely forgotten. "Follow me," Bethany instructed, and marched toward the chaos.

A chorus of yays and woo-hoos erupted from everyone in the group. Except Betsy.

"What time period is this supposed to be?" she asked in a vintage Betsy *something doesn't look right* tone.

"1717," replied Bethany. "This movie's about Black Sam Bellamy and the *Whydah*."

Betsy put her hands on her hip and stared at Bethany in disbelief. "Has anyone here ever read a history book?" Betsy's eyebrows were furrowed in annoyance.

As the Boggers followed Bethany to a nearby trailer, Maeve chatted up a storm, hoping to distract Bethany from Betsy's comments.

"This isn't my first movie, Bethany. Last winter I was in an original remake of *Roman Holiday*, you know, the classic Audrey Hepburn movie? . . . It was called *Boston Holiday*. Isn't that cute?" Maeve scrambled to keep up with the determined girl who marched forward like a U.S. marine.

"Anyhoo," Maeve went on . . . and on. "I wasn't the lead, even though the director wanted me to be . . . long story . . . it was a political thing, my dad said. You know how it is. I did play the supporting female lead, a charming little character called Nanny Nuna. Critics—mostly my mom and friends—said it was the most exciting portrayal of a kung-fu fighting nanny—"

Maeve stopped in mid-sentence. Two men in full pirate gear, surrounded by techies in black T-shirts, had passed behind the costume trailer. The pirates' faces were shaded by huge feathered hats. Maeve strained her neck to see . . . a familiar nose? She put her hand to her heart. *No, it just can't be. Not here on little old Cape Cod!* She would have heard about it . . . wouldn't she? After all Maeve Kaplan-Taylor was an official member of his fan club. *Somebody surely would have contacted me!*

"Sooo," Bethany said vaguely, completely ignoring Maeve's starstruck look. "Costumes are in here. See Corrine; she'll suit you up. Once you're dressed, go to that trailer for hair and makeup. And hurry, please . . . we don't have much time . . . and thanks for doing this, kids. Ozmond, he's the director, would have had a serious meltdown if I hadn't found you little lost-in-the-woods lambs!"

"No prob, Bethany!" Fabiana replied, leading the way into the trailer. Suddenly, the girl who couldn't find her map was in her element and in charge. Fabiana introduced herself to the costumer and directed the Boggers to line up. "Come on, guys. Chop, chop. These people have a movie to make."

"Ozmond?" Isabel snickered to Maeve. "That's such a weird name. Do you think he's as weird as his name? Maeve . . . what's wrong?"

"Oh, nothing, I just thought . . ."

Maeve was off in her own little world, which Isabel couldn't understand because they were standing right in the middle of the dreamiest trailer. Costumes were everywhere. They were practically hanging from the ceiling. The effect was dazzling.

Isabel's artist heart was enchanted by the racks of colorful silky dresses, rows of leather boots, slippers with ribbons, and boxes full of bonnets and felt pirate hats with big feathers. She wished she could paint the mix of colors and strange objects. And she especially wished Katani was here. The two of them would have a BSG blast creating outfits.

Corrine, the costumer, was a pale girl with choppy bright blue hair, and looked right at home among the wild outfits. She smacked her bubble gum noisily and tapped her foot as she scanned the Cranberry Boggers.

"You! Scullery maid," she barked, dumping a maroon and brown folded pile into Isabel's arms. "You, kitchen wench." She handed Fabiana some green and brown fabric and examined Danny and Riley.

"Just so you know, I was in my camp play *The Man Who Came to Dinner*," Danny shared proudly. "I played THE MAN."

"Awesome," Corrine responded dryly. "Now you'll be the cabin boy." She turned to Riley. "And powder monkey," she pronounced.

"Cool!" breathed Riley. "I guess once a monkey, always a monkey, right?"

"You're the coolest mustard monkey I know," exclaimed Maeve. Riley's band, the Mustard Monkeys, was his pride and joy, so he gave her a high five.

Corrine tilted her head at Maeve and Betsy.

Betsy prodded Maeve in the back. She blinked and gave Corrine her camera-ready smile. If Maeve got a starring role, she *might* get to meet those two pirates face to face! And if one of them was who she thought he was—well, life would be beyond perfect. But first things first.

"So Corinne," she informed the costume mistress, "my best colors are magenta, light magenta, hot magenta, and French rose. Red hair, you know the deal. If there's maybe a princess part . . . or some kind of Tinker Bell fairy-ish role . . ." Maeve raised her eyebrows hopefully. "I do a *great* fairy princess."

Corrine loudly snapped her gum. "Well, today you'll be cleaning the poop deck as a *great* cabin boy."

"The poop deck?" Maeve's face turned green.

Danny leaned over and explained, "The poop deck is a small deck that's also the roof of a cabin near the back of the ship."

Corinne ignored him and nodded at Betsy. "You too, cabin boy." The rest of the Boggers snickered as Corrine placed a pile of dirt-colored clothing into Maeve's once hopeful arms and handed an identical costume to Betsy.

Maeve raised her eyebrows. "I'm sorry, it sounded like you said 'boy'. . . ."

Corrine nodded. "I did."

"Well, that won't work. See, I'm a girl." Maeve held up a long, curly strand of hair to prove her point.

"No problem. That's what these are for." Corrine held up two short-haired brown wigs.

Maeve gulped. Brown was so not her color!

"You see," Corrine continued, "We asked for two female extras and the rest were boys. I'm sorry, but I'm fresh outta girl parts."

"That's okay," said Betsy in a haughty voice. She placed the costume on a chair. "I have three things to say. A. I am not an actress. While I regard the craft of theater as a noble talent, I myself am more invested, first and foremost, in academics. B. I would never *dream* of participating in a historical reenactment that peddled such—such well, let's face it, historical inaccuracy." She paused to take a breath.

"Honestly, there are tepees out there, tepees! And frankly, Corrine, anyone with half a brain KNOWS that the Native Americans in Massachusetts and Rhode Island were Wampanoags, and they didn't live in tepees, they lived in *wetus*."

Betsy sighed and tossed a braid behind her shoulder. "And C. Corrine . . . I *don't* do wigs. Gosh, haven't you people ever heard of head lice?"

The rest of the Cranberry Boggers' mouths dropped open. Even Maeve had to admit, it was a pretty impressive performance. She was about to jump in and explain away Betsy's unique world view, when Isabel interrupted.

"Me too. I mean, not me too for the same reasons, even though, Betsy, your reasons were very, very good ones. . . ." Isabel bit her lip and put the dress costume on top of Betsy's. "I just, I'm really, um, not big on . . . you know, acting or being filmed. I want to be an artist someday." Isabel let out a *whoosh* like she had been holding her breath the whole time. Maeve felt for her. Isabel hated to make speeches in public.

Her hand shot up. MKT would save her friend from the horrors of being an actress. "I can take her place!" she volunteered and ran over to Isabel, dramatically clasping a grinning Isabel's hand. "I will be the scullery maid that you . . . could not. I will make you proud."

"Oh boy, aren't you something!" Corrine tossed the maroon dress at Maeve, who clutched it to her like a brides-maid cradling the bouquet. "Okay, girls, you change here.

Boys, go to the trailer to the left labeled—big shocker—MEN. I need you in hair and makeup in five. You two"—she pointed at Betsy and Isabel—"come with me."

"That means five minutes," Maeve explained as Corrine, Betsy, the boys, and one very relieved Isabel hustled out of the trailer.

Maeve and Fabiana were both in love with their costumes, which had glorious white puffy sleeves, tight waists, aprons, and long, flowing skirts complete with fake rips and patches.

"It's called *distressed fabric,*" explained Fabiana.

"I'm kind of worried," Maeve confessed, tying a dark blue bandana around her red curls. "What if Betsy and her hysterically correct speech about this movie gets us all in trouble?" she asked.

Fabiana burst out laughing. "The word's *historically,* Maeve!"

"Whatever," Maeve said as she twirled around to see how far out her skirt would spin. "The point is that Betsy was kind of obnoxious—the movie crew people might not like that."

"It'll be fine." Fabiana assured Maeve. "Drama types love take-charge people. It makes it easier for them to concentrate on their craft."

Maeve pondered that wisdom for a second.

"Well, okay, "she said, "But personally I think that Corrine girl was kinda snobby, don't you?" Maeve asked confidentially as she looked around to make sure no one was listening.

Fabiana agreed. "Well, she sure wasn't what I'd call Miss Congeniality, but I still think that people who really care about what they do appreciate some honest feedback. And Betsy definitely shot her some of that!"

"You know, Fabiana, when you lost that map I thought maybe we were in trouble, but you really are a very sensible girl." "Sensible" was the word Maeve's mother used whenever she was complimenting someone. So why wasn't Fabiana beaming? "Did I say something bad?" Maeve hated hurting people's feelings more than anything.

"No, it's just . . . well, I felt bad about that map," Fabiana confessed as she looked over at the clock. "We'd better get over to hair and makeup." At that both girls burst into giggles. Hair and makeup and a real movie set! Maeve and Fabiana were in heaven.

When she and Fabiana arrived at the hair and makeup trailer they found a very distressed Riley and a displeased Danny, both of whom were surrounded by lipsticks and brushes and jars of potions and lotions. Corrine was practically on her knees pleading. "Come on, guys. It will only take one minute," she said.

"No makeup." Riley shook his head.

"Dude, no one will even be able to *see* it," Fabiana assured him, catching on to the problem. "Trust me, I hate wearing makeup too. But when you're under those bright lights, if you don't have makeup you look like a sickly ghost."

"*Real* pirates don't wear makeup." Danny jumped up. "Shiver me timbers, ye swabbies!" Danny brandished his arm about like it was a sword.

Maeve, who had no problem with makeup, jumped right into a whirly chair and sang, "Time to put my face on!" as a brown-haired girl swooped in with a soft puff filled with sparkling powder and gracefully fluffed Maeve's cheeks. "See, Riley!" Maeve explained, "It's fun! You'll feel like a real movie star. . . . I promise."

"Well, technically you are!" The brown-haired girl smiled. Maeve liked this girl a lot more than that grouchy blue-haired Corrine.

"So . . ." Maeve asked as the girl brushed her hair back, "who are the other real stars in this movie? I mean, the story of the *Whydah* totally deserves Hollywood's top talent!"

"There's Lindstrom . . ." Corrine started.

"Lola Lindstrom!" Maeve nearly fell out of her chair, and Fabiana let out a strange, high-pitched whine.

"Lola Lindstrom," Corrine repeated in a singsong voice. "Let me give you all a heads-up. That girl is mean as a snake and my advice is to stay away from her. . . . I mean it," she cautioned when she saw Maeve's disbelieving face. Lola was one of Maeve's favorite actresses and she didn't believe for one second what Corrine the iceberg was saying.

Zoe (that was the brown-haired girl's name) took advantage of the moment to smear creamy tanned makeup and fake dirt smudges all over Riley's face, which launched starstruck Maeve into a fit of nervous laughter.

"At least it's makeup *dirt*," he mumbled. "Dirt is okay."

"Don't you get all wacky over Lola, girls," Corrine warned. "She's not even supposed to be shooting until the wedding scene tomorrow."

A Nack-Crow-Nizzem

Isabel shifted back and forth nervously in front of the head of set design, a young man named Patrick, and his assistant, a curly-headed mop top named Poppy. Corrine had kindly dropped off Isabel with them, but hustled away without a word of explanation or an introduction. The two designers were staring at Isabel with expectant expressions on their faces.

A very embarrassed Isabel tried to explain. "Um, I'm Isabel and I thought I could just, well, watch what you do on the set," she said quietly. "I'm really into art and design and my friends are going to be extras . . . and I can't act . . . and, well, I have a passion for color. . . ." Isabel's voice trailed off. She hoped these two "movie types" didn't think she was a total geek.

"We could use an extra hand today," Poppy said coolly. "Couldn't we, Patrick?"

"Sure. We'll show you around," a nonchalant Patrick said as if it was no big deal to have some strange twelve-year-old involved in his work.

And soon, instead of sitting in a corner just watching the action, Isabel found herself wandering around a real live movie set, helping touch up the thatched roofs and walls in the village. Patrick even taught her how to turn on a set light—with his help, of course—and how to adjust the brightness as the clouds and sun changed. She couldn't wait to tell her mother and sister about her lucky day.

"I used to be a lot like you," Patrick confessed to Isabel as they poured some paint to fill in a crease in the Styrofoam of a wall Black Sam was supposed to burst through.

"Really? You liked art classes too?" she asked.

Patrick chuckled. "Um, no, I was one of those AV geeks. Totally into filming and video editing. But then I majored in film in college and took a lot of classes on set design. Poppy here was the art nerd."

"That's right, Isabel. My clothes were covered with splotches of paint every day." He shrugged, and held out one arm. It was already covered with yellow blotches and they'd been painting for only five minutes!

"Me too!" Isabel exclaimed, showing off her own splattered sleeves. Then she took a good look around and observed, "Well, this set looks pretty cool to me."

Patrick squinted and chewed the end of his pencil. "Eh, there are a couple of elements we need to tweak. Apparently your pal Betsy over there is consulting with the director now on how we can eliminate some of the anachronisms."

"What's a Nack-Crow-Nizzem?" asked Isabel, who, as a hard-core bird lover, would have noticed if there was a crow called a Nizzem flying around.

Patrick smiled. "Anachronism . . . um, something that is out of place for a time period. It would be like if there were a movie about Paul Revere and if instead of riding a horse and shouting 'The British are coming,' he rode a red convertible and just sent an e-mail."

Isabel clapped her hands. "I get it!" She made a note to tell Charlotte, who adored fancy words, about that one later. She was also busy making great use of her time with Patrick and Poppy to scratch a few items off the bonus list. She managed to take a picture of a little prop fox in the long grass, and finding something pirate-themed was a piece of cake.

As she snapped a picture of an abandoned pirate hat and cutlass lying in the grass, her friends came running over to show off their costumes. Isabel captured all the ridiculousness with the Cranberry Boggers' team camera. Lastly, Betsy sauntered over looking extremely pleased with herself.

"See that?" She pointed at a bunch of crewmembers breaking down a tepee. "And that?" She gestured to a group of actors getting their long pants hemmed into shorter britches. "All me! Ozmond is thrilled." She waved to an older man in a pair of bright red golfing pants and a white suit jacket who was presiding over the hemming of the pants and waving a notebook around.

"Ozmond told me to check and see if there are any other things on the set that don't make sense for this period in history," Betsy proudly shared with everyone.

"They're called anachronisms," Danny added. Isabel squared her shoulders, happy to have known that. "That's so cool, Betsy!" Danny went on.

Betsy seemed shocked by his response. "Really?"

He nodded enthusiastically. "I wish I got to be a consultant." His voice turned into a hush when he added, "But after that awesome speech you gave, you totally deserve the job!" The corners of Betsy's mouth turned up a bit as she basked in Danny's admiration.

"PLACES!" shouted Ozmond, and the entire notebook went flying out of his hands. A panicked assistant lunged for it, landing face-first in the dust just inches from the Styrofoam wall Isabel and the set designers had just fixed up. The wall quivered slightly as the assistant raised up the rescued notebook.

Ozmond barely seemed to notice. "Cameras roll in five!" He instructed in some kind of weird fakey British accent.

"Oooh! Here we go!" squealed Maeve, and with that the Cranberry Boggers-turned-extras scampered off to their places on the set.

"Ozmond's such a wonderful director." Betsy sighed and then looked around to see if anyone important was listening. "He has a minuscule budget on this film, you know. That's why he needs extra help on the set," she whispered conspiratorially to Isabel.

Betsy carried the notebook over to Ozmond, and placed it back in his hand. "Betsy Fitzgerald rides again," Isabel whispered.

8

Why Wookiees Can't Surf

With the sun streaming down on their backs, the Beach Barnacles raced down the bike path. By the time they reached Nauset Beach, they were hot, sweaty, and totally wiped out. But Team Barnacle's mood lifted considerably when they saw the sparkling blue ocean stretched out across the horizon before them. To Avery the blue water dotted with sailboats looked like the most inviting thing she'd ever seen . . . or at least the most inviting thing she had seen today.

"Check out the surfers!" she gushed, staring at the kids gracefully riding the waves down below. "Ooh! I would give my right foot to get on a surfboard right now!"

"Ha!" laughed Yurt. "Without your right foot, you wouldn't get very far."

Avery smiled. "Come on, Yurt. It's me! I can do *anything*. . . . One foot, two foot, red foot, blue foot . . ."

"Betcha can't beat me to the water!" Yurt challenged his feisty friend.

"You are on, dude," Avery retorted as she and Yurt sent up a sandstorm blasting off to the waves, Road Runner–style.

"My dermatologist says salt water isn't good for my complexion," announced Kiki. "I'm going to go work on my tan." She swished off to find a clear spot to lie down on the sand. A grinning Yurt decided to give Avery the race and follow Kiki instead.

"I'm pretty sure she has that skin stuff backward," Chelsea confided to Ben.

"When she's forty, that girl's gonna look like an alligator!" Ben agreed as he slathered on some suntan lotion. "Me, I love salt water. I dig it. I can't get enough, in fact. Ready, Chels?"

He began to run in the direction of the ocean, but stopped when Chelsea shouted, "BEN, WAIT!"

"What? This sand's *hot*, Sis," he grumbled as he jumped from foot to foot.

Chelsea laughed but her voice was full of urgency. "Ben, it's like, one o'clock already. Don't you think you're forgetting something?"

Ben stared into her face, looking puzzled, then he burst into a smile. "Oh, duh! The reason why I was so excited about coming to this beach in the first place. Blue slush!"

"Ben." She stamped her foot. "That's not what I meant."

But her brother was off and running to the snack bar. Left alone on the dune, Chelsea shook her head, convinced that her brother was a 12-year-old boy dressed up in a high school suit.

The Beach Barnacles are turning into scavenger hunt disasters! Chelsea felt like pitching a fit as she watched all her team members take off down the beach. The adventure that she, Charlotte, and Nick had worked so hard to prepare was spinning out of control. *Am I the only one on this team who even cares about winning this scavenger hunt?* she asked herself as she continued to huff down the beach.

The worst part was that not only was the hunt falling apart, everyone on her team was wearing a bathing suit underneath their clothes—except her, of course. Even though she had lost weight and worked really hard on getting into better shape, Chelsea still hated bathing suits. She just couldn't help feeling like a whale in a tutu even though Katani had taken her shopping and helped her pick out a flattering green suit with shorts.

When she tried it on, Katani had exclaimed, "Chelsea—you look so . . . athletic!" Chelsea almost hugged the Queen of Style for that comment. But today she didn't feel like wearing a bathing suit at all, especially with Kiki Underwood sitting around catching rays in the most stylin' two-piece suit she'd ever seen. *Grrr!*

Surf Bunnies and Barnacle Blues

Oh, yes! Avery was in luck and impressed. The East Coast surfers were catching some super rad waves. The coolest surfer was this one blond girl wearing a blue wet suit. Not only did Miss Blue Crush totally dominate those waves—she made it look easy! "Hey, you!" the girl called, running out of the tide. "You got a board?"

"I don't have it with me," Avery said. "I'm on a school trip, but I love to surf . . . and skateboard . . . and snowboard." She counted on her fingers.

"You're on a school trip to the beach and you are mad for boards? That's too cool." The girl grinned, offering up a high five. Then she introduced herself.

"I'm September . . . and I like your style." September was a bit taller than Avery, but definitely short for her age—just like Avery was.

"Sweeet name!" Avery gave the surfer a thumbs-up.

"Thanks," laughed September. "I like it too. September's my favorite month . . . and my birthday month."

"I love September too!" Avery agreed. "It's when soccer season starts."

"Down here the water can still be warm in September, all the tourists have left, and we own the beach. Plus, September on the Cape—well, it has super gnarly surfing conditions." The girl clutched her board and looked away dreamily as if it was September right now and she had just caught the perfect wave.

Then September said the magic words, "You want to borrow a board? I mean, the water's kind of icy today, but I don't mind. Plus I try to spend as much time as possible *above* the water—not in it . . . if you know what I mean. Not like Chewie over there."

She cupped her hands around her mouth and shouted, "Hey, Chew! It's a surfboard, not a diving board, buddy."

"His name's Chewie?" asked Avery as she tried to control her excitement. "Do I want to borrow a board? . . . Oh, yeah!" She started digging her foot in the sand to keep from jumping in the air.

"Well, Chewie's real name is Aaron Feldman but we call him Chewbacca 'cause he looks like a big Wookiee."

As Chewie bobbed up from the water, Avery almost burst out laughing. He had the biggest, craziest fuzzball hair Avery had ever seen . . . even worse than Henry Yurt's. He really did look like a Wookiee! "Oh, I get it. And what's *your* real name?" she asked.

September gave her a weird look and replied, "September."

Chewie, the Wookiee, ran in, covered in sand and seaweed, clutching his board. "That was mad harsh, dude." He held up his hand and the two slapped a high five.

"Hey, Wooks! What's up, fool?" September greeted him. "This is my new pal Avery. She's gonna be a triple threat."

"Whoa, that's bad!"

"Totally," Avery agreed.

"Don't you just love surfer lingo?" exclaimed September. "I mean, it's so much fun. 'Bad' means 'good,'" she continued. "'Sick' means 'right on.'"

"'Gnarly' means 'awesome,'" the Wookiee piped up.

"The important question is, will you be able to handle

this puppy?" She grabbed the board out of Chewie's hands and tossed it to Avery.

"Is it okay?" Avery glanced at the hairy kid.

Chewie shrugged. "Yeah, man. Go for it."

Avery grabbed the board but it was immediately apparent to everyone that it was way too big for her. Her heart sank. The waves were calling.

"Oh." September made a sad face. Then suddenly she snapped her fingers. "Wook man, go get Snow Bunny's board and wet suit. The Bunny had to go back to work and she's not too much bigger than this munchkin here."

"Dude, you shred brilliance!" With that, the boy with the giant fuzzball took off and ran toward the snack bar.

September turned out to be as awesome a teacher as she was a surfer. Before they even went in the water, she started giving Avery some helpful tips on catching the waves properly. Avery was a little annoyed with September's "short joke," but she hung on to the aloha girl's wave wisdom. Avery could surf, but she wasn't an expert just yet.

"The currents can be weird off this beach," September explained. "You have to catch the wave perfectly or you'll miss it.'"

By the time the Wookiee returned with the board and the wet suit, Avery was practically drooling. The surf was definitely up and the cresting waves were calling her— *Avery, Avery*. When she finished suiting up, she and September raced down to the water with their boards.

"Nauset Beach is famous for its freezing water!"

September shouted as she dove into the waves. "Brace yourself!"

Avery had never surfed on this side of the Cape before. "Yikes!" she yelped as she jumped in. September wasn't kidding about the water—it was like swimming at the North Pole! Her toes felt like they had turned into ice cubes, while her skin that wasn't in the wet suit had morphed into major porcupine mode. But Avery didn't care. In fact, the cold was downright refreshing after her long, hot bike ride.

She and September swam out and treaded water as they waited for the perfect wave. September gave a thumbs-up to the lifeguard who paddled past her. "Hey, Nicky, go save a seal, will you!" she teased. Avery liked this September girl!

"A huge part of this sport is being a great watcher. You need to know the difference between the good waves and the duds. That's Chewie's problem. He always gets way too eager to ride off and he goes for the duds. Then the wave dies and he crashes and burns in front of everyone . . . and I laugh." September winked. "But I'm his best friend."

"Cool." Avery nodded. She was totally into having guys as friends. Hanging out with Dillon and the Trentinis at home was a blast times seven.

"Hey, let's rock this one," Avery pointed toward a big swell coming toward them.

September shook her head. "Not with these currents. You wait. By the time it gets here, it will be nonexistent." Sure enough, the wave peaked just before it got to Avery and September, but it did manage to leave them soaked in its wake.

"Okay, this is our guy," September said, pointing. "See how small it is. Watch!"

As the wave approached, Avery waited for it to get bigger and bigger, but it still looked like a pathetic little thing. "Are you sure, September?"

September smiled. "Are you questioning the master?"

Avery grinned back. "Of course not, Yoda."

September laughed but then her face got very serious. "Can you handle this? It's gonna be a long ride." Avery nodded. September looked over her shoulder and added, "When I say go, paddle like there is no tomorrow, okay?"

Avery was about to say *okay*, when September cried out, "GO!"

Avery used all her arm strength to boost herself onto the board just before the swell hit them. Then the whole thing came together like a jigsaw puzzle. She remembered it all: *balance, position, direction*. The wave wasn't gigantic at all, but it sure was strong. Avery glided down the crest, loving the sensation of speed and power rolled into a thunderous surge of water—it was like the ocean showed up to give her its own personal amusement-park ride.

As they rode, Avery cut back and forth, showing off some of the tricks she had learned with her father. When they surfed all the way into the shore, the kids on the beach offered a ripple of applause. "Whoa, girlfriend, you sure had me going. You're an experienced wave rider!" September exclaimed as they leaped off their boards.

Avery could feel herself glowing. "Thanks! My dad

and brothers and I have been surfing in Hawaii for the past three summers."

"Hawaii?" September exclaimed. "I would just *die* for a chance to surf the big waves!"

"It's gnarly all right, but this surfing today was better than anything I could have imagined. I mean, who knew a little wave like that could give you such a great ride."

"Ah, young Aloha-Jedi, remember," September said, putting her arm around Avery's shoulders. "It's not the size of the wave; it's the motion of the ocean. Never underestimate the small ones."

Avery pointed her thumb at herself. "Trust me. I never do."

"Aloha-Jedi! Groovy surf name, little sister!" The Wookiee came running over to give Avery a high five.

"Wanna do it again?" asked September.

Avery nodded eagerly. She could surf all day! *But where were the rest of the Barnacles?* When she looked around, Ben Briggs and Yurt were having a blast splashing around on the shore. They didn't even see her totally rocking the surfboard. That was okay by her. After catching such an awesome wave, Avery felt like the only person in the world . . . or the ocean, for that matter.

She and September grabbed a few more waves with the Wookman, and Avery didn't even realize that she'd been surfing for an hour until she came up on shore to hear Chelsea yelling at Ben, "This is crazy. The day is flying by and we haven't gotten a single point yet, Ben. Not *one*."

Avery felt a stab of guilt. She thanked September and

the Wookiee and jogged over to her teammates. "Yo, chill out, Chels. It's all good."

"All good?" Her voice rose up about ten octaves. "We're going to lose this scavenger hunt and look like the biggest losers in the class." Chelsea stared at her brother, then at Avery. "This is bad, Avery. Bad."

September waved. "Haven't you heard? 'Bad' means 'good.'"

Ben grinned. "I like it."

"But you guys . . . ," Chelsea objected. "Charlotte and Nick are going to be so upset with our team."

"We'll work on it tomorrow," Avery promised. "They'll understand."

"What if they don't?" Chelsea countered.

"Would you quit with the nervous Nellie routine?" Ben demanded. "You're the only person on this trip who isn't having fun!" Chelsea almost cried but managed to gulp back her tears. She wasn't going to let her annoying brother get her upset anymore today.

"Fine. Do whatever you want." And she turned to march away.

"*Chelsea*," Ben groaned. "Don't be like that."

"I'm fine. I'm fine," Chelsea called but she wouldn't turn around. She regretted the moment she'd ever asked Ben to come. She should have known that her fun-loving older brother would do what he did best . . . have fun.

And she *wasn't* a nervous Nellie either. She was the only Beach Barnacle doing exactly what she was supposed to be doing.

Chelsea charged along the shore mumbling, "I'm not a nervous Nellie. . . . I'm not." *If they won't do this scavenger hunt,* she thought, then I will! *There must be some bonus items around here.*

Chelsea pulled the bonus list out of her backpack and set off to do what she came to Cape Cod to do: HUNT.

9

Once a Monkey, Always a Monkey

Maeve's role in the movie was Girl in Crowd 2, a scullery maid. Fabiana was Girl in Crowd 1, a kitchen wench. As the crewmembers ran around the set like chickens with their heads cut off, Maeve was working on getting into character. *Just who really was Girl in Crowd 2?*

"I'm an orphan," she whispered to Fabiana.

Fabiana gave her a weird look. "What?"

"My character. Girl in Crowd 2. My parents were lost at sea when I was a baby. I had to go live in this horrible orphanage, run by the most horrible, mean, grumpy lady. She yelled at me a lot. Can you believe her nerve, Fabiana? Anyway, all I had from my parents was a locket with a picture of them. I never gave up hope that maybe my parents were still out there somewhere and we'd all be together again. Then this guy adopted me."

"Let me guess . . . he was rich, right?" Fabiana smiled, not quite believing how wrapped up in her made-up story Maeve had become.

Maeve shook her head. "No. He was poor. Very poor. And he stole a loaf of bread to feed me. Then he got arrested and I ran away and hid in an old opera house where this weird man in a mask taught me to sing and I turned into a big star. And when he took off the mask, guess what?"

"He was a phantom?" ventured Fabiana.

"No! He was scarred all over from a shark bite. *Can you believe it?*" She drew her finger along her cheek and over her eye. "And even though he's, like, totally hideous, he had my eyes—Girl in Crowd 2's eyes."

Maeve was starting to choke herself up a little bit. "And then I realize that he's my father and he's been with me the whole time . . . well, like, half the time."

"But if he was wearing a mask, couldn't you already see his eyes?" asked Fabiana.

"It wasn't that kind of mask," Maeve replied.

"And if you're a big opera star reunited with your scarred voice-teacher father, then why are you washing dishes on a pirate ship?"

Maeve adjusted her bandanna and said primly, "Because Girl in Crowd 2 lost her voice after her father was so overcome from hearing her sing on stage for the first time that he, you know . . . passed away. So she got fired and had to go back to being a servant girl. It was like a totally terrible situation," she ended with a sigh.

Maeve was getting a little overwhelmed by her story at

It's a pirate life for me!
Yo
Ho
Ho
He's got Piratitude!
What's with him?
Isabel M.

this point. So when Ozmond yelled, "Hey! Girl in Crowd, quiet on the set!" Maeve was relieved. Although, she was very miffed that Betsy Fitzgerald put her finger to her mouth for Maeve to be quiet. *The nerve of that girl*, Maeve thought as she stuck her nose in the air.

As the pirate scene unfolded before her, Maeve thought that if Ozmond knew what was good for him, he'd at least give her a line or two. Girl in Crowd 2 was way more interesting than any of the goofy pirate people running around waving swords at one another.

Suddenly two of the pirates who were brandishing their swords at each other turned around and clashed their swords together right before her eyes. One of them winked at her!

She grabbed Fabiana's arm. "Oh, I can't believe it . . . look." Her finger shook as she pointed.

Fabiana swung around to look at what Maeve was trembling about. Fabiana's eyes widened and she began to stutter.

"Maeve, is that who I think it is?" She was shaking too.

"Yes! It's . . . it's *Simon Blackstone and Ontario Plume!*"

"Maeve, they are the biggest stars in the whole world," Fabiana gushed. "Oh, I can't believe it. . . . Simon Blackstone is coming this way! I think I'm going to faint."

Maeve wore a grin the size of Texas. Simon remembered. He totally remembered her from that time she was lost in New York City and he showed her the way to the *Teen Beat* fashion show!

"Maeve, me darling," he addressed her in pirate speak. "I can't believe it's you!" With that, Simon swooped Maeve up and twirled her about in a big bear hug. "What are you doing here?" he asked when he put her down on her feet.

"Well, my friends . . . we were on this little scavenger hunt." Maeve saw Fabiana's smile fade and she herself felt a little stab of guilt, but Simon grinning in front of her was just too fabulous. Guilt would have to wait. Staring up at Simon's handsome face, she continued with her tale. "We sort of stumbled on to the set when we were lost, and they asked us to be extras because the real extras never showed up . . . and here we are!" she gushed.

"Fight scene, take seven!" called Ozmond. "Have your little happy reunion later, Simon. We must press on! We have a movie to shoot. . . . Betsy . . ."

Simon tipped his feather pirate hat, winked at her, and said, "Later, Maeve."

"You know Simon Blackstone and you never told me?!" Fabiana yelped.

Maeve whispered, "It's a *long* story." She could tell that Fabiana could barely contain her excitement.

At Ozmond's direction, all the actors on the set, who had been frozen and silent, began shouting and performing the moves that had been finely choreographed. A few of them kept stealing glances at Maeve, probably wondering, Maeve thought, how a lowly extra like her was friends with the heartthrob of the century—Simon Blackstone! It was all so very thrilling. Maeve had to hug herself to keep from dancing a two-step!

Maeve and Fabiana were directed to stand behind the mast of the ship and cower. Maeve could do cowering. She reckoned Girl in Crowd 2 had cowered a lot back in the orphanage.

Simon was playing Black Sam Bellamy, the bad guy hero known as the Prince of Pirates. In the scene they were shooting, Black Sam had just burst through the wall Isabel had helped paint and now he was engaged in a fierce battle against the crew of the *Whydah* for all the loot and treasure on board. Ontario Plume was playing a young member of the *Whydah* crew trying to defend his ship by fighting off the pirates.

Isabel couldn't believe that Simon remembered Maeve. She herself wasn't fascinated with movie stars the way Maeve was. She was more interested in how the scene was coming together. With the cameras rolling, Isabel felt like she was watching a storybook come alive. She could almost hear the loud explosions and music . . . even though they would be added later.

When she relayed her impressions to Patrick, he nodded and smiled. "I understand—it's why I love my job so much."

Isabel agreed. "It's like seeing your imagination come to life right before your eyes. Does that sound cheesy?"

"Nah!" Patrick assured her. "I get it."

Isabel had been Patrick's helper all day, and it was one of the best days of her life. They spent almost two hours building wetus and repainting the figurehead of the boat a "more authentic color" (according to Betsy). Even though

Isabel had to listen to the actors complaining about their hot costumes the whole time, she was ecstatic that she got to sit on a blanket in her shorts and tie twigs together with some fellow art lovers. Who else would sit with her and talk about how different shades of blue could make you feel sad, happy, cold, or warm?

When the director finally announced, "That's a wrap, actor people!" the whole cast let out a collective sigh, including the stars. They were "being whisked off to some lux trailer where they could lie down, eat whatever they wanted, and listen to music," Betsy explained. She seemed to have the total skinny on this movie set. Danny, Maeve, and Fabiana were also positively charged. "We are now officially movie stars," exclaimed an effervescent Maeve.

Riley was less enthusiastic. "I feel like a total dweeb," he said, tugging at the puffy hat he had to wear.

"Actually," Fabiana commented, tilting her head, "You look more like a muffin."

Riley let out an audible groan. "I'm gonna have to quit the band!" he lamented. "The rest of the Mustard Monkeys are never going to let me live this down."

"You're in a band?" giggled a tall, thin girl. She and another girl who was shorter and pudgier circled around him. They both had blond hair (that Maeve was convinced was sooo not real!).

"Yeah, I mean, it's no big deal." Riley was trying to look casual even though his cheeks were turning bright red.

"What do you play?" asked the shorter girl.

"Guitar and lead singer," he replied bashfully.

"That's hot," said the tall girl without much emotion, tossing her hair behind her shoulder. "Isn't that hot, Michele?"

"Totally hot. My dad's a music producer," said Michele, the shorter girl. "He could, like, totally hook you up!"

"He's, like, famous," the taller one added. "You should give Michele a demo. And your phone number . . ."

Maeve's ears were burning. Who were these two blond starlets circling around Riley?

"Riley," Maeve tried to interrupt.

"My dad's, like, totally funding this movie," the tall girl interrupted. "Funding movies is hot, isn't it, Michele?"

"Totally hot, Michelle."

"Wait, hold on. You *both* have the same name?" Maeve asked loudly. No, she did not like these girls one bit.

Tall Michelle glared at Maeve then smiled sweetly at Riley. "Like, NO! I'm Michelle with two Ls. She only has one."

Michele pulled Riley's hand up, whipped out a pen, and scrawled her number on it. "When you get a demo tape together . . . call me." She winked. "I'll talk to my dad and see what I can do."

The two Michelles—or rather Michele and Michelle— waved coyly at Riley and sauntered away.

Riley looked pale. "That was truly frightening."

Maeve couldn't help it; she burst out laughing. "Oh, Riley, you'll get used to it. I think you just survived your first groupies!"

Suddenly Betsy ran over. She seemed totally petrified. She was holding the walkie-talkie away from her and waving it around like it was on fire. "Somebody! Take it! Take it! I can't stand the pressure anymore."

Maeve wrinkled her eyebrows. "What's going on?"

Betsy dropped her voice to a whisper and informed them, "It's Ms. O'Reilly. She's trying to buzz in to check on us and I don't know what to tell her."

Maeve shrugged nonchalantly. "Oh, Betsy! Just make something up."

Betsy was stunned. "Make something up? Are you suggesting I *lie to a teacher*?"

Maeve rolled her eyes. "Not *lie* exactly, Betsy. It's called improv!"

Ms. O'Reilly's voice sounded through the speaker. "Cranberry Boggers? Are you there? Over! Darn, is this thing broken? Over. Over. Over."

Maeve reached over and plucked the walkie-talkie out of Betsy's hand whispering, "*Watch.*" She pressed the talk button and said calmly, "Hey, Ms. O. What's shakin'?"

"Oh, thank goodness. I was just checking in to see how the hunt was going."

Maeve glanced around the action-packed set of the movie and replied, "It's going great! We're having the most amazing time."

The Boggers nodded. That was definitely the truth.

"Oh, excellent," Ms. O'Reilly commented. "So are you finding any clues?"

"Clues?" Maeve waved her hand for help.

This was Isabel's clue to jump in. "Um, well, we're a little short on actual clues, but we're getting a lot of things on the bonus list!" She proved her point by holding up the preview screen on the team digital camera so everyone could see the pictures she had gathered around the set. The rest of the group gave her an approving, and relieved, thumbs-up.

Fabiana then took her turn with the walkie-talkie. "See, Ms. O'Reilly, sometimes having fun and learning new things is more important than coming in first, ya know?"

They heard Ms. O'Reilly laugh. "Kids, I couldn't agree more. Well, stay safe and I'll see you at the barbecue."

"Bye!" sang a chorus of Boggers.

Fabiana tossed the walkie-talkie back to Betsy, and slapped Maeve and Isabel a high five. "And that," Maeve stated, "is how improv is done." Except she didn't feel as great as she sounded. Charlotte, Nick and Chelsea were suddenly front and center in her mind, but Simon Blackwell's greeting was still tap dancing in her head: *"Maeve, me darling!"* Maeve just didn't know how to feel.

10

Salty Cods on the Run

an, I dig Cape Cod sea salt and vinegar chips. They are like . . . the work of some kind of mad food genius," Dillon pronounced as he tossed a handful of the tangy snack into his mouth. The rest of the Salty Cods agreed as they scarfed down the last of Dillon's bag of potato chips and enjoyed the ocean view from their perch on the rocks.

Munching on a chip, Charlotte suddenly began to feel a little anxious. "Don't you think it's a little weird that we haven't seen any of the other teams even though we've found two clues?" she asked.

"You know, I was just thinking about that myself," Nick answered as he munched loudly.

Katani, in a best friend tune-in, immediately caught on to what Charlotte was thinking. "What if the other teams got here first? It's already four o'clock. What if we're way behind?"

"Impossible!" Dillon scoffed. "We were riding like champions! There's no way the Barnacles and the Boggers are going faster."

Katani gulped. "Maybe they found a shortcut . . . and remember Lance wannabe Armstrong," Katani reminded Dillon. "The Barnacles have Avery on their team."

Patrice, who had actually dozed off for a few minutes, was suddenly alert. "Team Salty Cods, we can't take any chances!" She jumped up and ordered everyone to get moving. "Come on, troops. Let's get cracking here." She pulled envelope number three out of her bag and read.

Beside a pool all full of brine stands a
structure stuck in time. Search among the
ponds with care and you will find this wheel
of air.

The Cods were completely stumped. No one said anything until Dillon finally asked, "Who has a pool on the Cape?"

"Dude, it's a metaphor," Patrice said.

"What?" Dillon's face wrinkled in confusion.

"Metaphor. You remember from English class? Something that means something else," Charlotte explained. "Like when Ms. Rodriguez says that the classroom is a zoo. She doesn't *actually* mean that the classroom is a cage full of animals. She means everything is crazy."

"Oh, I get it, as if we're all acting like animals . . . not me personally, of course," he said, grinning.

Nick gave Dillon a noogie and grabbed his last chip. "Let Charlotte finish, dude."

"It means that the pool in the clue is code for something else!" a very intent Charlotte continued.

"But for what?" Katani asked.

"Like a pond!" Nick snapped his fingers. "Let's check out the map."

Patrice unfolded the map and everyone peered at the area surrounding Rock Harbor.

"Okay, so I gotta know. What's a pool full of brine? 'Cause if that is, like, a code for garbage or something . . ." Dillon trailed.

"Brine is like salt," Nick answered. All the Cods, including Charlotte, looked at him, impressed.

"What are you, some kind of Albert Einstein, Nick? Who actually knows that stuff?" Dillon grabbed Nick in a friendly headlock.

"My parents own a restaurant, dude!" he said as he twisted his head out of Dillon's arm. "They use brining stuff all the time to preserve the meat for Montoya's famous breakfast sandwiches!" Nick looked at Charlotte as if she were the only one whose opinion mattered. Their eyes locked for a split second, and Charlotte felt like she was dancing.

"So, then, we're looking for a salt pond?" Katani asked. "Well, isn't that a salt pond right there?" Katani used her perfectly manicured nail to point out the tiny letters that read SALT POND in an area not far from Rock Harbor.

"Nice one, Kgirl!" Charlotte cheered.

"Sis, you've got the eagle eye." Patrice smiled, giving her sister a hug. Katani squeezed her sister back. It felt good to be part of Patrice's team now.

They quickly boarded their bikes and zipped off, everyone on the team convinced that the Salty Cods were unbeatable. Within ten minutes the salt air was as strong as if they were still by the sea, and the Salty Cods knew they were close. They braked in front of a scenic vista overlooking the beautiful, marshy Salt Pond.

"Whoa, dudes! Check out that mad old windmill!" Dillon gaped.

The team turned to look at the windmill, which was like an illustration from a history book. And then, just like that, a light bulb went off in Charlotte's head. She turned to Nick. "That's it! See, there's the flag! It's a 'wheel of air' that's totally 'stuck in time.'"

"Way to go, Char!" Patrice cheered. They all ran over to the flag and posed as Katani took the camera and snapped their picture.

Charlotte felt Nick squeeze her hand just as the camera flashed. *I wonder if these pictures will go in the school newspaper.* Charlotte experienced a fleeting flicker of concern. She liked her special friendship with Nick but she didn't want to broadcast it all over the school.

"It's almost time for dinner," Patrice noted. "Cods, are we ready to call it a day?"

The group gathered in a circle and bumped their fists together. "Three clues down, three more to go!" The Salty

Cods had given the scavenger hunt 100 percent of their effort and now visions of chicken wings and watermelon danced in their heads. They mustered up what was left of their strength and pedaled off to Kiki's house.

Barnacle Bluff

In exchange for letting Avery borrow her friend's surfboard, Avery allowed September and Chewie to break into the package of chocolate-chip granola bars that she had packed. Avery had decided that the granola bars would be the perfect thing for keeping her energy up on a fun-filled bike trip. September, Chewie (aka the Wookman), and the rest of the Barnacles were especially grateful for her planning.

"I haven't munched one of these since I was in junior high!" September admitted. "I used to make quadruple-decker granola bar sandwiches stuffed with peanut butter. They were the cheese!" she said as she stuffed a piece in her mouth.

"Mgghmmgg." Chewie tried to get some words out but it was an impossible task as his mouth was full of granola bar crumbs. When he smiled he looked like a cartoon hillbilly who'd lost half his teeth. Avery and the Barnacles doubled over with laughter. Even Kiki, who had mellowed out from her day in the sun, let out a big hoot, but she wasn't looking at Chewie.

"You think that dude over there has been out in the sun yet this century?" she quipped to Yurt, pointing to a pale teenager trying to get up the courage to step into the freezing water. Yurt held his hands over his face like a mask and intoned, "Another beachgoer falls victim to the Sunscreen Slasher!"

"Oh, shut up," Kiki griped. But she was smiling when she said it.

Just then Avery felt the force. She was magnetically drawn to anything having to do with sports, like she had a sixth sense or something. In fact, her powers had come through again. Behind her, a group of kids were setting up a volleyball game.

Avery spun around and ran as fast as her legs could carry her.

"Hey, you guys need another player?" she hollered, again completely forgetting about anything to do with the scavenger hunt.

"Totally," replied a dark-haired girl with a wide smile and hazel eyes.

A blond girl with short curly hair frowned. "I don't think—!" she whined.

"What? We *do* need another player." The dark-haired girl interrupted her friend and smiled at Avery. "Just ignore Tracy. The more the merrier!"

"You know how to play?" asked another kid, a tall boy with lots of freckles and brown hair.

"Do I ever!" Avery barked, and launched the ball into the air with a superpowered serve.

The volleyball kids cheered. All but Tracy, who lunged to hit back Avery's serve and missed completely. "I didn't even want to play volleyball," Tracy groaned. "We were *supposed* to be extras in a movie!"

"It's shooting in the middle of nowhere in the woods somewhere on Cape Cod," explained a boy with a Red Sox hat on.

"Yeah. Turns out, they were sooo in the middle of nowhere that my mom couldn't even find the dirt road to the set!" Tracy said sarcastically. "We drove all over the place and finally got to this beach. By the time we called the movie people they said they'd found some other kids to replace us," explained the girl huffily. "So now here we are on this gorgeous beach, but with no bathing suits, no towels, no anything."

"But we had a volleyball and there was already a net," added the boy. "That seemed like the next best thing."

"So, let's do it!" Avery commanded. Soon, a full-on volleyball game was in motion. Avery played water volleyball every summer at her father's, in the annual Telluride, Colorado, Volleyball Tournament. (She had three MVP trophies!)

"You know," she had explained to Charlotte, "if you have two brothers you just have to be into sports or you'll be left doing the dishes. And I hate doing dishes. I mean, if it wasn't for saving the environment and all, I would eat on paper plates every night and it wouldn't bother me at all."

Champions of the Beach

"Ahhh, Avery," shouted the Yurtmeister after a full hour of intense volleyball. "That last serve was absolutely killer." Then he proceeded to do a Henry Yurt–style dance complete with war whoops around the net. The Beach Barnacles had beaten the pants off the movie-extra kids.

As Avery went to shake hands, she promised herself that she would be sure to thank her brothers, Scott and Tim, for all their great volleyball tips. Avery also made sure to give Ben Briggs a thumbs-up. Who would have guessed the big football player had such grace when it came to leaping for the ball and tapping it across to just the right place? Kiki also surprised them all by not only playing, but also by stopping more than one spiked ball with her quick reflexes.

It seemed like nothing could ruin the Beach Barnacle's perfect mood. That is, until they heard a muffled noise starting to sound from Avery's beach towel.

"EARTH TO BARNACLES, OVER!" suddenly blared out of the walkie-talkie.

Avery stared at the walkie-talkie like it might detonate and blow up into a million tiny pieces. Kiki's eyes danced with mischief and she dove for the little yellow device. "Hi, Mrs. Moore!" she sang. "Ooover!"

"Are my young Barnacles discovering many a clue?" asked Mrs. Moore in her version of an Old English accent.

"But of course!" Kiki gushed. "We're on fire, Mrs. Moore. I think the Beach Barnacles might even win."

Avery gave her a look. She didn't mind evading the truth a little bit, but Kiki was doing more than just evading. They'd spent the entire day playing and hadn't found a single clue! There was no way they could win.

"That is mooo-arvelous news," replied Mrs. Moore, switching back to her comfort zone of cow talk. "I had a feeling this mission would be udder-ly perfect for you Beach Barnacles. "Haven't lost anyone yet, right? Ha ha ha, I'm only kidding, of course. Okay, well, I'll see you at your place in an hour, Kiki. Over and out."

After Kiki put down the monitor, she took a gander around the beach. "Come on, we've got to get back to my place! So . . . where's Chelsea?"

"Um, did anyone see her leave?" Ben's volleyball-victory expression drained away as the Barnacles glanced guiltily at one another with Ben and Avery looking guilti-est of all. Avery felt bad that Kiki Underwood, Empress of Mean, had noticed that Chelsea had gone missing before she had. Ben felt even worse because Chelsea was his own sister, and he was supposed to be in charge.

"Geesh! Where did she go?" Avery demanded.

Ben scratched his head. "Um, I thought she was just wandering around her with her camera. Maybe she went for a walk, but I didn't think she'd go that far. . . ."

"Okay everybody, stay calm," Yurt ordered. For a tiny boy, the president of the seventh-grade class had a way with demanding trust and attention. "She's gotta be on this beach somewhere. We just have to find her. Avery, you and Ben go left. Kiki and I are going to go right."

Avery chuckled. *Poor Yurt*—he had a huge soft spot for the glamour-type girls, no matter how atrocious their personalities. Then she remembered. He did go to the

Valentine's Dance with Betsy who was sooo serious. That kind of ruined her Yurt/glamour-girl theory.

Ben was starting to get frantic, so Avery jogged beside him as he ran hollering Chelsea's name up and down the beach. Both were silently blaming themselves for having fun and totally forgetting to look out for Chelsea.

"I'm, like, the worst chaperone and the worst brother rolled into one," Ben confided to Avery.

"Don't worry, we'll find her!" Avery picked up the pace, even though her throat was aching from half an hour of screaming nothing but "Chelsea! Chelsea! CHELSEA!"

Suddenly, Avery noticed a jetty of large boulders with a small pool of water siphoning in and out just ahead of them. "Hey, isn't that a tide pool?" she managed to shout at Ben. "That's one of the thingies on our bonus list."

She and Ben ran over to get a closer look. As they rounded the jetty, a flash of yellow sweatshirt caught Ben's eye. "Chelsea?" he blurted.

Chelsea, in a much better mood after her day of strolling the beach and taking pictures, looked up and smiled. "Oh, hey, guys! You won't believe how many bonus items I got."

Avery stood still as if she was staring at a ghost. Ben ran up and grabbed his sister in a giant bear hug. "What?" Chelsea laughed. "You guys are being so weird."

"Chelsea, we've been worried sick!" Avery exclaimed. "The whole team's running around the beach looking for you!"

Ben stopped hugging Chelsea and suddenly grew

stern. "How could you disappear like that and not even tell me?"

Chelsea's mind was boggled. "Are you kidding me? All I've been doing all day is trying to help our team. All *you two* have been doing is goofing off and having fun and now . . . you're getting on *my* case?"

Avery couldn't really argue that—she'd had a fantastic day surfing, swimming, and kicking a major win in beach volleyball.

"What's wrong with having fun?" Ben asked.

"It's okay, but we are *supposed* to be solving clues for a certain scavenger hunt. I thought you'd be happy that I've been working! Geesh!" Chelsea muttered.

Ben, who still looked guilty that he hadn't noticed Chelsea's absence, confessed, "I am happy, Chels; it's just . . ."

Chelsea began to storm back to the team, where she was greeted by a whole new slew of frustrated and angry faces.

"Geez, Chelsea, it's bad enough that we had to lie to Mrs. Moore in the first place, but now you made us late for the barbecue! We're never going to get away with this!" Kiki moaned.

"What?" Chelsea said defensively. She was the only one who had stuck to scavenger hunting and now everyone was blaming *her*! Plus, *she* had never lied to a teacher in her life—except for bending the truth to get out of gym, and she was sure that couldn't possibly count. *I mean,* she thought, *I think there's some kid universe rule that getting out of gym is considered okay.*

"You all did nothing all day . . . and lied . . . to a teacher," Chelsea accused the whole team.

Yurt shrugged. "Well, we didn't exactly lie . . . just kind of stretched the truth." He pulled his gum out of his mouth into a long, blue string on the word "stretched." Everyone, even Chelsea, cracked up. "Chels, we didn't want her to get mad at us for blowing off the scavenger hunt thing and not getting any points."

"It just wasn't the *whole* truth," Avery pointed out.

Chelsea shook her head. "Well, it *was* stupid. "'Cause what are we going to say at the barbecue when people ask us what we did all day? Did anyone even think about that?"

Obviously, no one had, because the Barnacles just looked at one another sheepishly.

Ben grumbled. "We should have said something else!"

Chelsea bonked her brother on the head with her sweatshirt sleeve. "Totally, dude. But, the day is not completely lost. I got a bunch of points while you slackers were playing beach bunnies."

"You did?" Yurt exclaimed. "How?"

"Bonus points . . ." Chelsea replied.

"Well, just *how many* could you have possibly gotten so that it would even make a difference?" Kiki demanded in a haughty tone.

Chelsea took an envelope out of her backpack and a list with nine checks. "All but one!" she declared proudly. "There's even a street on the other side of the beach named after an animal—Deer Path, and someone actually had a towel covered with foxes. I figure that is close enough." Now it was Chelsea's turn to be haughty.

No one said anything for a second. Everyone knew that if it weren't for Chelsea, the Barnacles would be toast!

Ben gave her a huge bear hug while the team let out a loud cheer and took turns slapping Chelsea high fives and patting her on the back—except for Kiki, of course. Unfortunately, there wasn't any more time for celebrating. The Barnacles were already running super late.

"We have to get to the barbecue fast or we're gonna be in so much trouble!" Avery concluded.

Kiki smiled. "You forget . . . it's at my house!"

"Sooo . . ." Avery insisted on pulling it out of her.

"Soooooo, I know a shortcut!" she said curtly.

The Beach Barnacles finally pedaled away from the beach, dreaming about (or desperately needing, in Ben's case) some delicious grilled grub dripping with barbecue sauce. Only Chelsea was still wondering what she would say when Mrs. Moore or Charlotte and Nick asked her about their day at the beach. She could lie . . . or as Yurt put it, stretch the truth. But somehow neither felt right.

Part Two
The Race Is On!

11

Yo Ahoy Ahoy What Up?

The sun, turning from bright yellow to warm honey, fell onto the trees like a giant beach ball. Everyone on the set was sipping iced tea, and congratulating one another on a hard day's work on the set.

When Mr. Moore buzzed through on the walkie-talkie to tell the Cranberry Boggers it was getting close to dinnertime, Maeve felt a little sad. She had been daydreaming about Ozmond asking her to stay on as a full-time member of the cast.

"Why, Ozmond, dear," she would say after he asked her to expand her part. "I'd be delighted!"

She had already planned out how she would decorate her dressing room: all pink with lots and lots of sparkling jewels and feathered boas. Hey, she'd throw in a top hat too, just for good measure.

Even though she'd gotten a huge glob of superglue on her new sneakers when she and Patrick were assembling the wetu, Isabel had enjoyed every moment of her day as well. It was worth it just to have gotten to contribute to a real movie set. Isabel decided to cherish that little glue glob as a free souvenir.

Poppy gave the Boggers directions back to the bike path, which, as it turned out, they had actually been riding alongside the whole time! As the team headed out on their bikes, they heard someone running behind them.

"Hey there!" It was Bethany. "You guys wouldn't be interested in shooting again with us tomorrow? We have one more crowd scene, and it would totally help me out." Bethany looked like she was about to get down on her knees and beg them to come back.

"Bethany! It would be our honor!" Maeve blurted before anyone else could say anything. She covered her mouth when she realized she had spoken for all the Boggers. Seeing their shocked faces, she backtracked a bit. "I mean . . . I guess."

"But Maeve, don't you think tomorrow we need to start working on this scavenger hunt?" Isabel prompted. "I don't want to get in trouble . . . or let Nick, Charlotte, and Chelsea down. They worked so hard at putting it together."

But everyone paused for a moment to think about Bethany's offer. "Well, Isabel . . . this *is*, like, a once-in-a-lifetime opportunity," Danny offered.

"You know, we can always do a supercharged clue

hunt when we're done," argued Betsy, who believed in the power of planning. "Bethany, will this crowd scene take place first thing in the morning?" she asked.

"No prob, Bets," Bethany assured the film's historical accuracy consultant. "I'm sure Ozmond would agree to that. I'll tell him you kids can only do it then," she said with a wink.

After almost gagging at Betsy's pleased-as-punch smile, Maeve grabbed Isabel's hand and gave it a squeeze. Izzy was the sweetest girl, and she didn't want a fellow BSG to feel bad about the team's decision.

"Where are you shooting?" asked Fabiana, taking out her map.

Bethany showed the Boggers the location—two miles up the coast.

"Hey, isn't that on our scavenger hunt route anyway?" asked Betsy, who had spent some time carefully mapping their path.

"You're right!" Danny exclaimed. "Always on target, Betsy."

Maeve whispered playfully to Isabel, "I think Danny and Betsy could be the best love match since 'Isabel and Danny in the Museum.'" Isabel made a face and yanked one of Maeve's curls.

Fabiana agreed that since the location was on the way, they could afford to squeeze in "a few more hours of movie time . . . but no more than two!" she warned. After carefully taking down the directions from Bethany, she placed the map safely in the side pocket of her bag.

"Would you like me to be in charge of the map this time?" Betsy volunteered.

Maeve was proud of how Fabiana coolly replied, "Thanks, Betsy, but I got it covered." And then Nick's sister did the funniest thing.

"Cranberry Bogger alert! Everybody check out where I am stashing the map! Map in the pack," Fabiana sang as she waved her hands around like a bandleader.

"Map in the pack," she beckoned for everyone to join in. Betsy looked at her as if she were an alien. "Hi-ho, the derry-o, the map is in the pack!" the team sang. At the close, there were high fives all around. No way was Fabiana going to lose another map.

"Well, I guess that should do the trick," Betsy said sarcastically.

Wow! Betsy cracks a joke, thought a bemused Isabel.

"Ha ha, Betsy!" Danny slapped his knee. "You are too funny!"

On the ride to Kiki's, Maeve regaled Isabel with all the details of what it was like to be filmed on a real movie set. "I personally enjoyed it," she noted, "but Annabella did not."

"Who's Annabella?" asked Isabel.

"Oh, my character . . . her childhood was very difficult, you know." Maeve's voice dropped to a whisper. "I think she might be afraid of crowds."

"Oh," Isabel said. At this point in her friendship with Maeve, she knew that sometimes the best way to deal with Maeve's fantasy worlds was to just go along . . . as though everything that came out of MKT's movie-star-in-training mouth actually made logical sense.

"Yes," Maeve continued as they rode along. "Annabella is a very complex character. I really have to work at remembering her issues when I scrub the deck. I mean, should I scrub with vigor or with regret?"

Isabel, who had other things on her mind besides Maeve and Annabella, nodded vaguely. She was still feeling a little guilty about how the Cranberry Boggers had spent their day. No one on the team had gotten a single clue. Not one. The only points they'd earned were the few items from the bonus list that she'd found on the set.

"Hey, look," Riley suddenly shouted. "Squirrel Lane. Isn't a street named after an animal one of the things on the bonus list?" he asked.

"Riley, you get an A plus!" Isabel said with relief. She quickly hopped off her bike to snap a photo. A little while later they found themselves riding alongside the lovely ocean shore, and Isabel captured a shot of a sand dune. In total she had four bonus-point items—the prop fox, the pirate-themed thing, the street, and the sand dune.

Still, Isabel only felt a smidge better about the team's predicament. It was the same sick-to-her stomach feeling she got when she left a big paper to write the very last night before it was due. *No bueno!* She knew she would feel terrible the minute she saw Charlotte. Would she have to lie to her friend?

"So when everyone asks us what we did today, just

what exactly are we supposed to tell them?" she asked Fabiana who rode up alongside her.

"We tell them exactly what we did. We had fun . . . found a lot of bonus point stuff . . . and we're going to concentrate on clues tomorrow."

"It *is* the truth . . . sort of," said Betsy, who caught up on Isabel's other side.

But the truth, Isabel knew in her heart, was that no one wanted anything to get in the way of their being in this movie. Maeve and Fabiana were thrilled to be in a real live movie with Orlando Plume and Simon Blackstone. Even Betsy and Danny were getting a feel of the stardom rush—Danny with his role as an extra and Betsy as Ozmond's preferred historical consultant. And Isabel had to be honest. She loved hanging out with Patrick and Poppy . . . much more than trying to win a scavenger hunt.

Only Riley would have probably been just as happy to never put on that goofy costume or makeup again, but he was so easygoing that he wasn't complaining. Instead, he and Maeve were laughing hysterically as they rode their bikes next to each other and belted out a rap song that Riley was making up on the spot.

I'm hanging out with pirates, yo ahoy ahoy what up?
You better look out, mates, ahoy, or yo, I'll steal your cup!
My mates are kinda raggy, hey, but that's just how we row.
The captain's all 'What up, homies? The landlubbers lie down below!'

"Well, one thing's for sure," an adamant Isabel said to Fabiana and Betsy. "We can't tell the Adventure Club leaders that we blew off the hunt they've been working so hard on—I mean, Charlotte would be totally crushed if she knew we skipped out on scavenger hunting today."

Overhearing the conversation, Maeve stopped rapping to solemnly concur, "Yes, you're *so* right, Isabel. We have to think about their feelings."

"That's really nice of you guys," Betsy said, sounding surprised.

Maeve and Isabel looked puzzled. "Well, obvi—that's what being friends is all about," said Maeve, who didn't go on to say that that was what being in the BSG was all about. She didn't want to seem cliquey. But from the expression on Betsy's face, it was clear that Betsy had no idea *what* the BSG was all about. Maybe in Betsy's mind the BSG were like the Queens of Mean. *That would be terrible,* worried Maeve.

After all, cliques are sooo yesterday, she reasoned, remembering how a group of girls in third grade made fun of her red hair and wouldn't sit with her. She flashed her best megawatt smile at a dazzled Betsy.

"Maeve." Isabel leaned in so no one else could hear her. "Do you think we are really lying?"

"I don't think so," Maeve said, then thought for a minute before adding. "We're just not telling the whole truth to spare our friends' feelings."

"I guess so," Isabel responded. But if it was okay, why did she feel so upset about not telling Char what they did all day?

Katani was hot again. Really hot. The sweat was pouring down her face and her back. She couldn't understand what kind of bad luck had fallen on her that she got stuck in the group that insisted upon riding their bikes at absolute super speed to every single destination. She could understand if she were on Avery's team or something, but the person mostly responsible for this constant torture was her very own flesh and blood—Patrice—her competitive, intense sister.

Katani had to admit, however, that all the extra effort came in handy when they rolled up to a mailbox with Kiki's address number and balloons on it at five o'clock sharp—right in time for the barbecue. She couldn't wait to slurp down tall lemonade and collapse in a chaise lounge. Katani loved the sound of "chaise lounge." When she had her own house, she promised herself that she would have a hundred chaise lounges . . . in different colors!

"Well, here we are," Patrice announced. She hopped off her bike and turned into the driveway entrance lined with thick shrubbery.

"Uh, cool, but where's the barbecue?" Dillon asked. He didn't see a grill anywhere, let alone a house.

"*This* way." They heard Patrice shout. She jumped back on her bike and as she peddled away shouted back, "Uhhh . . . you might not want to get off your bikes quite yet."

The Cods followed Patrice down a long road covered in crackly white seashells, until the driveway became a large circle with a lovely courtyard of flowers in the middle.

Kiki's house wasn't just a house—it was a mansion . . . on the beach!

A classic Cape Cod style, Kiki's house was sided in gray cedar shingles, and the trim and shutters were painted a rich, creamy white. There was a main house, and then another smaller (not even *that* small) house next to a swimming pool that looked like it was falling into the ocean.

"I think we just landed in Disneyland," Dillon quipped.

"They're here! They're here!" sang a voice from the porch. "Kiki's friends, do come in. Kiki has so been looking forward to this barbecue." Kiki's mother and father were standing by the front door looking like they had just stepped off a magazine page.

Mrs. Underwood had on a bright lime shift dress with tiny watermelon-colored turtles embroidered on it. Mr. Underwood was wearing blue-and-white seersucker pants with a white shirt. His perfectly brown wavy hair had been combed straight back (and didn't move at all), and neither did Mrs. Underwood's wavy blonde bob.

Katani gave them both a fashion A-. If only they would let their hair loose, she might up it to an A+.

Katani was a little embarrassed because her Salty Cod team was somewhere around a D-. . . . They looked like they had literally been purged from the sea and dragged in with by a fishing net. They were sweaty, dirty, and definitely not dressed to impress.

"Boy, do I feel like a fish out of water," Charlotte whispered to Katani.

"Ha ha," Katani replied dryly as Mrs. Underwood waved them closer.

"Well, let's not be strangers, everyone. I'm Kiki's mom but you can call me Sienna, and this is Dexter, Kiki's father."

"I believe I met some of you at the school talent show." Dexter held out a beefy hand to each of them to shake. "When I filmed Kiki's act," he reminded them.

Charlotte, Katani, and Nick nodded and exchanged looks, unsure if they were really expected to say, "Hello, Sienna and Dexter. Thanks so much for inviting us to your mansion."

"Now, who's been here before?" asked Sienna Underwood with an expectant smile on her face. Katani wasn't sure what fantasy world Kiki's parents lived in where they thought she regularly invited over the kids from AAJH. Didn't they realize that Kiki only hung out with the Queens of Mean and various upperclassmen that she deemed cool enough?

When it was determined that this was a first-time visit for all the Salty Cods, Mr. Underwood insisted on giving them the "grand tour" and Mrs. Underwood went to check on the caterers they'd hired to cook the barbecue so that they could "enjoy their time with their daughter and her friends."

"Wow, I feel like we are on a movie set!" Nick exclaimed to Charlotte and Katani.

"Yeah, a movie called *The Empress of Mean Has a Barbecue*," shot back Katani.

"Katani!" gasped Charlotte. "You need to jump in that pool and cool off . . . now!"

Katani sighed. "You're right, Charlotte. I don't know what's gotten into me." Katani resolved then and there to put on a happy face and enjoy the party. *Nobody likes a crankmonster at a party,* she told herself.

Kiki's house was luxurious, full of rooms and wings the likes of which Charlotte had seen only in magazines. There was a game room complete with a pool table, a pinball machine, and single-lane bowling alley. And the cherry on the sundae—the Underwoods had a small movie theater complete with red velvety chairs and a popcorn machine! *Wait till Maeve sets her eyes on this!* Charlotte imagined her friend having a total fantasy breakdown.

Across the hall, Mr. Underwood ushered them into a room filled with CDs, speakers, and recording equipment from the floor to the ceiling. From the way Mr. Underwood went on and on about his collection, it was clear he loved his job as a music video producer. Riley would be in seventh heaven when he saw this, figured Charlotte when she caught sight of all the technical equipment.

Patrice was pumped to check out the gym and sauna, and Dillon was impressed with the greenhouse and connecting sunroom. He said it reminded him of "a small jungle where tigers might roam."

But Charlotte's favorite place was a quiet meditation room overlooking the ocean. She had never even heard of one of those before, but concluded that when she grew up, no matter how small her house, she would dedicate a little corner for her to unwind, think her deepest thoughts, and record them in her journal.

Katani went out of her way to tell "Sienna" what a beautiful job she had done decorating. Kiki's mom was very pleased and described to a fascinated Katani how she chose all the different fabrics, and how she picked soft colors and patterns "so no matter what room anyone goes in they will feel happy and content." Katani was impressed with Sienna's decorating flair and how nice she was being to "Kiki's little friends."

"Now, I hope you kids brought your suits, 'cause I heard this was supposed to be a pool party," Dexter informed them when they had concluded the tour.

The Salty Cods couldn't wait to play in the Underwoods' beautiful swimming pool overlooking the Atlantic Ocean.

"There's something so *über*cool about the idea of having two kinds of water right in your backyard," Katani said.

"Whoa, Dexter, killer water slide, dude! And a jacuzzi, too! Sweeeeet!" an enthusiastic Dillon complimented his new pal Dexter.

Everyone rushed to change into their suits and, as they ran outside, the sight of Mr. Underwood doing a huge cannonball into the pool caused them all to cheer.

"You are the man, Dexter!" Dillon shouted as he ran up the water slide ladder. Charlotte, Katani, and Patrice opted to unwind in the Underwoods' jacuzzi. As the scent of delicious barbecue grew stronger in the air, Charlotte began to think that this party at Kiki's was turning out to be pretty cool after all. There was just one thing: *Where was everybody else?*

	Salty Cods	Beach Barnacles	Cranberry Boggers
Clues 3 pts each	Camping Yurts Rock Harbor Eastham Windmill		
Bonus Items 1 pt each	Coyote Street scallop shell tide pool sand dune	fox towel surfboard sandpiper Deer Path scallop shell sailboat tide pool sand dune park ranger	prop fox Squirrel Lane pirate hat sand dune
DAY 1 POINTS	13 points	9 points	4 points

CHAPTER

12

❁ Mermonster from the Blue Lagoon

Fist of all, Beach Barnacles, this is the pool!" Kiki gushed, doing a half spin in front of the pool. "But I like to call it the *lagoon*. It's not much, but to me, it's summer."

Chelsea felt her antisnob reflex kicking in. *Who calls their pool a lagoon?* Annoyed, she snapped a picture of Kiki posing by the *swimming pool*.

Kiki *insisted* on giving the weary group of Barnacles a complete private tour of the "mansh" as she called it. As the Barnacles followed Empress Kiki around, roaming from beautiful room to more beautiful room, Chelsea had to admit that the house gave off a very welcoming feel. And, of course, Kiki's bedroom with its four-poster bed, powder blue walls, and spectacular view of the ocean was to die for.

Maybe Kiki will let me lie down on her princess bed for a few minutes, a suddenly exhausted Chelsea thought fleetingly. Kiki must have read her mind because the Empress kicked off her sandals and flopped down on the end of the bed, sighing. "It's so relaxing lying here and staring at the water. . . ."

"Kiki, can we go swim now? I'm so hot," pleaded a yawning Avery. A chorus of "me too"s followed.

"Why didn't you just say so in the first place?" a miffed Kiki said as she hopped off the bed and led them down to the pool house to grab towels.

Before they could join the Salty Cods in the pool and jacuzzi, who should show up but the Cranberry Boggers— looking a little scattered and out of breath.

"So sorry we're late," an out-of-breath Fabiana apologized as she sidled up to Ben. "Finding clues, you know? Tricky stuff."

Ben nodded. "Totally hear that. How'd your day go?"

Chelsea had to bite her cheeks to keep from laughing. Her brother was clearly taken with Nick Montoya's sister.

Fabiana shrugged and said coolly, "Fine. Totally normal. How about your day?"

Ben gave her one of his cool-guy looks and replied, "You know. Same. All things fab. Just did a lot of scavenger-hunt stuff, mostly."

"Cool. Cool," said Fabiana.

"Nice pool," Ben commented, gesturing toward Kiki's "lagoon."

"Nice? It's absolutely *Lives of the Rich and Famous!*" said

Patrice, making her way to her fellow captains wrapped in one of the pale yellow beach towels the Underwoods had handed out. "A seriously welcome sight after a *long* day of serious scavenger hunting! I gotta have a swim . . . now!" Patrice threw off her towel and dove into the pool.

"Scavenger hunts take it right out of you . . . don't they?" Ben agreed in a somewhat higher than normal voice.

"They sure do. . . ." Fabiana said, fanning herself with her hand.

"And now it's time to chil-laxxx and have fun!" Maeve announced, cutting her leader short before she could give anything away.

After a day spent in long, thick, heavy fabric (that, puhleeze, did not breathe at all!), Maeve was more than ready to chill out in Kiki's pool. From the way Riley, Danny, Isabel, and even Betsy were dashing toward the changing rooms, Maeve could tell she wasn't alone.

Charlotte and Katani were already kicking back in the hot tub drinking the tastiest frozen drink, an icy blend of pineapple and coconut juice with whipped cream and a cherry on top. Dexter (Charlotte simply adored that name) called them Pineapple Dreams, "In tribute to one of the Underwoods' favorite vacay places—Hawaii!" he'd explained as he handed out the yummy-looking concoctions to the thirsty Cods.

"I love the way Mr. Underwood talks. It's like he's a TV spokesperson or something," Katani observed in between slurps.

"What's up with the Beach Barnacles? They aren't even swimming," a suddenly curious Charlotte observed. "Have you ever seen Avery Madden pass up on a pool?"

"Are you kidding? That girl would go swimming in the North Pole for Christmas," Katani joked. They watched Avery, who instead of swan-diving off the board (her usual plan of attack) was dangling her feet in the water.

"Ave, better get in line," yelled Yurt and waved her over to the buffet table.

"The Barnacles are circling that table like a bunch of piranhas waiting for prey," Katani quipped.

"It's like they've been lost in the wilderness and are ready to sit down to their first meal in weeks!" Charlotte laughed.

"Would you look at Maeve and Betsy?" Katani pointed to the two girls frolicking in the deep end. "I've never seen those two swim so fast—not even in gym class." The two Boggers, along with their extremely energetic teammates, Riley, Danny, and Isabel, were playing a spirited game of Marco Polo.

"It's like we've landed in upside-down land, Katani," Charlotte noted, as she sank deeper into the jacuzzi. "We did so much biking today that all I want to do is sit in this hot tub and reeeeelax."

"Cheers to that!" agreed Katani. "I am barely moooving," she mimicked Mr. Moore.

Suddenly, they both sat straight up as a creature emerged from the water before them. At first, the creature appeared to have Ariel of *The Little Mermaid* qualities:

long ravishing red curls, alabaster skin, turquoise bathing suit. But when the creature wiped the hair out of her face, Katani and Charlotte cringed in horror.

It wasn't a mermaid—it was a mer*monster* . . . formerly known as Maeve. Streaks of tan and pink ran down her cheeks and neck. Her black-rimmed eyes made her look like the ghost of a redheaded panda.

"What happened to you?" a confused Charlotte asked.

"Huh? What do you mean?"

"Maeve, I say this with love." Katani shook her head. "*You look terrible!* Like the creature from the black lagoon! You better find a mirror."

Maeve tossed her soaking hair back and tried to flash her friends a confident smile, which to Katani and Charlotte still came across as bad-movie creepy. Maeve reached for a towel to wipe away a little black gunk from under her eyes, but that only made the look worse. Now she looked like a crazed raccoon, and there was a giant smudge on the Underwoods' designer towel.

"Gosh, Maeve, I don't remember you wearing makeup this morning," Katani said suspiciously. "You, uh, must really know how to apply it well, huh? Cause I gotta say, you looked pretty natural."

If Maeve had learned anything from her improv classes it was how to think on her feet. "Oh, you know me," she said jokingly. "Always trying a new look. Uh, gotta go!"

She slithered out of the pool and made a beeline for the bathroom in the pool house. Maeve was determined to look presentable as quickly as possible. She didn't want Dillon or Riley, her former and present class crushes, to see her like that. Besides, she could feel Charlotte's and Katani's penetrating eyes following her as she ducked into the bathroom and she didn't want to answer any more questions about her day.

When she emerged a few minutes later, Sienna Underwood waltzed over to the pool wearing high heels. "Yoo-hoo! Dinner time!" she called out as she rang a huge bell to get everyone's attention.

"*Mom!*" an embarrassed Kiki groaned in frustration.

"What, dear? The dinner bell is an Underwood family tradition." Sienna Underwood laughed. "Your grandmother rang it, my grandmother rang it, and someday, when you're married with kids, you'll ring it too."

"I guess Kiki's human like the rest of us," joked Avery to the BSG who had gathered in their towels. "Now let's eat. . . . I'm so hungry I could snarf that whole table!"

As Kiki looked like she might drop dead out of sheer mortification, the BSG shared a secret glance. It was a little fun to see the Empress of Mean so positively unglued.

Barbeque Underwood Style
The barbecue was a monster hit. Dillon's eyes popped open at the corn on the cob, grilled chicken, corn bread, coleslaw, and burgers. Avery and Yurt were creating space aliens out of hamburger buns and corn cobs, Isabel and Katani were discussing Mrs. Underwood's fabulous interior-decorating choices, and everyone was basking in

the orange glow of the setting sun. Charlotte was thrilled to be with all her friends again in such a gorgeous locale and couldn't wait to find out about all the adventures the other teams must have had as they hunted for clues.

"Hey, the teachers are here now," Avery said as she waved. The Moores had arrived toting a cow-shaped cake for dessert, and Ms. O'Reilly brought a plate of veggies that Yurt immediately raided to make tentacles for his space alien.

"We came so close to getting a fox." Charlotte walked over to Isabel and Katani. "Patrice had us running through the woods to find the little guy."

"Boy, did she ever," giggled Katani.

"We got a fox!" blurted Isabel.

"Oooh, let's see!" Charlotte urged.

But then Isabel remembered that her picture wasn't a real fox, it was a prop fox, which might win them the point in the end, but certainly would unearth a whole Pandora's Box of questions from the Salty Cods that she did not want to get into. *Where did you see a fake fox? Why were you there? What were you doing?* No, Isabel clearly couldn't risk it.

"Sorry, guys . . . I am sworn to secrecy," she said, feeling uncomfortable that her words bordered on a fib.

"Oh, okay," Charlotte answered softly, suddenly worrying that maybe the Cods were behind. "How about you guys?" she asked Chelsea.

Chelsea really wanted to show off her ten photos. She was quite proud that she had accomplished finding all the bonus items on just the first day. But she also knew that finding all ten things on the first day looked a little suspicious. *How could she have possibly found everything between looking for clues?* So Chelsea just shrugged and said coyly, "Us too. Sworn to secrecy. Go team!" She tried to laugh but it came out kind of weak.

"Um, I'm going to go get seconds," Isabel announced. "Anyone want anything? No? Okay, then." She quickly got up and hustled away.

"I'm, um, going too," Chelsea said, following Isabel.

Charlotte was all for team spirit, but her classmates were acting so *weird*. As Isabel walked away, Charlotte, whose brain was wired for detective work, spotted a large odd-looking blue glob adhered to her shoe and some yellow splotches on her sleeve. She had no idea where the Cranberry Boggers' journey had taken them, but Charlotte had a feeling that they had gone on a very different kind of scavenger hunt than she had been on.

"Here, they brought out watermelon!" Isabel said as she and Chelsea came back with extra slices for Charlotte and Katani.

"Watch out for flying seeds," Chelsea warned, just as Dillon let one loose.

"That's a new record!" Avery whooped. "Let me try again."

Thankfully, Sienna Underwood stepped in the middle of the seed-spitting contest with a box of graham crackers in one hand and bags of marshmallows and chocolate bars in the other. "Who likes s'mores?" she asked, and watermelon seeds were completely forgotten.

As everyone licked their sticky fingers, Dexter Underwood stood up. "Now, who here is up for a rousing game of water polo? We've got a net we can put up across the pool!"

The Cranberry Boggers had their hands up before anyone. Charlotte couldn't figure out how they were so lucky to have gotten their second wind. She was absolutely zonked. Just then she learned she had an unexpected ally.

"I am one hundred percent POOPED!" Avery declared. I couldn't serve another volleyball today if you paid me." She received a round of weird looks from everyone who was not on Nauset Beach to witness her impressive display earlier. "I mean, a volleyball other than the zero I served already, which was my limit."

"I am with Avery all the way. You should have seen the Salty Cods today! Man, we were on *fire*," Patrice announced proudly.

"You were?" asked Avery.

"So check it out. We got Charlotte who's, like, a human dictionary and knew all the hard words on the list. Nick and Katani who are, like, masters of the map, right? And Dillon and me to motivate everyone to go as fast as they can. Between the five of us, the Cods are unstoppable!" Patrice beamed at her team and winked at her sister. Katani was surprised and pleased that her sister mentioned her map skills.

Avery felt a pang of jealousy. Even though she'd really enjoyed her day at the beach, Patrice's enthusiasm had triggered her competitive streak. *Okay, it wasn't so much a streak as it was a full-blown lightning bolt.* She would have to get the Beach Barnacles on the ball! *Tomorrow,* she promised herself. *Tomorrow!*

"We worked so hard getting clues today, I bet all my fish are ready to rest," Patrice shared.

"Is this true? Does everyone feel that way?" asked Mr. Moore. Hands raised included the Cods and the Barnacles nay, the Boggers yay. Majority ruled, and Charlotte was thrilled to be exempt from an opportunity to embarrass herself in a fast-paced game in the pool. But she couldn't help that nagging feeling . . . the one that said it was strange that Avery didn't want to do an athletic activity. *There is something rotten in the state of Cape Cod!* Charlotte remarked to herself.

"What about a ghost story?" Nick suggested. "My family always tells scary stories when we go camping."

"Yeah!" Fabiana agreed. "Sometimes we even act them out."

"WOOOooooOOO!" Yurt jumped up, waving his hands in the air. "I'm a ghost!"

"That will be enough, Henry." Ms. O'Reilly put a hand on his shoulder before he went spinning straight into the hot grill. "Who has a tale that they would like to share?" she asked.

Maeve's hand shot up. "I have one!"

Ms. O'Reilly shook her head. "Why am I not surprised? Maeve, go ahead."

Maeve took a deep breath and began, "High on a hill

lived a lonely goatherd, lay-ee odle lay-ee odle lay hee hoo. . . ." She was yodeling.

"Um, Maeve, is this, like, a song from a musical or something?" asked Avery.

Maeve nodded. "I borrowed it from *The Sound of Music*."

The group shifted uncomfortably. "Can we just hear a regular spooky campfire story instead?" Avery followed up bluntly.

Maeve sat down, looking only slightly wounded. Leave it to Avery to make a comment like that. However, Avery's honesty was welcome to the rest of the group. It was obvious by the looks on everyone's faces that no one particularly wanted to hear Maeve's yodel story, except for Isabel who said, "I love *The Sound of Music!*"

"Okay, scavenger hunters. I've got a good one," Mr. Moore announced.

"It'd better not be about cows," Dillon whispered to Maeve, who, even though she was still smarting from Avery's comment, managed a tiny smile.

But Mr. Moore's story, thankfully, had absolutely nothing to do with cows. It was about—much to the Cranberry Boggers' delight—pirates. "Once upon a time, in the deep, blue waters of Boothbay Harbor in Maine, lived three merry pirates. These pirates didn't have much to speak of in terms of treasure . . . and they weren't much to look at. There was Old Googles McFlanagan, who would've been a rather handsome lad if it weren't for his one googly eye and his propensity for spitting when he spoke. Very unfortunate, really. Then there was Red "Lettuce Head" Johnson. Crazy pirate was an organic vegetarian! Have you ever heard of anything so preposterous? Very hard to maintain that kind of diet on the Seven Seas, I'll have you know."

The kids giggled. Mr. Moore was turning out to be a very entertaining storyteller! "And finally, we had the leader of the pack—Four-Eyed Charlie. Yeah, they weren't really that creative back in the day. Four-Eyed was small, but he was the only pirate the other two goons listened to, because he was the only one giving any sensible orders. Anyway, these three pirates were an odd band of fools, you see—a motley crew, a mishmashed bunch. All the other pirates in Boothbay Harbor would laugh at them as they sailed around with their fancy boats. But the crew of the *Wamalama Ringding*—that was their boat—didn't let the laughter of the competition get them down.

"They were underdogs, see. They knew that they didn't have the largest crew or the biggest boat, but they had something that the other pirates did not. Who can guess what that was?"

Betsy's hand shot up. "Heart. They had heart."

"Wrong!" Mr. Moore declared. "Anyone else?"

"Brains?" Danny ventured cautiously.

"Yes, but everybody has a brain, Daniel. Your body needs one to live. No, the crew of the *Wamalama Ringding* had keys to the local perfume shop. That's right! You see, Four-Eyed Charlie's mother owned the store."

Riley raised his hand. "Um, Mr. Moore, why would pirates want perfume?"

"Exactly! That's what was so brilliant about it, Riley. No self-respecting pirate would want to be caught dead in his mother's perfume shop. But every night it was Four-Eyed Charlie's curse to have to lock up the store and dust the store windows. Oh, it was the most dreadful form of torture. The store was right next to the dock, and all the other pirates would go around the harbor and laugh at him. They would call him Flower Four-Eyes and Charlie Cologne . . . *oh, the laughter*. Lettuce Head and Googles were powerless to stop the evil pirates.

"Well, finally Four-Eyed became fed up with whole thing and decided to put a stop to the tormenting once and for all. The crew of the *Wamalama Ringding* decided to get their revenge. They were going to take a whole basketful of eggs from Lettuce Head's organic farm and when the clock stuck midnight go down to the docks with a superpowerful egg catapult that Four-Eyed invented and just go nuts. Imagine! Eggs everywhere! Oooh, the smell! The SMELL!"

Mr. Moore rubbed his hands together deviously. "All those evil pirates would beg for perfume and Charlie wouldn't give them ANY!" The science teacher was so into his story, Maeve could sense the anticipation of the audience. Would the crew of the *Wamalama Ringding* succeed?

"But then . . . on the night of their fatal attack . . . disaster! Four-Eyed's mom got a shipment in of ten extra boxes of exotic pink lotus blossom bubblegum scent."

"Hideous!" Katani murmured just as Maeve uttered a wistful, "Awesome!"

"Four-Eyed's mother had no room for the boxes in her tiny store. 'You must do something with these,' she ordered her son. 'Honestly, I don't care what you do with them, but I can't keep them in this attic. Not only is it a fire hazard, but I'm afraid the weight might cause our roof to cave in.'

"Four-Eyed was, at heart, a good pirate, and he did not want to see his mother's store destroyed by surplus bottles of flowery bubblegum-scented perfume, so he agreed to help her out. As he was dragging the first box out the back, and wondering how he was also going to get rid of 419 eggs now that the catapult plan was off, a single bottle fell out of the bottom of the box and started rolling toward the harbor . . . and that's when Four-Eyed had an infinitively more brilliant epiphany.

"Four-Eyed got the crew of the *Wamalama Ringding* together and the three pirates spent the entire evening . . . baking. They stirred and mixed and measured like they'd never baked before."

Nick raised his hand. "Uh, Mr. Moore, *had they* baked before?"

Mr. Moore rolled his eyes. "Don't forget, at least one of those pirates had an organic farm. . . ."

Nick and Charlotte giggled.

"Anyway, they baked until just before sunup. They almost didn't think they would finish! Finally, they carried their *magnum opus* down to the harbor and left a little gift on the deck of every single ship in that bay. As the dawn started breaking they sat on the beach to wait.

"'I'm starving!' Googles declared. He was always the first on the *Wamalama* to want to eat something, and they *had* spent the entire night cooking.

"'What about all those eggs I've been saving in my fridge?' Lettuce Head suggested.

"With that the three merry pirates scuttled back to Lettuce Head's farm and not only collected their eggs, but picked a whole bunch of fresh veggies and brought them back down to the harbor. At this point it was light out and the rest of the pirates were gathering on the decks of their ships, cheering and wondering whose birthday it was. For the crew of the *Wamalama Ringding* had baked cakes for every single ship.

"But when the meanest, most evil pirate of them all, Fritz Fang, sliced his cutlass through the cake, what should explode all over his ragged crew but the overwhelming stench of lotus blossoms and bubblegum! That's right, the cakes were just a disguise baked around a thin bag full of the hideous perfume.

"All the other townsfolk were also waking up and they wondered what that horrid smell was. Why, word spread, and there were villagers from ten, twenty miles away making the journey to catch a whiff of the Boothbay Perfumed Pirates!

"Now, Lettuce Head, see, he was pretty handy on the grill, so he broke out his grill and a pan. Next thing you know he's making the most delicious veggie omelets you've ever seen and selling them to the tourists at four bucks an omelet. In today's economy, that'd be around twelve bucks each. So, true to his pirate creed, he was essentially robbing the villagers blind. And that morning was the start of Lettuce Head's House of Organic Omelets and Produce, which still stands in Boothbay Harbor to this day. And, might I add, still overcharges the townsfolk."

"And what happened to the other pirates? The ones who got perfumed?" Maeve asked.

Mr. Moore shrugged. "Fritz Fang and his gang tried tomato juice, they tried jumping in vats of ale, they even tried washing—none of them had had a bath in twenty years—but no matter what they did, they still smelled like flower-scented candy. And they never messed with Four-Eyed Charlie again, I can tell you that right now!"

The kids and adults started clapping, and as Mr. Moore took a bow, Mrs. Moore announced, "Ladies and gentlemen, may I present to you, Four-Eyed Charlie in the flesh . . . my husband!"

The crowd laughed and Mr. Moore turned a little pink. "Well, I was a bit of a merry prankster back in the day. But remember, kids, not a single pirate was harmed, and not vial of perfume was wasted. We recycled all the glass bottles."

"That's very nice, Charlie," Ms. O'Reilly said with a chuckle. "You know, I heard that there's actually a bit of a pirate craze hitting Cape Cod right now as we speak. Yes, apparently a major studio is shooting a movie here about Black Sam Bellamy. I heard that Simon Blackstone is going to be playing Black Sam! Can you believe it?"

Charlotte wasn't sure, but she thought she noticed

Maeve giving Isabel's elbow a little pinch. She was positive she heard a sharp intake of breath from Riley.

"Black Sam is the man!" Yurt cheered. "I read up on him after Danny mentioned him in class. Turns out he was like a Robin Hood dude, and would steal from the richer pirates and give the loot to the poor. Every time he got a bigger ship, he would give his old one to the captain whose ship he was stealing. That's kind of cool, isn't it?"

Before the kids could begin to discuss the moral dilemma of a Robin-Hooding pirate, Mr. Moore announced, "Okay, kids, I hate to break this party up, but it's getting late. Nick, Charlotte, Chelsea? Who wants to announce where we're going to be bunking down for the night?"

"We all will," Charlotte said, motioning for her friends to stand and join her in the middle of the circle. "Nick, you want to tell?"

Nick stood up and announced, "You guys are going to love this! We have arranged to stay in an old Coast Guard station called the NEED Building. It's the coolest old house and it's been converted into, like, a hotel for school groups to stay in."

"Not really a hotel," Chelsea went on to explain. "I mean, don't expect to find mints on your pillow or tiny shampoos in the bathroom. But it does have bunk beds, and it's right by the ocean!"

"It also has a kitchen with cooking utensils. I think it'll be sweet!" Nick continued. "Like if we all lived together in a house by the sea in the 1800s. Pretty cool, if you ask me!"

"Dude, is it haunted?" Dillon asked.

"Probably with the ghosts of those perfumed pirates." Yurt pinched his nose and made a *whooo* sound that came out in a funny squeak.

"Are you *sure* I can't just stay in my own house?" Kiki whined to Ms. O'Reilly.

"No way!" Nick, Charlotte, and Chelsea chimed in together. "We came on this trip together, we stay together!"

Isabel was feeling a little nervous. Staying at an old house by the ocean seemed exciting and all, but she also thought it sounded a little spooky. She wanted to check in with Charlotte to make *sure* that there weren't any rumors that this place could be haunted, but she was afraid someone would hear her and think she was a major scaredy-cat . . . which she was. But she decided that now was as good a time as any to practice being brave, and so she took a deep breath and boarded the cars with her friends.

Kiki gave her parents a hug good-bye before she left, and as she did, her mother whispered, "It was so nice to meet all your friends! These kids are such a refreshing change from the usual bunch. If I have to hear Anna McMasters and her 'duh' one more time . . . You should have these kids over more often."

"I agree, Pumpkin," Charlotte heard Mr. Underwood proclaim. "That Avery girl is a hoot. And Maeve Kaplan-Taylor . . . what a character. Oh, and Yurt, was it? Real stand-up guy."

Kiki nodded. "Okay, great. Good night, guys."

"Oh, and darling?" Sienna Underwood added, "Your father and I are so proud of you."

"Parents just don't get it!" Kiki muttered tragically.

"Come on, Keeks," Yurt teased her. "You know you can't wait for tomorrow."

Kiki turned her head, but Charlotte could tell she was smiling.

13

Creepopalooza!

Why do all the girls have to be on the second floor?" Maeve griped as she dragged her heavy sleepover bag (Maeve's sleepover bags were always the heaviest) up the creaky wooden stairs at the NEED Building.

"Come on, Maeve, you can do it. All that dancing has made you Super Maeve!" Charlotte cheered on Maeve as she huffed and puffed up the stairs.

"That's not it!" Maeve retorted. "I just kind of imagined that we would all stay up late telling ghost stories together. It would be so much fun! I bet some of the guys have some really funny stories. It could be like a party!" she gushed.

"Well, that's never going to happen!" scoffed Katani. "Everyone's too tired, including me. Come back to planet Earth," she said, tugging on Maeve's backpack.

"Well, it sounded fun, right?" exclaimed Maeve with an infectious smile. "I hope all the BSG will at least be able to room together," she whispered to Charlotte.

Maeve detected a little *something something* in Charlotte's look when she turned to answer. "Actually, Maeve, I had my dad call the NEED Building in advance to ask about the setups of the rooms. They said that whoever took the downstairs would all be bunking together in one huge room, but the upstairs people would have to break down into smaller groups. The largest room up here . . ." Charlotte ran ahead, dramatically opened a door, and ushered her friends inside. ". . . has exactly five beds!"

"Yay!" Isabel squealed, clapping her hands together in short little energetic bursts and running over to claim the lone twin bed.

Avery rushed to the bunk beds, crawled up like a monkey, and threw her sleeping bag down like an explorer marking newly discovered territory. Charlotte was also partial to the top bunk, which was fine with Katani and Maeve, who preferred the lower.

"This is almost like camping in the wild! I love it," Charlotte declared. Sure, the mattress might have been a little weathered and worn, and yeah, maybe the floors were a little dusty, but this is what roughing it was! When the pitter-patter of plump raindrops began sounding on the roof above, Charlotte was positively in heaven. Could she have asked for a more perfect evening?

But some of the BSG were a little less excited.

"This does remind me a little of Montana. . . . It's kind of spooky," Avery murmured. Over the winter, Maeve, Charlotte, and Avery had gotten stuck in an abandoned—well, almost abandoned—mining town in Montana with Charlotte's dad.

"Bite your tongue, Avery." Maeve nodded toward Isabel, who had begun to chew on her finger.

"I can't even imagine if I had been out there with you guys!" Katani shivered, remembering the huge storm that had them stranded for days. She and Isabel had been worried sick at the hotel, waiting for their friends to show up!

Just then, the doorknob turned.

Isabel nearly jumped out of her skin, but it was just Chelsea. "It's a little too quiet and creepy in my room," she said. "Betsy is reading and Kiki went to shower."

"Okay, everyone," Charlotte assured them all. "Patrice and Fabiana are in the room right next door, Ms. O'Reilly is across the hall, and Ben Briggs is staying with the boys downstairs. We're totally safe!"

"I wouldn't be relying on Ben if I were you." Chelsea shrugged.

"What do you mean, Chels? Your brother sure looks like the big and strong type. I would trust him to wrestle down a little old ghost," Maeve said with a nod, confident that a star football player like Ben would defend his sister and friends against any evil that might befall them.

"Normally, I would agree with you," Chelsea answered. "But didn't you see how he stumbled into his bedroom yawning like a giant lion? I promise you, my brother is probably already out like a log," Chelsea said. "As a matter of fact, I'm pretty tired too. See you guys in the morning."

She yawned and headed back to her designated room, feeling better that she was surrounded by friends.

"Where are Mr. and Mrs. Moooore sleeping?" mooed Avery. She had become quite fond of the crazy cow man and his adoring wife.

"Oh, Ave." Charlotte explained, "Since there was no room here, Mr. and Mrs. Moore are staying at a breakfast-and-bed inn near here."

"What?" Charlotte stared at her friends, wondering why the BSG were looking at her like she was from another planet.

Finally, Katani took pity on her. "Char. It's bed and breakfast."

"Isn't that what I said?" she asked in confusion.

"Ahh, no, Char. You did not," Avery said with a devilish twinkle in her eye. "You said breakfast-and-bed. Therefore, I'm sorry to say, you must be punished." With that, Avery, pillow in hand, jumped off her bed like a flying squirrel and began to chase a shrieking Charlotte around the room. As Charlotte ducked in and around the screaming BSG, Avery pretended to stalk her like a marauding ninja.

"Go, Avery, go, Avery," rocked Maeve.

"Go, Charlotte, go, Charlotte." Isabel and Katani chanted as they stomped around the room in unison.

When Charlotte ran behind the cheerleaders, Avery, with a devilish gleam in her eyes, charged through and tried to bonk Charlotte with the pillow. For once Charlotte was the quick one and ran to her bed for her own pillow.

But when she turned around, Avery was nowhere to be seen.

"What's going on here?" Charlotte asked. Her heart pounded as she tried to control her breathing. "Where is that little imp?" she demanded of wide-eyed Isabel, Maeve, and Katani, who stood before her, their arms locked, innocent expressions plastered on their faces.

Suddenly Avery burst through from behind the girls and began pelting a hysterically laughing Charlotte with her pillow. Charlotte unsuccessfully tried to dodge the pillow-mashing as Avery shouted, "Take that you word-masher."

While Charlotte shrieked and the BSG screamed uproariously, Maeve began to sing, "Girls just wanna have pillow fights."

Their antics were abruptly interrupted by a loud bang from the stairs. "Elephants, please be quiet or there will be trouble," shouted an obviously tired Ms. O'Reilly.

Giggling, the girls collapsed on the beds.

"You know, guys," Charlotte said when she could talk, "this really is a safe place, except for the presence of a certain person who has been sighted for repeated pillow-mashing. Here . . . listen up."

Charlotte began reading from a pamphlet she had pulled from her backpack. "'NEED stands for National Park Service residential environmental education program. The goal of the program is to provide a *safe* place for school groups to stay and learn about the environment while visiting the Cape.' So except for the danger presented by the notorious Brookline pillow-masher, known as Avery Koh Madden, I don't think we have to worry." A grinning Charlotte propped herself up on one elbow and directed, "On to the showers, campers!"

Comforted, the BSG took turns showering. Afterward, Maeve put on her fuzziest of flannel nightgowns and, climbing into her sleeping bag, declared, "I feel like a million bucks!" The rest of the BSG agreed. "There's nothing like a hot, soapy shower after a day pedaling around Cape Cod on bikes to make one ready to snuggle up and head for the land of Nod," announced Charlotte as she stood by her bunk.

Or playing on the beach, Avery thought secretly.

Or sweating in polyester costumes, Maeve also thought secretly.

Once Avery, Maeve, Isabel, and Katani were all zipped up in their sleeping bags, Charlotte produced a flashlight from her backpack, turned it on, and placed it on the floor. It sent a dim light to the ceiling, breaking the absolute blackness. After Charlotte climbed up to the bunk above Katani and squeezed the drips out of her wet braids, she asked, "So what was the best thing that happened to you guys today?"

There was dead silence.

This is getting too weird. Charlotte lay back on the pillow.

Maeve longed to share how exhilarating her experience on the film set was, and how adorable Orlando Plume was in real life, but she knew that letting her team's secret slip would be a horrible mistake. So she just said as nonchalantly as she could manage, "Nothing *too* exciting. Except it looks like old Danny Pellegrino's in love again. . . ."

Charlotte sat up again. "Oh, that's terrible. Has he been annoying you all day, Iz?"

"No," Isabel confessed. "It's Betsy that Danny has his eye on now."

Avery, Katani, and Charlotte gasped in unison. "No way!"

Maeve assured them in a higher-pitched voice than usual. "It's true! You should have seen *them* today. Seriously, Char, Danny was mesmerized by Betsy's encyclopedia-like pirate facts!"

"Pirates?" Charlotte held her pillow tightly against her chest. What *was* Maeve talking about? Maeve tried to regroup, but the excitement of the long day was making it impossible to keep everything in. "Oh, you know Betsy, she knew absolutely everything about Cape Cod, and anachronisms, and wetus . . . wetus!" Maeve fell back on her bed suddenly exhausted.

"Yeah!" Isabel jumped in, nervous that Maeve was really close to getting their team in big trouble. "You wouldn't believe the Betsy Fitzgerald *Book of Facts About Everything.*"

Charlotte peered down at a loopy, giggling Maeve. "You Cranberry Bogger ladies need to spill. What's going on with this Betsy–Danny thing?"

"Yeah!" Avery piped up, glad no one had asked her about *her* favorite part of the day, which was obviously surfing.

"Well, it's not really a *romance* thing," pronounced. Maeve, who thought herself somewhat of an authority on the subject. "It's more like someone is finally paying attention to all those braggy comments Betsy's always making and they're *both* loving it."

"Like how?" probed Charlotte, feeling somewhere in her foggy, sleepy mind that she was still missing something here.

"You know, like when Betsy got that special job as the director's consultant—"

Isabel threw a coughing fit to get Maeve's attention. A totally sleepy Maeve was spilling all right—their big secret *everywhere*.

"What special job?" asked Katani.

Isabel listened, baffled, with no idea how to stop the madness, as Maeve continued on, completely oblivious to Charlotte and Katani's growing suspicion.

"She got everyone to make wetus! And they had to be his-tor-i-cal-ly ac-cur-ate." Maeve enunciated every syllable separately in her best academic voice. "Can you believe it? They're just like these round tent-house things that people lived in a long time ago. . . ."

"Maeve!" Isabel admonished, then realized Charlotte was grinning.

"Oh! Like yurts. We saw those too . . . the first clue, right?"

"Yes!" Isabel agreed. She didn't know what had just happened, and she never got a chance to find out how yurts and wetus were related, because at that moment their door burst open and three shadowy figures in white stood in the frame. "Thank goodness, you're up!" It was Kiki along with Chelsea and Betsy. They were wearing long white T-shirts and shaking like leaves.

"Come on in!" beckoned Avery. "What's wrong with you crazy cats?"

Betsy gulped as she and the other two timorously sat down on the lower bunks. "Nothing is wrong. I'm convinced there is a logical explanation. . . ."

Chelsea shook her head vehemently as she sat on Maeve's bed. "No! You guys, something really weird happened."

"Trust me, I wouldn't be here if I wasn't totally creeped out," Kiki asserted.

"It's okay," Maeve wrapped her arm around Chelsea's shoulder. "Tell Auntie Maeve."

Kiki began, "Well, on my way back from the shower, I overheard the boys talking in the game room and then these girls just happened by. . . ."

"*Ahem,*" Chelsea said loudly, giving Betsy and Kiki an accusatory look.

"Okay, we were sort of kind of spying on them," Betsy admitted.

The Beacon Street Girls were speechless. "Betsy Fitzgerald misbehaving? This is one for the history books," a surprised Charlotte finally blurted out.

"What?" asked Betsy. "It was only a joke. . . ."

The BSG had no problem with spying on boys, especially Maeve, who was feeling a little jealous that she hadn't thought of it first. It was just that the thought of Chelsea Briggs, Betsy Fitzgerald, and Kiki Underwood crouching outside the game room and up to mischief like the best of friends was almost too crazy to imagine.

"Well, I wish I'd never done it!" Chelsea declared. "Now all I can think about is that terrible story. . . ."

Betsy explained, "We heard Danny Pellegrino telling the other boys that, like, ten years ago a kid about our age"—her voice became so quiet the girls could barely hear her—"*died here.*"

Isabel covered her mouth. "No way! Ew, that's so creepy," she shuddered as her foot began to shake.

Chelsea was pale. "It gets worse. Apparently he went night swimming with his friends and disappeared. . . . He must have drowned or something. Then they had to close the building down afterward."

Charlotte frowned. "I don't remember reading anything about that. Chelsea, do you?"

Chelsea shook her head. "No, but I don't think that that's something they'd put in the brochure, you know?"

"I suppose not," Charlotte mumbled.

"Tell them the rest," Kiki demanded.

"There's more of this Creepopalooza!?" Avery didn't know how much more she could handle before bedtime. Let alone how much more Isabel could handle—she was starting to look really weirded out.

"We think . . . we think we saw something," Chelsea uttered finally. "Out . . . out by the beach."

"What did you see?" asked Maeve, awestruck.

"It looked like"—Betsy pursed her lips and whispered—"a little boy."

Isabel, Charlotte, and Maeve gasped, but Katani just rolled her eyes. "Oh, please. You guys are crazy if you think you actually saw a ghost out there."

Isabel looked relieved. "You don't believe in ghosts?" she asked Katani in a timid voice.

"No way!" Katani shook her head. "My dad, who is really smart, said there is no scientific proof of ghosts, spirits, or anything like that. It's just people's crazy imaginations."

Kiki folded her arms. "If you think I'd make up something like that then *you're* the one who's crazy."

"Ahem!" Avery said, sounding like a lawyer. "She does have a point, Katani."

Charlotte pulled her journal and pen out of her bag. "Okay, can you describe to me exactly what you saw?" She didn't want to miss out on the description a real ghost, if there was one.

Betsy, not surprisingly, was the first to volunteer. "He was a small boy, younger than us, I think. He was dressed in—well, I couldn't really tell because it's so dark out—but it looked like he was crying."

Charlotte was intrigued. "Crying, like how?"

Betsy bent over and placed her head in her hands and Chelsea, very cautiously, began to tiptoe over to the window. Isabel grabbed her arm to stop, but it was like Chelsea was in a trance. When she got to the window she let out a yelp and cried, "He's here! He's here! Come see for yourselves!"

The girls leaped up and rushed over to the window. Sure enough, there was a tiny person kneeling by the dune. At once, all eight girls let out a hair-raising, blood-curdling scream. And the screaming didn't stop until Ms. O'Reilly and all three chaperones appeared at their door-way. Ben's eyes were still half shut and Fabiana hovered in the doorway behind Patrice, but Ms. O'Reilly strode right into the room.

"What's going on in here?" she asked, genuinely con-cerned.

"G-g-g-*ghost*!" was all anyone could blubber. Even Katani looked a little shaken.

When Chelsea and Isabel burst into tears, Ben Briggs snapped into action.

He stormed up to the window, huge hands locked on his hips. "That's no ghost!" he growled. He jiggled the lock on the window, effortlessly pushed it open, and stuck out his head. "HENRY YURT! YOU GET YOUR FUZZY-HEADED SHORT SELF IN HERE!"

Then he turned to Chelsea and gave her a giant bear hug. "It's okay. I'll teach those boys not to pick on my sister and her friends!"

The "crying" person stood up and started running at lightning speed back to the house. Suddenly, from out of the bushes, four more runners appeared. "Looks like we had more than one ghost haunting the beach," Ben grumbled. "Don't worry, Ms. O'Reilly. I got this one."

"Are you sure?" asked Ms. O'Reilly.

"Oh, yeah. There's only one thing scarier than a ghost in the middle of the night. . . . *ME!*"

Ben stomped down the creaky stairs to greet the merry pranksters upon their return. The girls scampered behind him, at once furious and dying of curiosity. Maeve couldn't help admiring how dashing and debonair Ben seemed, defending the honor of the ladies of the house. *How positively heroic,* she thought fondly.

Isabel sniffed up the last of her tears and felt her horror washing away. Now that she knew it was all a joke, she almost felt sorry for the boys.

"Nick, Dillon, Riley, Danny . . . and look who it is . . . our little ghostly friend, Yurtmeister!" Ben crouched down to look Yurt in the eye. "I just have one question for you punks: WHAT IN THE NAME OF ALL THINGS SANE WERE YOU THINKING?"

The boys hung their heads, as the girls stole secret glances of smug satisfaction. The boys all looked so guilty and ashamed of themselves. *This is awesome,* thought Avery, who couldn't wait to tease them tomorrow.

"Now I think you owe these young ladies an apology. Before me and the guys on the football team start owing one *to you!*"

"Sorry," the boys all mumbled. Charlotte noticed that a chagrined Nick was making eye contact with only her, as if to say, "Yeah, that was really stupid," and she gave him a smile to show her forgiveness. It was impossible to stay angry at *him*. Besides, no one really got hurt or anything and . . . it was kind of funny. She'd have to write up the whole story in her journal later. Maybe she'd even share it with Nick.

Dillon and Riley seemed to be seeking Maeve's approval, but Maeve was completely immersed in her role as the wounded damsel in distress. She just flounced the skirt of her nightgown, gave a little high-pitched, "Hmph!" and marched back up the stairs.

"You know we were totally kidding," Danny confided to Betsy as she passed. "I'm real sorry."

Betsy gave him burning snake-eyes. "You are not forgiven," she sniffled.

"Poor Danny," Isabel said to her as they climbed the stairs. She knew there was nothing Betsy detested more than being wrong, and she had definitely been wrong about the ghost in the yard. But it was obvious that Danny felt absolutely terrible about what happened. He had kept trying to get Betsy's attention, but she had refused to look at him.

"Betsy," said Isabel, who believed in the power of forgiveness to solve problems. "He said he's sorry."

"Ha! He deserves no sympathy, trust me," an indignant Betsy charged.

"Wow, Betsy, isn't that a little cold? I mean, wasn't it just a joke and all?" Avery asked, then ducked into the BSG's room, leaving Betsy and Isabel alone in the hallway.

Betsy squinted in confusion. "What is she talking about, Isabel? You were really scared! And that trick was obviously *his* idea. He was the one telling the stupid ghost story."

Isabel smiled. She was no expert in boys, but she knew Betsy had a lot to learn. "That trick was the idea of *all of them*. Haven't you heard that expression, 'boys will be boys'?"

Betsy harrumphed. "I doubt it. Danny's the only one of that bunch capable of coming up with something so deviously clever!"

"You think he's smart?" asked Isabel. She was surprised Betsy was willing to call anyone else clever. Even in her anger, it sounded almost like Betsy was impressed!

Betsy shrugged. "Not as smart as"—she bit her tongue—"other people. But yeah, I guess he's pretty smart."

"Well, Danny obviously thinks pretty highly of you," Isabel said as they stood outside the door of Betsy's room. "He was practically drooling on the movie set today," she added in a hushed voice.

"No!" Betsy objected, but she looked interested.

Isabel nodded. "Yes. And I bet he feels pretty terrible after how angry you were."

Betsy swallowed. "I'm not really *that* angry, I guess."

"Me neither," Isabel confided. "You know, Danny's a sweet guy. You guys could be friends. Maybe think about being a little extra nice to him tomorrow."

Betsy smiled. "Okay. I'll think about that."

Isabel and Betsy said good night. As Isabel made her way to her bunk, it occurred to her that this scavenger hunt wasn't just about having fun with her best friends and going on an adventure; it was bringing people together in all kinds of new ways.

14

The Cods and the Compass

Charlotte woke up the next morning feeling peachy fine. She'd dreamed that the Salty Cods had found 1,000 clues, including a humpback whale living in the Underwood's swimming pool, and somebody from the *Guinness Book of World Records* had called! After a big cat stretch, she squinted at the lovely sunlight streaming into their little room through the open window.

"Yum." She breathed in the dewy, salty scent of the sea air. The fresh smell reminded her why she loved writing, traveling, and daydreaming.

She looked down from the top bunk at a sleeping Isabel and Maeve, then across at Avery, who had one arm hanging down the side of her bunk. Little chortling snores came from Maeve's sleeping bag. Charlotte thought it was kind of cute, but she knew Maeve would just die if she ever knew she was a bit of a snorer. Charlotte got up and headed to the bathroom, where she found Katani already dressed and brushing her teeth.

"I just talked to Patrice," Katani informed her. "And here's the plan. Nick and Dillon are already awake. They're playing soccer in the backyard. Patrice says if we hit the road now we'll have, like, an hour edge over the other teams."

Charlotte smiled as she admired her own freshly polished pearly whites. "Your sister is such a leader. Do you think we really have a chance at winning this thing?"

"Maybe . . . if we get an early start," Katani replied as she put her toiletries away in a stylish yellow pouch. "Besides, if we don't win, I'm never gonna hear the end of it. Believe it or not, my sister isn't the greatest loser. So let's get a move on."

Charlotte feigned a look of shock. "A Summers sister . . . an unhappy loser. NO WAY!"

The girls packed up quickly, careful not to disturb their sleepyhead friends. Whatever noise they ended up making didn't matter because the rest of the BSG were out like lights. Charlotte wondered for a second if they were doing the right thing—not waking the other three girls.

They knocked on Ms. O'Reilly's door across the hall, just to let her know they were heading out. She was dressed, and had a mystery novel in one hand.

"I was just going to wake you girls after I finished this chapter."

"Make sure you get some breakfast in the kitchen,"

she reminded them as they walked off. "And keep your walkie-talkie turned on. Good luck!"

After gulping down some cereal, Charlotte walked outside and caught sight of Nick Montoya. What was it about a big old camp T-shirt and backward Red Sox cap that made him look so cool? Charlotte used to think about herself and Nick as just good friends. But now his face lit up whenever he saw her.

"Morning, Char," Nick greeted, kicking the soccer ball to her.

"Hey," she replied, feeling her cheeks growing a bit pink. Charlotte jogged over to the ball, but as she bent her knee to kick it, she completely lost her balance on the wet grass and proceeded to wipe out on the lawn. *Oops! Charlotte "the Klutz" Ramsey strikes again.* She cringed.

Maybe if she just lay there, she hoped, somehow the horrible moment would just magically disappear,

"Nice one, Char." Nick was standing over her offering a hand. "What number is it now?"

"Could we just pretend that I am a graceful dancer and they just polished the floor but no one told me?" Charlotte asked as she grasped Nick's hand.

"No prob." Nick smiled as he helped her to her feet.

If Maeve had seen the moment, Charlotte knew she would have deemed it extremely swoon-worthy. Charlotte was just grateful Nick never made a big deal over her wipe-outs.

As Charlotte brushed wet grass off the seat of her pants, Patrice sauntered over waving an envelope. "Okay,

Cods, we must be in the lead. So let's not blow it now."

Katani shook her head. "That's motivational, Patrice—'let's not blow it'?"

"What do you mean? I don't know about you guys, but I didn't come this far to lose in the homestretch," Patrice stated matter-of-factly.

"I'm with Patrice! Let's open up that clue and get this show on the road," commanded Dillon. "I want to kick the competition to the moon!" he shouted as he raised his fist in the air. "And before I forget—nice splat, Charlotte."

"Thanks, Dillon," Charlotte answered, shuffling from one foot to the other.

"Okay, let's focus, people!" Patrice said as she opened the envelope and read the clue.

Directly north of where you slept is
where this landmark thing is kept. Alone it
stands all red and white, known for miles by
its strong light.

"That's easy! A lighthouse," Katani said as she folded her arms.

"Cool, but this is Cape Cod. There are like a gatrillion lighthouses!" Nick replied.

"Oh . . . so how are we supposed to know which it is?" asked a perplexed Dillon.

"Well, here's what we know. It's red and white. And it's directly north of the NEED Building," Charlotte contributed. "There must be a lighthouse on the map that's close."

Katani, who was turning into quite the budding cartographer, quickly located the NEED Building on the map and used the map key to find the lighthouse symbol. She then pointed out that there was indeed a lighthouse directly north of the NEED Building, and there appeared to be a path leading right to it. The only problem was that there were about six different paths departing from the NEED Building. . . . So which one was the one that went north to the lighthouse?

Dillon scratched his head. "Okay, I know how to figure this out. I got the ocean on my left, and the sun is riiiiight there, which means north is . . ." He spun around like a top, faster and faster and faster, and when he stopped, his arms were directed smack in front of a bike path shooting off into the woods. ". . . there!" he concluded proudly.

Nick gave his friend a light shove, and Dillon, dizzy from his spinning, toppled over like a Jenga tower. "This is a scavenger hunt, not spin the bottle, brainiac," Nick joshed.

"I was solving it the old-fashioned way," Dillon defended as he picked himself up.

"Or we could just check the compass," Katani suggested.

She pulled Patrice's Outward Bound compass out of the pouch on the back of her bike. Everyone gathered round to watch the needle. Charlotte patted Katani on the shoulder, and Dillon gave her a thumbs-up when the needle pointed exactly the way he had indicated.

"Wow! You got some mad skills on that compass, Sis,"

Patrice said admiringly. "Now, enough goofing around, people. We have a scavenger hunt to win!" The rest of the Cods didn't need to be told twice and climbed on to their bikes with their eyes on the prize . . . whatever that was!

Barnacle Maneuvers

Avery felt a surge of energy shoot through her as soon as her eyes opened. She sat up in bed, so eager to start her day that she completely forgot that she was on the top bunk of a bunk bed and whacked her head on the ceiling.

"Yowch! Now I get why you guys wanted the lower bunks." She yawned. "You guys . . . *you guys*?" She hung over the side of the bed. "What?" She was puzzled when she realized that she was the only one of the BSG left in the room. "This is a first," Avery mumbled as she pulled on her clothes at lightning speed, trying to ignore the aches she was feeling as a result of her surfing adventure the day before. As an athlete, Avery knew that muscles you haven't exercised in a while could be sore at first. "This better not ruin my biking," she said out loud to the empty room. "*Today* we have to get some clues!"

The halls were so quiet when Avery slipped out that she wondered if maybe everyone else had already gone. What if they'd forgotten about her? *Forget about me?* Avery had to laugh. *What, am I crazy?*

Indeed, no one had forgotten about Avery at all. Outside, the Beach Barnacles were sitting around the picnic table, chatting and munching on cold cereal and yogurt. Kiki, in sunglasses and a bathing suit, flipped through a fashion magazine, and Henry Yurt was carrying a pair of old flippers and snorkel that he'd found in the game room of the NEED Building.

"Finally! We thought you were going to sleep until noon," said Kiki, closing her magazine. "Now can we go, Ben?"

Avery rubbed her hands together. "Ooh. Why didn't you wake me up? What's the plan? Where are we going? Have we solved another clue?"

Chelsea, who had been quietly reading through an historical book about Cape Cod, looked up. "No!"

Avery frowned. "What do you mean, *no*? We gotta get this wagon train a-movin', people!"

Chelsea looked sullen. "They said they don't feel like doing the scavenger hunt." She motioned at the rest of the Beach Barnacles, including her brother. "They said that we don't have a chance of winning at this point anyway, so we might as well just go back to the beach."

Kiki rolled her eyes. "I mean, why not?"

Chelsea was appalled. "No! No way! The point of this thing is to do a scavenger hunt that we worked really hard on and explore Cape Cod and *have fun* on the way. I don't want to let Nick and Charlotte down. It's not fair." Chelsea stared at her brother as hard as she could, hoping she might be able to bore a hole in that thick skull of his.

Ben shifted uncomfortably. "Chels, I get that you worked hard and stuff, but we're so far behind, and everyone else kinda wants to just hang out, so—"

Avery stamped her foot. She had to intervene, even if

her heart secretly longed to get back on a surfboard. "Hey! No way can we give up. First of all, thanks to Chelsea over here"—Avery gave her a high five—"we nailed the bonus list yesterday, which means the Beach Barnacles are still in the running. I'm not sure, but it sounds like the Cranberry Boggers weren't exactly hardcore with getting points yesterday, either. I wouldn't be surprised if we were in second place."

A look of pleasant surprise went around the picnic table. "Chels," Ben said as he banged his fist on the table, "you're the chief, and Avery, you're a shaker! Barnacles, we might actually have a shot at winning this thing if we get cracking!"

"Yeah!" Avery cheered, starting to get revved up. "Besides, when I heard the others going on and on about finding the clues . . . well, I *really want to beat the pants off them*!" Ben, Chelsea, and Yurt burst out laughing. For such a tiny person, Avery's competitive spirit was off the charts.

"Oh, lame!" Kiki proclaimed. She fanned herself with her magazine and looked bored. "Can't we just go back to the beach and have, like, a chill day?"

"No," Ben defended the group decision. "We have to give this scavenger thing a shot. I mean, I'm supposed to be keeping you guys on track . . . and if we go back to the beach, we're always going to wonder if we could have done it if we'd put in some effort . . . besides looking like complete losers."

Kiki yawned loudly. "Not me."

Avery glared at her. "Won't you feel guilty for coming on the trip in the first place?"

Kiki smiled. "Not even a little bit." Kiki Underwood was a mystery to Avery. How could her parents be so nice, and Kiki be nice around them, and now it was like the Empress of Mean was back and worse than ever. "Well, if you guys don't want to go to the beach, that's okay. I can go alone. I know the way," Kiki said coolly, leaning back.

Avery put her hands on her hips and snapped, "No way, José. If you won't go on the scavenger hunt, you can go home!"

"Please, Keeks," Henry Yurt begged as he got down on one knee. "The scavenger hunt won't be the same without you." Kiki completely ignored him.

Ben smiled and picked up the walkie-talkie. "Or I can just ask Mr. Moore if he needs an assistant for the day. . . ."

"Hey, that's no fair!" Kiki yelled.

"But I'm sure he'd *love* to go to the beach," Avery said with a giggle.

Ben picked up the walkie-talkie. Avery could tell he was enjoying the panicked look in Kiki's face almost as much as she was.

"Wait, stop! If you call Mr. Moore, I'll get real detention for sure," Kiki pleaded.

"I am sick of this. . . . Just call Mr. Moore," a frustrated Chelsea complained.

Avery was shocked. She'd seen Chelsea stand up to her brother, sure, but standing up to Kiki Underwood was quite another story. Avery was impressed. She gave Chelsea a shoulder shrug in appreciation.

"No! I'm sorry. I'll be good. I'll participate and everything," Kiki begged. "Just let me come. *Please!* I *want* to come. . . . I'm allergic to detention!"

Ben paused as if deep in thought and then put down the walkie-talkie. "Well, okay." Team Beach Barnacle was back in the game! And Kiki looked like she'd just been pardoned from walking the plank of a real pirate ship.

15

⚑ Dancing and Divas

By the time the Cranberry Boggers hit the road, they were already thirty minutes late, and it was a fifteen-minute bike ride to the set. "It's cool," Maeve assured the Boggers. "They expect stars to be fashionably late."

"Maeve, I hate to burst your bubble," retorted Betsy, who had been the only one of the team to be up on time. "But I don't exactly think anyone here would qualify as a *star*."

"Ahhh, Betsy, if you don't think you are a star, you'll never be a star," explained Maeve cheerfully.

When they finally arrived at the set, it seemed that Bethany shared Betsy's opinion. "Where have you all been!" she fumed. "I was about to try to call those kids from yesterday!"

"We rode as fast as we could. We're on bikes, remember?" Danny Pellegrino spoke up. Though Betsy was still avoiding him after the incident last night, Isabel noticed their eyes meet. *Mmm*, thought Isabel, *Betsy must have for-given Danny. Maybe things will actually work out between them, and I will be free of Danny Pellegrino forever.*

Unfortunately, at that moment, Danny turned and said, "It's not like we're getting paid for this, right, Izzy?" He practically winked as he looked right at her. Maybe she had spoken too soon; Isabel cringed as she gave him a little half smile.

Betsy's little smile faded into a look of pained discomfort. Any more of Danny's over-the-top confidence could get them kicked right off the set!

"I'm going to pretend I didn't hear that." Bethany took a deep breath and began to pace back and forth like a worried sandpiper. "We're shooting the wedding banquet scene, when Black Sam Bellamy interrupts the dinner to save Princess Polly from her loveless marriage to the brutish Sir Eric Bonewagon," Bethany explained. "Maeve, you are going to be a flower girl. Fabiana, you're a wedding guest."

"A flower girl!" Maeve gushed as she twirled around in her imaginary flower girl designer dress. She had always wanted to be a flower girl, and she could only imagine what the dress was going to look like! *Perhaps light pink lace layered over white? Or maybe dark rose with a scalloped neck? Did flower girls wear crowns back then?*

"Riley, you're reprising your role from yesterday as the powder monkey," Bethany informed him. "And, get this, Ozmond even wrote in a few lines for you. Everyone thought you looked 'appealing' in your little pirate outfit!" She smirked.

Maeve's dress fantasies were rudely interrupted by a twang of jealousy—both for Riley getting a speaking role, and that someone other than she (certain blond girls, probably) thought he was adorable.

Life is so unfair. She gritted her teeth. Maeve was supposed to be the only one who knew and appreciated Riley's adorableness. That was the whole point of having a crush on the *band cutie who no one ever noticed until you did.*

"What about me?" Danny asked.

Bethany looked at her sheet. "Um, I don't need any more extras today. Thanks anyway, though!"

Danny looked completely crushed. "But my historical outfit was perfect, except for the shoe buckles, and I had an idea about those—"

Betsy spoke up before he could get them in even more trouble. "Danny can help me with the consulting today," she told Bethany. "He has a wealth of historical information at his fingertips."

Danny gave Betsy such a look of puppy-dog adoration that Isabel was happily convinced that she would be safe from a Danny Pellegrino crush for the rest of her junior high days. Now she could actually be pleasant to Danny and not have to worry that he would glom on to her like superglue ever again.

Bethany didn't look too impressed, but she answered. "Hey, I'm in wardrobe, so I'm going to go ahead and say why not."

"Although," she added, as she checked her wardrobe list, "I personally don't get why Ozmond wants you kids following him around, but then again no one understands a thing a crackpot does. . . ." Bethany strode off with her clipboard, muttering to herself.

"I guess I'll go find Patrick and Poppy," a relieved Isabel announced, running off to search for her favorite set designers.

Maeve let out a big sigh of relief as a grateful Danny sidled up beside Betsy. "Thanks for letting me help," he said as they wandered around the set looking for Ozmond, who was supposedly off somewhere getting coffee.

"Well," Betsy said. "That girl was not nice. I mean, you just can't take everyone from a group and leave one person out. . . . It's highly inappropriate social etiquette . . . but movies are a business. We have to go with the flow, you know."

"Betsy, you are something special, you know?" Danny looked at her again, this time his eyes wide with fascination.

Betsy giggled. "Maybe she was afraid that if she gave you a part, they'd have to pay you a zillion dollars or something!"

Danny's eyes sparkled. "Maybe they do! Maybe they have to pay everyone! Ha ha, just kidding. Man, I'd do this for free any day."

"Well, if it's any consolation, helping the director is fun stuff," Betsy assured him.

"Really?"

"Oh, yes. Ozmond totally listens. He wants things to

be right. Maybe we could even add this to our list of extra-curriculars."

Danny's face brightened. "So I can just tell him about a couple of anachronisms I've noticed?"

Betsy blinked. "Yes! Isn't that the greatest thing ever?"

Cranberry Boggers Dance a Jig of Sorts

It was taking the film crew absolutely forever to start filming. There was some sort of technical difficulty or something.

Fabiana asked everyone if they wanted to wait it out or get going. Maeve was conflicted. What she did know is that for the first time ever she was having the most amazing time *not being* filmed, but what about her friends? Fabiana asked for a show of hands—no one wanted to leave.

Maeve couldn't help voting to stay. She was thrilled because the flower girl (not just an orphan anymore!) got to do a little jig with the powder monkey boy. *Dance a little jig . . . with Riley.* That was what the script said.

Maeve was hoping the jig was interpretive and maybe she could convince the director to let them do a ballroom dance instead, but Danny (grrr) said that that would be completely unrealistic. So . . . a little jig was exactly what she and Riley were practicing.

I had no idea that a little pirate jig could be so much fun! She and Riley spun each other around and around until they began staggering from dizziness. Maeve's heart leaped when Riley reached out his hand to steady her. Or, was it she who offered her hand to Riley? He was, after all, beginning to turn a rather alarming shade of green.

"Riley," a suddenly concerned Nurse Maeve said, "you really don't look very well. Maybe we should try something different, so you don't get sick," she said sweetly.

Riley nodded gratefully. *It really doesn't matter as long as we keep dancing . . . together,* she thought happily.

Maeve patiently showed him a few dances she remembered from her week of Irish step dancing lessons. Although the lessons were a long time ago, Maeve's natural talent for dancing helped her recall a few simple moves.

In fact, after a few tries, she and Riley, who also had natural rhythm, were completely in sync, and the pirate crowd was going wild. They formed a circle around them and clapped, while the musicians on set played some Irish music on their guitars.

"Wheee!" Maeve shouted giddily when the music picked up pace.

"What is going on here?" demanded a shrill voice. The crowd stopped clapping and the music fizzled out as everyone cautiously cleared a path for a young woman wearing a fluffy red bathrobe. "I mean it! Will somebody please tell me why I'm *still waiting* in hair and makeup?"

Maeve gasped and leaned over to Riley. "Oh, that's her. . . . Lola Lindstrom . . . superstar!"

Riley's eyes widened. "Dude, you're right! I almost didn't recognize her with that black wig." Lola Lindstrom was huge . . . mega huge, and famous for her long fire-engine-red hair (Maeve had always felt a kinship), a penchant for dating foreign princes, and her oh-so-infamous, on-set temper tantrums.

"This is the best day of my life, Riley!" Maeve clasped her hands to her chest while she whispered. "To witness a Lola Lindstrom temper tantrum! It just doesn't get any better than this." Maeve squeezed Riley's hand.

"Like I told you, there are just a few kinks the director is trying to work out. . . ." Bethany began.

"Still?" Lola groaned. "For Pete's sake, by the time they're done I'm going to be *middle-aged*! I can't believe I turned down *Safari Game Park* for this."

"Don't worry, Miss Lindstrom," a visibly nervous Bethany tried to assure her. "The director is working with some historical consultants, and everything should be ready shortly. Why don't you go back to the trailer and put on the Princess Polly wedding dress?" By the end of her little speech Bethany's voice had begun to shake.

Lola crossed her arms and sniffled. "No."

"Pretty please," Bethany tried again, sounding strained.

"Hmm . . . no. I hate that hideous outfit. The fabric makes my skin itch."

Lola's face looked like she had just smelled something very stinky. Maeve was affronted. How could someone who had so much look so annoyed and unhappy over a little itch? It seemed . . . well . . . unprofessional. *Still, Lola's diva attitude is impressive*, she thought.

"Look, Riley. This is the stuff of entertainment."

With a raised eyebrow, an unimpressed Riley watched

a quivering Bethany turn to Lola and say, "Pretty please, Lola, with sugar on top?"

Was this groveling mess of nerves the same girl who had dismissed Danny with such indifference earlier? Maeve could not believe what she was hearing.

Lola frowned and uttered a dramatic, *"Fine."* She started back to the trailer, then paused. "But I *need* my cappuccino *yesterday*, Beth, or whatever your name is. And make sure it's *nonfat* this time. Last time they said it was, but it tasted too good to be. Make sure this time it doesn't taste so good. Everyone is just trying to get me fat!"

They all watched as Lola flounced off to her trailer, while a spent Bethany, who had averted a crisis with her star, shot dagger eyes at the temperamental superstar's back.

Finally, Riley whirled his finger around his ear to signify that he thought Lola Lindstrom was completely bonkers. Maeve had to agree.

"Boy, Riley," Maeve said, fanning herself. "I have to admit, star or no star, I don't want to get anywhere near someone who is freaking out about a cappuccino that tasted great."

Isabel, who had wandered over to witness the dramatic star's rantings, whispered to Maeve, "If you become a star and ever act like that, the BSG will have to have a trial and sentence you to a hundred pillow-mashes till you come to your senses!"

Maeve held up her hand and promised "to never act like a crazy diva with a bad attitude to anyone, even to someone who brings me fabulous-tasting coffee." Maeve and Isabel collapsed in a sudden fit of giggles.

"I sure hope Betsy and Danny fix those kinks before Lola Lollapalooza, or whatever her name is, bites someone's head off!" Riley warned Maeve and Isabel, who nodded in unison.

The Facts About Fireworks

At the far end of the set, Ozmond was standing with one white-sneakered foot directly in the middle of a patch of poison ivy and peering over his notebook at a few technicians unloading giant boxes labeled DANGER: HIGHLY FLAMMABLE from a truck.

"So we get rid of the fireworks completely?" asked Ozmond, tapping his pencil against the ragged pages of scribbled notes. "Are you quite sure about that?"

"Would I lie, Ozmond?" Danny nodded at the director and continued with his explanation. "One hundred percent. They're nice for special effects and everything, but they don't make any sense. Why would there be fireworks on an eighteenth-century pirate ship?"

"Bingo! Gosh, you are good." The director scratched something out until a rip showed through the paper, and chewed on the tip of his pencil. Then he tore the page out and let it flutter into the hands of one of the dozens of assistants running back and forth across the set.

As they walked back toward the giant pirate ship, Betsy and Danny could hear the technicians grumbling. They were loading fireworks back into the truck again.

Betsy had also tried to suggest losing the fireworks, but just as she'd opened her mouth to say something, Danny jumped in and took the rest of the sentence from her. She took a deep breath and racked her brain for another contribution.

"What else?" asked the director. "You two history buffs *must* know more! And more is what we need! More feeling! More history . . . more *truth*!"

Betsy raised her hand, "Well, you have Black Sam interrupting the wedding by swinging in on a vine to save Princess Polly," she began.

The director perked up. "Yes? Go on!" But before Betsy could finish speaking, Ozmond raised a hand and announced in a booming voice. "Listen up, everyone! These young people are fabulous! Historical people! Where are you?"

Betsy found herself suddenly surrounded by staring eyes. Two young men with frazzled faces emerged from the crowd.

"We must harness these young people's brilliance!" Ozmond gushed to the film's historical advisors. They shrugged in unison.

"If you say so, Ozmond."

"Well," Danny spoke up, "Betsy's right. The vines are completely unrealistic! We're in New England, for crying out loud, not the Amazon. Vines in this climate are not that strong. This isn't *George of the Jungle*, you know?"

"Duh!" The director bonked himself on the head. "I can't believe I missed that! Good find, Danny, my boy! Someone get him a chair."

The historical advisors jumped to obey. Two seconds later, Danny was sitting in a brand-new director's chair, beaming brightly. But Betsy's cheeks were red—and not in a good way. She planted herself in front of the director and flipped forward in the script.

"You know, the whole bride throwing the bouquet, and then talking about her honeymoon, and what she's going to wear, and going to Hawaii . . ." Betsy started.

"Uh-huh . . ." Ozmond urged.

"It's preposterous!" Danny bit his lower lip and gave Betsy a sweet smile.

What is wrong with you? she mouthed back, but he was already off and running, stealing her idea. "They're in Cape Cod! What, are they going to *sail* halfway around the world to Hawaii? The whole bride part is pretty ridiculous, Sir Ozmond. These lines sound like something from a modern-day chick flick."

The director smacked the table and beamed at Danny. "Young man, I had exactly the same thought on the read-through, but Lola's agent said we had to expand her part if she was going to sign. So we gave her even more lines. More distasteful, bad, poorly written chick-flick lines . . ."

Danny gagged. "They've got to go, Ozmond! The integrity of the movie depends on it." He gave the director a high five, and Betsy a thumbs-up.

But Betsy didn't notice. Lola Lindstrom was screaming at a gathering crowd outside. Betsy was shocked. Lola was actually throwing props at that Bethany girl and screaming, "This cappuccino is too delicious!"

"She looks crazy mad," Danny observed. He raised his eyebrows at Betsy. "Isn't helping out behind the camera so much more fun?"

Betsy swallowed and managed to squeak out, "A blast."

CHAPTER

16

A Meow in the Road

Charlotte felt like tap dancing—something she had never done in her entire life. But it was early and the Salty Cods had just solved another clue. The little red flag was right there in front of the lighthouse . . . with a note.

Super Scavenger BONUS! Since you came here first, here's a treat for your team. After all your hard work, you don't want to lose steam. Ride one mile north—it's right on the way to winning this hunt at the end of the day.

"That's it, Salty Cods," shouted an ecstatic Patrice. "We're kicking the Great Scavenger Hunt big-time!"

Katani was excited too, but she still wished her sister would tone down the competition thing. The Cods might have found the lighthouse first, but that didn't mean they'd cross the finish line at Drummer's Cove first. What if they didn't win? The team would be so disappointed. "Patrice, I think—"

"Let's celebrate!" Dillon interrupted her. "I don't know about you guys, but I'm ready for breakfast number two." He bent over and grabbed his stomach like he hadn't eaten for days. Then he staggered over to his backpack and pulled out a huge twelve-inch turkey sub as Charlotte's and Katani's mouths popped open. "What? I'm a growing boy!" he said as he chomped down on the humongous sandwich.

Nick grinned and broke out his mid-morning snack—a huge apple and a big bag of cheese chunks that he'd snagged at the NEED Building.

"You guys eat almost as much as Avery," Charlotte joked.

"Okay, Cod people, I think this moment calls for a picture," Patrice said. "Everyone march to the front of the lighthouse."

The group charged over to the lighthouse and happily looped their arms around one another as Patrice snapped away. Katani, who was usually the fashionista of any group, was wearing an oversize sweatshirt and loose-fitting sport Capri pants. The salt air, the ocean breezes—and the fact that her team might have a shot of winning this thing—had tossed the AAJH's Queen of Style's fashion concerns right out the window!

"Hey! You guys want me to get a picture with all of

you in it?" asked a tall, freckle-faced boy who was stand-ing around with what looked to be another school group of hikers.

Patrice grinned, "Gee, thanks . . . That's really nice of you!"

The group appeared to be about the same age as the Salty Cods. "What brings you all to beautiful Cape Cod?" asked Dillon the jokester.

"We were *supposed* to be extras in this movie," said a petite girl with curly blond hair. "But," she complained in a whiny voice, "my *mom* got lost. . . . We drove all the way from New Hampshire . . . and now we missed our opportunity."

Annoyed with her daughter's tone, the woman defended herself. "Good gracious, Tracy, I'm doing the best I can here. It wasn't my fault that the movie company decided to shoot in the middle of nowhere!"

Tracy, who in Charlotte's opinion sounded like a little bit of a brat, put her hands on her hips and continued to challenge her mom. "Thanks to you, *Mom*, I probably missed out on the biggest break of my career."

"I think you're exaggerating a bit, dear—being an extra doesn't necessarily equal stardom." Her mother smiled tolerantly at her obviously frustrated daughter.

"I like that mother," Katani whispered to Charlotte.

The freckled boy, who volunteered to take the picture, hugged his mother and gave his sister the "chill" look. "Trace metal," he teased, "Mom *did* take us to the beach yesterday. . . ."

"Which beach?" asked Nick.

"I can't remember the name, but it's just down the road." Tracy's mom pointed.

"We're from western New Hampshire . . . in the mountains," said another girl, "so going to the beach is such a treat. I think it's better than being a movie extra."

"Well, we're from a city called Brookline—it's near Boston, and we still think it's awesome to go to the Cape," Charlotte told the kids.

"No *way*," Tracy said and then turned to her friends. "Those kids we met at the beach yesterday were from Brookline too!"

"Maybe we know them," suggested Dillon. "A bunch of us from our school are doing this scavenger-hunt thingy this weekend. We ride our bikes all over the Cape looking for clues. It's pretty intense."

"Oh, I don't think these kids were part of your group, then," said the mother. "They were just chilling on the beach all day. None of them looked like they were searching for clues!"

"Yeah, there was this one girl with a long black ponytail who was really tiny, and she was amazing at beach volleyball. . . . You wouldn't believe her serve, *and*," the freckled boy shared, "she was an awesome surfer, too. How crazy is that?"

"Crazy," Katani mumbled. The Salty Cods glanced at one another, all thinking the same thing. There was only one girl they knew who could rock the house in two sports in one day: Avery Madden.

"Um, what did the other kids look like?" Katani inquired.

Tracy looked aggravated. "I don't know. I wasn't taking notes." Tracy's mother wore the desperate expression of a woman asking herself, *What am I going to do with this child?* Katani and Patrice knew that if they spoke like that in front of their parents they would be in serious trouble!

The friendly freckled-faced boy spoke up instead. "As opposed to my sister, I have a very good memory. One girl was blond and acted a little bit like my sister here." He pointed at Tracy. "She mostly just stayed on her towel and tanned all day. Then there was an older-looking kid, a big athlete type, who was kind of in charge; um, a short boy with crazy hair who kept cracking jokes; and then another girl who"—his voice dropped to a whisper like he was about to say something scandalous—"was kinda chubby." He returned to normal volume. "And she was mostly taking pictures."

"You should be a detective," Charlotte, admiring the boy's keen observation skills, blurted out. But she also felt dizzy. She had wondered why the Beach Barnacles were so tired last night . . . and now, it all made sense. *The Barnacles had spent the entire day playing . . . on the beach!*

"This is not okay," Katani spat. "Not cool. Not cool at all. I can't believe Avery."

Nick looked like he had just lost a friend. "They didn't even *try* to do the scavenger hunt?" he mumbled. "Not even Chelsea." He glanced over at Charlotte in disbelief.

"I'm sorry, did I say something wrong?" asked the freckled boy.

"Yo, *perspective*, everyone," said Tracy. "Missing a silly scavenger hunt is nothing like missing your first part in a *movie*."

Charlotte couldn't help herself. She shot dagger eyes at Tracy. Their classmates and friends had betrayed them, and this wannabe star was telling them to chill out?

Katani, who was about to say something, felt a hand on her arm. Patrice, holding tight, interjected, "I don't think you quite understand the situation, Tracy. My sister and her friends, Nick and Charlotte in particular, worked long and hard planning this trip. I think they have a right to be a little upset right now."

Tracy's mother gave Patrice a subtle thumbs-up while Katani and Charlotte stared at Patrice with admiration. Patrice had stuck up for them with a Queen of Mean stranger right in front of the girl's mom! That took some major guts.

Patrice turned to her defeated-looking team with a positive smile. "Come on, Cods. . . . We've got a scavenger hunt to win," she directed.

With a quick good-bye to the kids from New Hampshire, the Salty Cods climbed back on their bikes and headed out. The Beach Barnacles' betrayal had fueled Patrice and Dillon's competitive fire. The two of them zoomed ahead, chanting high school fight songs. "Come on Cods!" Dillon exhorted his team. "Let's hunt!" Soon Nick joined him yelling, "Salty Cods rock!"

Charlotte, however, couldn't seem to shake the feeling that someone had just let the air out of their tires. She was deeply hurt that Avery and Chelsea thought the activity she'd worked so hard to plan was so lame that they'd rather just blow it off. And worst of all, they lied to her about it.

Katani looked at Charlotte's downtrodden face and offered, "Don't be sad, be *mad*! It's much better that way."

"Are you mad?" asked Charlotte.

Katani scoffed, "Of course! They tricked us. Outdoor activities aren't even my thing. Don't get me wrong. I'm having fun, but the Beach Barnacles have the nerve, *the nerve*, to just blow off their responsibilities. They will *not* get away with this!"

Charlotte had to laugh a little. Katani looked like such a maniac whenever she got fired up. "Well, what are you going to do?" she asked to the furiously pedaling Katani.

Katani rolled her neck like she was preparing for a fight. "I am going to give those Barnacles a piece of my mind—Summers style. But first I'm going to do my best to win this thing. Let's pump it!" she yelled, sounding just like Patrice.

"Is that bad? . . . a piece of your mind?" asked Charlotte.

Katani raised an eyebrow. "Honey, you do *not* want a piece of my mind. . . . Believe me."

"How could they do this?" Charlotte shook her head. "It makes me not want to finish the hunt."

"Char, don't take it personally," Nick offered as he

rode up next to her. "I think they probably just got caught up in the moment." He gave her a half smile.

"You're not still mad at them, then?" she asked him.

"Well, I am a little, but I'd rather not think about that. Because," he said, grinning mischievously, "if they were playing all day yesterday, they've got to be way behind."

"You're right Nick." She nodded. "But I'm just not ready to stop being sad, or mad, or whatever, just yet."

"No giving up, team! The best revenge is to win!" Patrice suddenly shouted. "Let's teach those slacker Beach Barnacles a lesson they'll never forget."

"And what lesson would that be, Sis?" asked Katani, rolling her eyes. But this time she was smiling, too. Patrice's can-do attitude was lifting everybody's spirits.

"Winners rule and losers drool, of course. Now, are we going to do this?"

Suddenly Dillon stopped pedaling, nearly causing a four-bike pileup as Katani, Nick, and Charlotte scrambled to get out of the way. "Hey, a box! Isn't that the first thing on the bonus list?"

"No, dude," Nick laughed. "The list said *fox*! What do you think we were looking for aaall day in the park yesterday?"

"So I guess I didn't read that closely this morning," Dillon said with a shrug. "Sue me. But check it out, there really is a box over there in the grass . . . and it looks like it's . . . moving." He threw his bike down and jogged over to investigate. "Whoa!" Dillon yelled. "You guys have got to see this!"

The rest of the group dropped their bikes and raced over. They were anxious to see what was in the box. The Beach Barnacles were forgotten for the moment.

"Snap to it, Salty Cods," Patrice shouted, poised on her bike, and ready to put the pedal to the metal again.

Then Charlotte gasped, feeling her heart melt in her chest when she saw what was in the box—five teeny tiny brown and gray kittens!

Charlotte had a huge soft spot in her heart for cats. After all, her first kitty love was Orangina, a large cat who'd lived with her and her dad on their houseboat in Paris.

When Charlotte lived in Paris, she and Orangina were inseparable, but when she left to move to Boston, Orangina disappeared. Charlotte even went to find him in Paris after her friend Sophie said she had caught sight of the rascal cat. But when Charlotte spotted him on the back of a barge cruising down the River Seine, she knew he belonged in Paris the same way that she now belonged in Boston.

"We've got to help these little babies," Charlotte said as she reached into the box and gingerly plucked up a soft little ball of fluff. It was so tiny and warm, nuzzling into the palm of her hand.

"What should we do?" asked Katani. "We can't carry them with us."

Patrice rode over to see what all the fuss was about. "Oh, come on, you guys! We've got to get going."

"But these kittens are so tiny. . . . They need our help," Katani informed her sister.

Patrice groaned. "They *do not* need our help. Clearly they belong to whoever put them here. Besides, I'm not so sure you should be touching them. . . . They might be diseased."

"More like *abandoned them* here," Charlotte corrected. "Who leaves newborn kittens, which by the way are safe to touch, in a box in the wild? Especially near the beach with scavenger birds, dogs, and cars, and . . . coyotes!" Patrice almost jumped back at the fire in Charlotte's voice. "Well," she sputtered.

"Why don't we just call the Animal Rescue League?" Nick suggested. "When my sister found a stray puppy last year they saved him and found him a good home with a nice family."

"That's a great idea," Charlotte declared, hoping that the fact she thought Nick was a knight in shining armor right this minute was coming through in her eyes.

Patrice stamped her foot. "Guys, we are going to blow this hunt if we stop. What happened to 'Let's beat those Barnacles'? Is last place what you want? Is it?"

The Salty Cods stared up at a pacing Patrice, who was now making them nervous. One of her eyes was bugging out a little, and Katani could have sworn her sister's cheek was twitching. Someone had to chill Patrice out . . . and Katani knew she was just the sister to do it. She took a big swig of her water bottle and a deep breath.

"Are you nuts, Patrice?" Charlotte blurted suddenly.

Patrice looked startled . . . and so did Katani. "Huh?" they both gasped.

"There are five adorable baby kitties that need our help and you would rather worry about a *seventh-grade scavenger hunt* than save them?"

For the first time all weekend, Patrice was speechless. "Uh, um, well, I just thought—"

"What? This—this scavenger hunt," she stuttered. "It's only a game. These kittens . . . they're *real*," Charlotte said with conviction. "And I am not moving until I know they're okay."

You could have knocked Katani over with a feather. Easygoing, quiet Charlotte had the heart of a lion. Katani was proud of her friend. It took a lot of courage to stand up to Patrice—she should know. "Me neither," stated Katani.

"And me," Nick agreed.

"Ditto me, brother," added Dillon.

There. They had Patrice outnumbered four to one. Patrice let out a huge sigh and murmured, "I'm sorry, guys. I got a little carried away. Here. You can use my cell." She handed her phone over to Charlotte. "Walkie-talkie Mr. Moore first and let him know about the situation." Then Patrice walked away by herself and perched on a rock. Katani felt torn. Should she go to her sister?

"Hi, Mr. Moore. It's Charlotte Ramsey." She began to explain their predicament. Mr. Moore was very understanding. He said he was proud of the Salty Cods for taking the "moral high ground" as he called it. "And you won the treat for making it to the lighthouse first!" he applauded them. "Since you'll be waiting with those kittens, I'll just take your bonus treat to the finish line at Drummer's Cove.

The path you're on is actually a shortcut to the next clue, so you should be able to make up your time."

The Salty Cods waited for the Animal Rescue League to show up, and passed the time by cuddling with the cute little kitties. Nick and Katani were looking at their old friend with new admiration. "That was the awesomest part of the whole trip," Nick confided to her and squeezed her hand gently.

Blushing, Charlotte stuck her face into a little ball of fluff that was mewing for attention.

CHAPTER
17

 Captain Kiki
Rocks the Boat

W e did it! We did it! We—HOO HA—we did it!"
Avery jumped up and down and slapped the
air. Chelsea and Yurt joined in Avery's crazy victory dance, as Ben and Kiki looked on, laughing. Here
they were at the lighthouse—home of clue number four,
as confirmed by the telltale Abigail Adams Junior High
red flag.

"Hey, it's you guys!" The tall, freckled boy from the
beach the day before ran over and greeted the Beach Barnacles with a friendly wave. "So you're doing the scavenger hunt after all?"

Avery scratched her head. Even though yesterday was
a bit of a blur, she was pretty sure she hadn't said anything
about the scavenger hunt.

"Oh, I'm not psychic or anything," the boy quickly

explained. "We ran into your friends from Brookline. They were just here. They told us all about it."

Chelsea gulped. "And what . . . exactly . . . did you tell them?"

The kids shrugged. "Not much," said Tracy. "Just that we saw you at the beach yesterday . . . and that's about it. You did *not* look like you were doing a scavenger hunt yesterday. We told them that, too. . . . They took off down the road like they were on some kind of important mission," she added snidely.

Avery glanced at Chelsea who stared at Ben who suddenly looked very sorry for himself. "I have a feeling the cat's out of the bag," he mumbled.

"You think they know?" asked Chelsea.

Avery kicked a pebble and stared at Tracy. From the moment she'd laid eyes on her at the beach yesterday, she knew she was trouble. "Oh yeah, they know all right," Avery grumbled.

Chelsea felt a gnawing in the pit of her stomach. "What team do you think it was?"

"It could be either," Avery said, "But if I had to make a bet, I'd say four-to-one odds it's the Cods. You heard Patrice last night. They were on fire."

Chelsea gulped. That would be Charlotte and Nick's team—her fellow scavenger-hunt organizers.

"Ben, what are we going to do?" she asked her brother. "Nick and Charlotte are going to be so disappointed with me."

Ben put his hand on his sister's shoulder, but Chelsea

cried out, "I feel awful!" Whenever a situation in Chelsea's life got too crazy, it was her first instinct to enlist the aid of her big brother. Having Ben's support tended to be enough to get her through anything. But Ben looked as miserable as she felt, and feeling bad for themselves wasn't going to fix anything.

"Let's just forget this whole thing," Kiki whined. "If the Cods know already then what's the point? Let's just go back to the beach . . . and have fun."

Yurt looked temped by this idea—Avery could practically see the visions of beach balls dancing in his head. So she leaned in and warned him, "Don't even think about it."

Then she confronted Kiki. "What *don't* you get about this, Kiki?" Avery demanded. "Yesterday was play beach. Today is attack scavenger hunt."

She turned to Chelsea and added under her breath, "It's the only prayer we have of Charlotte forgiving us." She laughed.

Chelsea couldn't believe Avery was so cool about this. Maybe it was because the BSG were like best friends and Avery was sure she would be forgiven. But she, Chelsea, was just a school friend, so the BSG and Nick might never speak to her again. She felt her knees begin to shake and went to sit down.

But Avery's determination seemed to be all Ben needed to rally. "Come on, Chels," he ordered. "Short stuff here is right. Let's solve another clue. It's not over . . . until it's over!" Ben pulled an envelope out of his bag and ceremoniously handed it to Avery, who decided not to be annoyed by the short joke, and read:

Where the birds fly free and high, the water meets the open sky. Nature here is on display to show the world Cape Cod's array.

The normally enthusiastic Henry Yurt drooped in despair. "That clue's impossible. Nature is on display everywhere. . . . Hello, it's Cape Cod." He waved his hands in the air like the sky was falling.

"President Yurt, where's your scavenger-hunt spirit? Where there's a clue there's a way," Avery cheered. "We just have to put our heads together and think."

"Hey!" The freckled boy interrupted his Frisbee game with his friends to run over to the Beach Barnacles. "I'm a huge fan of scavenger hunts, and birds as it turns out. Did you know that birds are descended from dinosaurs? Ahhh, anyway . . . ," he continued, seeing their disinterested faces, "I think I have an idea of what that clue's talking about."

Suddenly the Beach Barnacles were all ears. There was no rule that said you couldn't use whatever means necessary to solve the puzzle . . . including seeking the sage wisdom of other kids who happened to be on Cape Cod. "Well, spill it!" Avery urged.

"I think it means the Wellfleet Wildlife Sanctuary. . . . It's the only place I can think of where tons of birds and other animals can just be free and also protected. I was there once a couple of years ago."

"It makes sense," Chelsea agreed. "Now how do we get there?"

The freckled boy wrinkled his nose. "That's the thing," he said, hesitantly. "We took a boat. I think there's some kind of bike path to get there . . . but I don't know. . . ." His voice trailed off.

"Is there a ferry or something?" asked Ben.

The boy shrugged. "My friend's dad took their boat. . . . I think it's just up the coast that way a couple of miles."

"Hey!" Kiki suddenly perked up. "I used to go up there with my family too. . . . It's not that far, only about ten minutes away from my house. I know how to get there by boat."

"You have a boat?" Avery gaped.

"Well, yeah!" Kiki looked at her like she was crazy. "It's the Cape, dude. People have boats here!"

Yurt's eyes glowed. "I'm down for some boat action. Let's go!"

"Is that okay? The teachers never mentioned anything about finding the clues using other forms of transportation," Chelsea pointed out.

"We're running low on time!" Ben argued. "All's fair in love and war . . . as long as we're scavenger hunting, and it's safe—oh yeah—Kiki, *is* it safe? I'm Captain Safety, here," Ben said in his big grizzly bear voice.

Chelsea smiled. *Big Ben is back!*

Kiki shrugged and said casually, "Duh! I took boating safety class. I've had my boating certificate since forever."

Her smile got a little bigger and she said softly, "I *love* boating!"

Avery had to admit—she was impressed. She couldn't wait to tell the BSG that there was more to Kiki Underwood than sparkly lip gloss and her evil entourage. But then she felt funny. Thinking of the BSG made her feel bad, like she had let her friends down. She vowed she would do her best to make it up to them today.

"Barnacles unite!" cheered Ben, and with that the team got back on their bikes, and, pedaling furiously, arrived back at Kiki's house in twenty minutes. Kiki's mother was so excited to see them she brought out a tray of lemonade and popsicles. Talk about a bonus item!

"Thank you, Mom!" Kiki kissed her mother on the cheek. *Surprise number two,* Avery ticked off in her head. Kiki and her mother really got along well with each other. "We can't stay and visit. I'm taking the crew up to Wellfleet Wildlife Sanctuary on the boat."

Kiki's mother pressed her hands over her heart. "How lovely, dear! I do love to see people enjoying the boat." She graciously led the kids into the garage and showed them where to leave their bikes so they'd be safe and out of the way. Then she and Kiki bumped their fists and kissed each other on each cheek while they said, "Safety First."

"It's just this thing we do," Kiki explained nonchalantly to her stunned classmates.

Avery almost couldn't believe her eyes. Seeing Kiki pal around with her parents at her Cape house brought out a whole new side of the Empress. If Avery didn't know any better, she would have said that Kiki Underwood was actually sort of . . . nice.

One thing was for sure: When it came to her boat — a fancy Boston Whaler with a serious motor — Kiki took her responsibilities as captain *very seriously*. She showed everyone her boating safety certificate. "Required by law to operate a boat if you're between the ages of twelve and fifteen," she shared. "I wanted you all to see so you'll feel safe. Obviously that's an important Underwood concern," she joked.

"Now, everybody grab a life jacket," Kiki ordered, pointing to a wooden bin inside the boathouse. "I mean it, if you're not fastened properly, you don't board this boat." Kiki went around and double-checked everyone's straps and one by one allowed them into the boat, giving them each a seating assignment.

"Arms and legs inside the boat at all times," Kiki instructed. "There will be no standing, no rocking, and no shouting, which doesn't really matter because . . ." Kiki turned the key and the motor started up at a disturbingly loud volume as she yelled over it, "I WON'T BE ABLE TO HEAR YOU ANYWAY!" And with that they were off!

Avery and Chelsea were thrilled by how beautiful the Cape looked from this new vantage point. They had ridden their bikes so intently, it was really fun to chill out on the boat. Inspired, Chelsea was snapping pictures madly while Avery turned her face to the wind which whipped her ponytail back and forth.

"*Holy bologna!*" Yurt suddenly cried. He pointed, while

trying his hardest not to rock the boat. "Ahoy, mateys! There's a pirate ship washed up on the shore!"

Everyone on the boat turned to look. Henry wasn't lying. There, in a little deserted patch of sand and forest, rested an enormous old-fashioned–looking boat, and on its mast waved a large black flag with a skull and crossbones right smack in the middle.

"Let's check it out," Kiki said decidedly.

"Wait! Are you really sure that's such a good idea?" Chelsea asked. "There really are modern-day pirates. I read all about them."

"There aren't any pirates on Cape Cod, *duh*!" shouted Kiki as she drove the boat closer.

"I hope you're right, Captain Kiki, 'cause I'd hate to have to take a whole ship of pirates down," joked Ben.

As the boat journeyed closer to the shore, a man carrying a large camera caught Avery's attention "You fruit loop!" She gave Yurt a gentle shove. "That's not a *real* pirate ship. Did you forget about that movie Ms. O'Reilly was telling us about last night?" Avery slapped her knee in hysterical laughter.

Yurt feigned indignance. "I beg your pardon. I certainly did not!"

"Yo, you did!" Avery teased as Kiki steered the boat away from the set and back on their course, "You said, and I quote, 'Holy bologna, there's a pirate ship washed up on the shore!'"

"I'll have to check my notes to confirm that," retorted Yurt.

Suddenly Chelsea exclaimed, "That looks like Maeve!"

The members of the boat squinted and indeed noticed there was a girl with curly red hair dancing around in the middle of the crowd. "Weird," Avery commented. "Too bad for Maeve *it's not*. Wait till she hears there was a girl who looked just like her who got to be in a movie on the Cape this weekend."

Chelsea's eyes widened as she pulled out her camera and quickly snapped a photo. "You guys!" she shouted. "That's the last bonus item—something pirate-themed! We have all ten!"

The Beach Barnacles cheered as the pirate ship disappeared from their sight. Then they whizzed on up the bay toward the Wellfleet Wilderness Sanctuary, led by Captain Kiki.

18

Waiting for Ozmond

Maeve lay sprawled out in the slightly itchy grass, beginning to wonder if they were ever going to shoot this movie today or not. *Who knew there was so much of doing nothing on a movie set!* The Cranberry Boggers had been on the set almost three hours, and not a single camera had rolled.

Lifting her head, Maeve scanned the yard for Isabel, who was staring at a computer screen and sipping iced tea with that Patrick guy and his assistant, Poppy. They were laughing and Isabel looked like she was having the time of her life as Patrick showed her some old candleholder thing.

Bethany had put Riley into dancing time-out under a tent out of the sun, because he was sweating so much (gross!) that his makeup had started to drip off his face. Maeve tried to wave to him, but his eyes were closed and he didn't see her. Danny and Betsy were nowhere to be seen, and Fabiana was sitting under a tree doing yoga, which she said relaxed her.

Maeve knew that making movies was harder than it seemed, but she was starting to stress out. *What if they never get around to shooting my scene today?* That would mean that she'd blown off the entire scavenger hunt for nothing. She rolled over and looked up at the sky . . . *At least this sun feels nice. . . .*

"Attention, everyone. Group meeting, right here, right now!" the director bellowed. Maeve jumped up. Finally! She ran over to join the group, which had encircled Ozmond, Betsy, and Danny. When the crowd was silent, Ozmond began, "I apologize, fellow thespians and technicians, artisans and actors, et cetera, et cetera . . ."

"Hmm," Maeve murmured to Riley, who had come to sit by her for the group meeting. "Ozmond sounds like . . . someone . . ." Maeve snapped her fingers. "Oh! It's Yul Brynner from *The King and I.*"

"Hey, you're right!" Riley answered.

Maeve was practically shaking. *I'm in the presence of brilliance and Riley actually appreciates it!* She clapped for Ozmond, who looked at her strangely.

"Where was I? Ah yes, this delay. As you know, in order to make this movie into a real work of art, it is of paramount importance that we try to be as historically accurate as we can on this shoestring of a budget they have given me." Ozmond glanced around for approval.

"I have decided that the whole hoopla surrounding the bride and her melodramas is a modern conflict that doesn't even make sense in the epic tale of Black Sam Bellamy. Which is why I have decided to cut Princess Polly's lines in this scene in their entirety. So that means, my dear Lola, you will not be speaking in the scene we are about to shoot. Okay, everyone, let's start filming."

Lola's face went from creamy white, to pink, to red, then redder, but Ozmond was in his own world and did not seem to notice. He wrapped his arm around Danny's shoulder and added, "And by the way, people, we have this visionary of a young man to thank. Everybody give it up for my young protégé, Danny Fitzgerald!"

Maeve's eyes almost popped out of her head. Wasn't *Betsy* Fitzgerald supposed to be the protégé who was helping the director? Maeve turned to see Betsy looking utterly mournful. The poor girl seemed to be on the brink of bursting into tears!

"Oh, Riley, I've just got to console poor Betsy. She must be devastated," Maeve exclaimed. But as she ran over to give Betsy a big hug, out of nowhere she heard a terrible, shrill cry of "*Aaaarrrgh!*"

From the crowd emerged a furious Lola Lindstrom with streams of black makeup running down her face. She came charging past Ozmond, past Betsy, right to Danny, and knocked him over like a football tackle. With her black Princess Polly wig hanging sideways off her head like some kind of wild witch hair, Lola stood over Danny with her fist in the air shouting at the top of her lungs: "Eeeeek! How dare you march in here with your . . . your historical *facts*! Do you know who I am? *Do* you? And do you know who cares about *facts*? Nobody! That's who. People will come to the movie to see me . . . Lola!"

Before anyone could do a thing, Lola Lindstrom stormed off, leaving a cowering Danny and a stunned crowd. Betsy's look of despair transformed to one of relief. As the whispers began, she glanced at Maeve with wide eyes and mouthed *Phew!* As they watched Danny stumble to his feet, Betsy sighed. "Poor Danny. He looks like a shell of his former self."

Maeve nodded in agreement, although Danny's face was, Maeve thought, starting to get some color. In fact, his face was getting red! "Oh, Betsy, I think Danny's mad!"

Suddenly, pandemonium broke out on the set, as all the cast members began mumbling that they had a runaway bride. Maeve's eyes followed an irate Ozmond who turned to walk back to his office. Maeve followed, beckoning Betsy and Danny to come with her too.

"The nerve!" Danny muttered as the trio darted behind trees. "And no one tried to stop her! I think I've suffered hearing loss. Could you say something quietly, Betsy? I'll tell you if I hear anything."

"I'll tell you what I think, Mr. Danny *Fitzgerald. . . .*" Betsy started.

"Shhh!" Maeve shushed them, straining not to miss a word of Ozmond's juicy phone conversation. Maeve couldn't believe it. *This drama is better than the movie!*

"That was the last straw," Ozmond shouted into his cell phone. "That diva is off my set! I don't care if she's the *Queen of England*. Bruce, there is simply no place for that kind of behavior in my movies. We are creating a master-piece on a pauper's budget, thanks to my wonderful consultants Danny Fitzgerald and . . . what's-her-name. The other one. They're brilliant, I tell you! Brilliant. Yeah, whatever, we'll put her check in the mail."

The director flipped his phone closed and dabbed the beads of sweat from his forehead. "Divas," he grumbled. "I swear, if they didn't make me millions I'd have every single one of them deported to Mars. *Now* what I am I going to do?"

"'What's-her-name'!" Betsy whispered. "That's all I am? '*The other one*'!" She didn't even realize she'd spoken out loud until Danny looked solemnly into her eyes.

"Danny Fitzgerald has a nice ring to it, don't you think?" He grinned. "Let's go see if they changed the rigging ropes from nylon to cotton like we suggested. Maybe Ozmond will put us in the movie credits: Danny Fitzgerald and Betsy Pellegrino, historical advisors . . ." Danny chuckled at his little joke mixing up the names. Betsy trailed after him, opening her mouth at least a dozen times. She tried to say, *It was my idea to be historical consultants,* but Danny never stopped talking.

Maeve was so engrossed in the drama that she didn't notice Betsy and Danny take off. Over by her trailer, Lola was piling a mountain of dresses, makeup supplies, and empty cappuccino cups into the arms of a hapless Bethany. The poor girl was staggering under all the weight and trying desperately to hold on to all the empty Styrofoam cups, which kept rolling away in the grass.

When someone tapped Maeve on the shoulder, she nearly jumped a foot in the air. "This is crazy!" Fabiana exclaimed.

"I know. Ozmond's going to have to pick someone on the set to replace her, and Fabiana . . ." Maeve took her chaperone's hand in hers and murmured, "I hope it's going to be me."

Fabiana smiled sadly. "I wish it could be you, Maeve, but Princess Polly is at least eighteen years old. Lola must have an understudy or something."

Maeve touched her heart and said, "You know when you want something really really badly, and if you really really believe it'll happen, sometimes it does?" Her voice hushed to a whisper and she concluded, "It has to be my turn."

Fabiana shook her head. "Optimistic thinking is good for you, but I don't think—"

Maeve lifted her chin in the air. "All I need is Lola's black wig and, snap! Princess Polly." Maeve turned and sauntered over to demand her rightful role as the heroine replacement, when—just like magic—the director looked right over in her direction and shouted, "YOU."

Maeve grabbed Fabiana's hand as Ozmond walked toward them in huge, deliberate steps with his arm extended, pointing straight ahead. Maeve wished she had prepared a speech of what to say when he offered her the part, but her thoughts were a jumble. *This is it! Maeve Kaplan-Taylor's big break! I wish I was wearing pink. . . . Oh, wait, I am. Should I shake his hand? Bow? Smile?*

When Ozmond reached the girls, he placed both hands on Fabiana's shoulders. "You. You look just like the raven-haired beauty that is Princess Polly. With a little careful film work, audiences will never know the difference between you and Lola. What do you say? Will you help save our little masterpiece and stand in for our misbehaving star?"

Fabiana glanced uncertainly at Maeve, "Um, uh, sir, I'm flattered, but quite frankly I don't know what to say."

"Well, that's easy. This is the opportunity of a lifetime," he announced with a flourish as he started guiding her toward the costume trailer. "Say *yes*."

"Yes!" she instinctively blurted, then turned to Maeve raising her hands in an apology of sorts.

Maeve couldn't respond. She felt like someone had knocked the wind out of her with a basketball. *Oh, the betrayal!* she thought in anguish. How could she ever look Fabiana in the face again?

She pointed her finger—which was trembling—at Fabiana and the director as they walked away and decried, "A plague on both your houses! A plague I say! Oh, woe is me! Woe is poor, pitiful Maeve. I was going to be somebody. . . ."

Riley, seeing this breakdown transpiring, ran over and said, in a voice full of concern, "Maeve, what's wrong? Are you okay?"

"Oh, Riley!" she cried. "Do I *look* okay?"

He shrugged. "No?"

"You're so right." Maeve gritted her teeth. "I'm not okay. Ozmond just chose Fabiana to stand in for Lola

Lindstrom in the wedding scene! Can you *believe* it?" She put her hands on her hips and shook her head. "You know, it's times like this, Riley, that I wonder if I'm cut out for this business. I mean, I just might be too sensitive! So, dude, what exactly happened here to destroy my once-in-a-life-time chance at stardom?"

Riley squinted and then smiled. "Oh, *dude.* I get it. From a distance, Fabiana looks *just like* Lola Lindstrom's character. Whoa! That's crazy. They could be, like, twins separated at birth or something!"

Maeve's eyes settled on Riley. She took a deep breath and sighed. "I guess the show must go on." A tear rolled over her cheek.

"Oh, Maeve, I'm sorry," he said. He stood there, looking petrified. The lesson Riley had already learned that day was that there was nothing more terrifying than a hysterical actress.

Thankfully, Maeve was not that kind of actress. "You know, Riley, I think I just have to go under a tree somewhere and chill out. Thanks for being there." And she ran off to sit under a weeping willow tree away from the maddening crowd and the cameras. But when she sat down, she heard a sob, followed by, "Stupid Danny Pellegrino!"

"Betsy!" she exclaimed.

"How COULD he?" Betsy blubbered.

"I thought you felt bad for Danny after Lola?" Maeve said as she sat down next to Betsy.

Maeve twirled the grass between her fingers as Betsy ranted. "It's like, I was just trying to be a good friend, and be supportive, and he didn't even apologize for not reminding Ozmond that the cotton ropes were *my* idea . . . even after I told him Lola was a horrible witch and he was a wonderful historian!" Betsy sniffed.

"Betsy," Maeve consoled her, "I know how you feel."

"They were all *my* ideas, too, and *he* got a director's chair!"

"It's like you're not paying attention, and they just go and steal your role right out from under you," Maeve griped.

"Yes, Maeve! Exactly!" Betsy agreed. She stopped crying and declared, "You think you have talent, you know? That you matter. One day, you're finding your place in the world—"

Maeve nodded. "—and the next you're yesterday's news. That's showbiz for you, Betsy." Maeve felt everything she'd been holding in start to well up and managed to utter, "It can be so cruel!"

"Oh, Maeve," Betsy said, putting her hand on Maeve's shoulder. "You can let it out. It's okay."

With that, Maeve lost control. "Why me? Why?" she wailed.

Ozmond, who was busy coaching Fabiana with some last-minute instructions, took notice of the commotion near the willow tree. "Why, that . . . that is just the kind of emotion that I've been looking for!" he remarked, signaling a cameraman. "Come, follow me."

He crept up behind Maeve, who was crying as loudly as ever. From the intensity of Maeve's tears you would have thought she had just found out her family had been abducted by aliens.

"Yes! Yes! That is it! You are sad, very sad. Pretend you have just had your teddy bear stolen—NO—your *starring role* was stolen. It is . . . the biggest tragedy of your young little life."

Maeve suddenly paused her sniffling long enough to realize what was happening. *She was being filmed . . . by not one, not two, but three cameras!*

"That is it! Magnifique!" the director exhaled. "That will be the perfect shot for the end of the movie, when the village mourns the death of our hero, Black Sam Bellamy. Young lady, I thank you. You have just convinced me that there is still hope for an Oscar. Now, back to the wedding. Take one . . ."

Maeve dabbed her eyes, adjusted her dress, and said to Betsy with a smile, "I never doubted myself for a second . . . and you shouldn't doubt yourself, either!"

CHAPTER
19

The Amazing Race

I think I'll call this one Pleather," said Dillon as he held a tiny strawberry blond kitten close to his face and rapped, "Yo Pleather! Yo Pleather! Who's in style? You are! You are! Kitty cat wild."

"Pleather?" Katani grimaced in distaste.

"Hey, Kgirl, don't dis the Pleather. It's soft, inexpensive, environmentally friendly . . . and very stylish," he said in his fake TV-announcer voice.

"Dude, you are so going to regret this," ranked Nick as Charlotte snapped a picture of Dillon posing like a British Invasion rock star . . . with a kitten plastered on the top of his head.

"No way, Montoya. Pleather and I are going straight to the top. . . . Aren't we, cat man?" Dillon's grin suddenly turned to a grimace as the kitten began to dig his tiny claws into Dillon's scalp.

Charlotte and Katani exploded into laughter at the

sight of the desperate Dillon trying to pry little Pleather off his head.

"Seriously, will somebody please get this killer tiger off me before I need a hair transplant?" he begged.

Nick, who had been watching his goofy friend lose his cool, took pity on Dillon, and carefully released the kitten's claws from his scalp. Nick set Pleather down on Charlotte's lap as Dillon fell to the grass in a heap, pretending he had been mortally wounded.

"What is taking those Animal Rescue people so long?" a frustrated Patrice groaned. She was pacing back and forth like a coach whose team was down by one point in the last quarter of the championship game.

"They'll come," Nick assured her. "Sometimes it takes a little while." When Patrice checked her watch for the zillionth time, Katani lost it.

"Would you *please relax*, Patrice?" she pleaded. "You're really stressing everyone out," she complained as she grabbed for the kitten that was attacking her shoelaces.

Patrice turned to face the Cods. "You kitten-loving people should be the ones feeling stressed out! If we don't get on those bikes soon we'll be hangin' our heads in shame—beaten by a bunch of Boggers and Barnacles."

The Salty Cods shifted uncomfortably, like they weren't quite sure how to respond. Finally, Charlotte said what all the others were thinking. "Umm, Patrice, we agreed it's more important to save these kittens than win the race."

Patrice looked like she had just been told she'd committed a terrible crime. Katani, rushing to her sister's defense, immediately stood up and sputtered, "Patrice just . . . she just wants to finish the race. . . ."

Patrice put her arm around Katani and made a motion for her to be quiet. "It's okay. Charlotte's right. We can wait . . . a few more minutes." A subdued Patrice knelt down and reached in the box for one of the kittens.

"Look at this monster here," she said, holding up the biggest kitten in the litter, a black one with white socks. "I think we should call you *Brontosaurus*! What ho, Bronty!" she said and began to stroke Bronty on top of his head. As the kitten began to purr, Katani watched her sister chill out about a hundred degrees.

"Look." Dillon pointed. An official white van pulled over by the side of the road, and a pleasant-looking woman got out of the car and walked toward them. "Hi! I'm Dory. Are you Charlotte Ramsey?" she asked Patrice, who was cuddling Bronty.

Charlotte raised her hand. "I am. You must be the Animal Rescue people."

Barnacles and Butterflies

"Hey, check this out!" a very excited Avery called out to her Barnacle Buddies. "There's a hummingbird and butterfly garden in this place! Can you dig it? Hummingbirds!"

Avery, lover of all creatures great and small . . . including snakes (she had one named Walter), wanted to check out every corner of the Wellfleet Wildlife Sanctuary. *Its lovely lush marshes and acres of natural habitat provide sanctuary for a spectrum of wild animals,* Avery read to herself on a plaque outside the entrance.

"You guys, we can't miss this!" Avery protested as she caught sight of a small bird whizzing by.

"We have to go, Ave," Ben yelled. "Remember, we're on a mission now!"

"Let's just quickly check out the hummingbird garden. . . . Five minutes, okay? Oh, man, I just saw a huge monarch!"

"Butterflies are not my thing, dude, but ask the rest of the team," Ben said with a shrug.

Avery turned excitedly to her teammates, sure that no one would want to pass up the chance to get up close and personal with some cool-looking hummingbirds and supersized monarch butterflies.

But before she could beckon her teammates to follow her, Captain Kiki took the wind out of her sails. "Come on, everyone, we just figured out a clue. Can't we just take a picture and move on? With all the bonus points Chelsea found, we might have a chance to win."

"*Five minutes,* Kiki. You don't like nature?" Avery accused.

"Of course I like nature. Only doodlebrains don't like nature," Kiki huffed. "But the longer we stay here, the more time we *won't* have to find the rest of the clues. Besides," she added with a sneaky smile (her specialty, noted Avery), "you don't want to let your friends down . . . do you?'

Yurt, Chelsea, and Ben turned to Avery—their faces all

expressing the same *she does have a point, dude* sentiment. "But . . . the hummingbirds," Avery protested weakly knowing that Kiki really *did* have a point.

"Okay, let's get this photo op done," an impatient Chelsea directed. She bunched the Barnacles into a picture overlooking the vast, creamy turquoise marsh. Everyone wore huge smiles—except for a disappointed Avery, who could only manage a tiny crooked smile. She had so been looking forward to having butterflies swirl around her head and maybe even land on her shirt!

"Come on everybody! Back to the boat!" Kiki ordered, clapping her hands together. The Beach Barnacles sprinted back to the Boston Whaler and struggled to clip their life jackets as quickly as their fingers could manage. "Great job, Yurt. Okay, let me help you into the boat, Chelsea," Kiki encouraged. "Give me your hand, Avery." She stuck out her hand to help Avery step down.

Being such a good sport herself, Avery had to hand it to Kiki. She really was an excellent boat captain. "You should join the Navy when you grow up, Kiki," she said as Kiki helped her untie the lines.

"That's a great idea," the Yurtmeister pronounced. "Kiki could be the first girl commander of a Navy destroyer or something. Let's hear it for Captain Kiki, everyone!"

The boat erupted in hoots and claps as Kiki started the boat and steered it away from the dock. Kiki rolled her eyes at Henry Yurt, but Avery could tell she was pleased. She kept biting her lip to keep from smiling.

What would happen if Captain Kiki ever used her powers for good instead of evil back at school? Avery wondered.

Herding Cats

"We better get these little guys boxed up and back to the Animal Rescue shelter. We need to give them all their shots and check them out," explained Dory as she began placing the mewling kittens one by one into a nice plastic cat carrier.

You could have knocked Charlotte over with a feather when Dillon, who was cuddling Pleather again, resisted. "Could I adopt him?" he asked, a hint of desperation in his voice, as Dory reached over to take Pleather.

Charlotte was even more surprised when Patrice put her arm around Dillon's shoulders and told him, "Dude, I'll call your parents and put in a good word for Pleather."

Dillon flashed Patrice a grateful look. "Word," he answered.

Suddenly sirens filled the air. Almost immediately the Cods were surrounded by flashing lights and TV cameras. "What the heck is going on here?" a bewildered Dillon asked as two policemen, followed by an attractive photographer, hurried toward them.

Patrice grabbed Katani's hand as she reached for Charlotte's arm. "Did we do something wrong?" Charlotte asked Dory nervously. She could see the headlines now: SCHOOL GROUP ARRESTED FOR TAMPERING WITH WILD-LIFE.

Dory shook her head and put her hands on her hips.

"That big policeman heading toward us is my own darling husband."

As the officers approached, the still nervous Salty Cods stood huddled together like the kittens they had just rescued. A grinning Dory called out. "What are you doing . . . checking up on me?"

The shorter cop said. "Nah, Dana called to see if there was any news for tonight's broadcast and we told her about the kids rescuing these little rodents here."

"They're not rodents. They're high quality kittens!" an indignant Dillon blurted out. Charlotte covered her mouth to keep from laughing as Katani whispered, "The Dillon Johnson we know and love is back."

In what seemed like a matter of seconds, Dana, the reporter and photographer from the town paper *Nauset Lighthouse*, snapped a picture (Dillon insisted on taking Pleather out of the carrier and putting him back on his head for the shot) of the kitties and the kids from Brookline who saved them, and promised to let the school know when the picture would run.

"I'll run it with an article about the Animal Rescue league and how people shouldn't abandon defenseless animals!" Dana informed them.

Charlotte hated having to say good-bye to her little gray kitty Gus, but Patrice was nudging them all toward their bikes after thanking Dory for coming to their aid. Dory, heading back to her white van, gave the group a grateful good-bye. "Remember, if you ever know of an animal in need or that has been abandoned, you can always call your local Animal Rescue League chapter. That's what we're here for."

"Good-bye, Pleather . . . I'll see you soon . . . I hope." Dillon, sounding tragic, waved as the truck sped away.

"That was a really great thing we did!" Katani triumphantly shared.

The others nodded, and Patrice said, "I agree. Now . . . Salty Cods . . . Are we ready to pump it?" This time, even Katani joined in. "PUMP IT UP!" they all shouted as they ran for their bikes.

"Patrice," yelled Nick as they pedaled wildly down the bike path. "Where *are* we going?"

The Perfect Sneeze

Fabiana paced back and forth in front of Maeve, who had recovered completely from her moment of theatrical distress under the willow tree. Now, she was back under the same tree trying to calm Fabiana, who was muttering to herself.

"Ontario Plume, I, Fabiana, apologize profusely . . . no . . . Mr. Plume, please accept my apologies. . . . Wait, is that too formal? Help me, Maeve!"

On about the gazillionth take of the wedding scene, Fabiana's dress—which was sprinkled with talcum powder and dirt stains to make it look like she'd endured a battle to be with her beloved—finally got the better of her and she sneezed all over her betrothed, Ontario Plume! They had to pause everything while hair and makeup fussed over the handsome superstar.

"These kinds of things happen in show biz," Maeve assured Fabiana, who was clearly mortified.

"My career is over before it even started!" Fabiana wailed. "I wish we'd done the scavenger hunt. What is Mr. Moore going to do to me when he finds out? I'll be suspended and I won't be able to do the musical, and—oh!"

"Ah, Fabiana, I think maybe you are . . ." Maeve was afraid Fabiana was about to lose it.

Just then, Betsy and Danny came walking over, and between them strode the young blond man who until today, Maeve had only seen on the poster above her desk. Now, Fabiana had not only married him on film, but also sneezed in his face. Could the day get any stranger?

"Good news, Fabiana!" Betsy announced happily. "Ozmond *adored* that last take!"

Fabiana ignored her and stared at Ontario. "I, um . . . apologies, I mean, I'm sorry profusely . . . oops, I—"

"No worries!" Ontario smiled. "That sneeze was just the right thing to give me the perfect startled expression! And Ozmond loved the look in your eyes."

"In other words . . ." Danny started.

"We're done!" Betsy snapped her fingers. "Now let's get crack-a-lackin' on that scavenger hunt!"

Maeve looked at Isabel. It was obvious they were both thinking the same thing. Betsy was *baaack*!

"Thank you, milady," Ontario said suddenly, spinning Fabiana around by the waist like they were still in the movie. "And good luck to you!"

"Where are we *going*?" Nick repeated at the top of his voice.

Laughing, Patrice brought her bike to a screeching halt. "Nick Montoya, you are a genius! Gather round, Cods. We need to regroup and make a plan."

"Well, I vote we forget clue number five and go right to clue number six," Charlotte suggested.

"I agree," said Katani. "It's a little crazy, but I think it might be our only shot of still coming in first."

"You decide, team." Patrice folded her arms and waited. Katani wondered what had gotten into Patrice— playing with the kittens had turned *her* calm and cool as a cat.

"Let's go to clue six!" Dillon said, and Patrice took out the envelope.

"Your eagle eyes spotted those kittens!" Patrice smiled at Dillon. "You be the announcer."

He opened the envelope and read in a loud, slow voice: "In fourteen hundred and ninety-two, Columbus sailed the ocean blue. But from this spot in nineteen-oh-three, macaroni signaled across the sea."

The group was silent. "Okay, would somebody like to tell me how a noodle can signal across the sea?" asked Dillon.

"Must be a pretty big noodle," Nick chuckled.

"Maybe it's a famous explorer?" Charlotte suggested.

Patrice sighed. "I think one of us would remember if we'd learned about a famous explorer named Macaroni."

"Well, if we can't figure this out, then what are we sup-posed to do?" asked Katani. She didn't come this far in her great outdoors exploration weekend only to spend the last hour slumped over her bike, completely stumped.

"Maybe we should head back to the final meeting place at Drummer's Cove and try our hardest to come up with an answer on the way," Nick offered. "That way, if we don't get the points for winning the clue, at least we'll get them for coming in first."

This sounded like the most logical plan yet, and the Cods pedaled off on the bike path.

"Who signaled America in 1903 with macaroni?" Char-lotte asked out loud. "This is definitely the weirdest clue of all!"

Nick, who had been staring off into a clearing beside the bike path, suddenly hit the brakes. "Whoa! Check this out, guys! There's a huge pirate ship over there."

"That must be where they're shooting the movie Ms. O'Reilly was talking about," said Charlotte. She couldn't resist her curiosity. "You want to go check it out? Just for a second?"

"If we don't get back to scavenger hunting soon, I swear, *I am gonna lose it!*" joked Patrice as she followed her team across the clearing. An enormous wooden pirate ship lay at dock, surrounded by dozens of platforms and cameras. Some of the cameras were even suspended in the air to capture the shots from above.

"This is so awesome!" breathed Charlotte as she saw several actors in pirate gear swinging from the mast of the ship. She took out the team camera and snapped a photo. They'd still needed something pirate-themed for one of their bonus items!

"What can I say, Char. . . . When you're right, you're right," agreed Katani. Then suddenly her face turned sour. "YOU HAVE GOT TO BE KIDDING ME!" she spouted.

"*Shhh!*" shushed the four other Cods. Katani's mouth opened and closed like a fish as she pointed at the boat. "It's . . . it's . . . it's . . . '" she stuttered.

Charlotte's eyes widened and she finished, "MAEVE AND FABIANA!"

✿ Yurt Alert

Ben broke out the last clue as Kiki's boat roared away from the Wellfleet Animal Sanctuary. He had to shout to be heard over the rumbling motor:

In fourteen hundred and ninety-two,
Columbus sailed the ocean blue. But from this
spot in nineteen-oh-three, Marconi signaled
across the sea.

"We're on the sea, and I don't see any signals!" Chelsea moaned.

"Wait," Avery said, perking up a little bit. "What time is it, Kiki?"

"Four thirty-five!" the captain responded.

"That gives us twenty-five minutes to either look for this clue, or race to the finish line!" Avery shouted, suddenly energized. "That Marconi thing is only three points, but finishing first gets us ten!"

"Let's go for it!" Kiki cheered.

"But," Chelsea protested, "we have only *two* clues out of six!"

"Three!" Suddenly Yurt plucked the camera from Chelsea's bag, smiled, and pressed the button. He proudly handed the camera back to Chelsea and pointed at the preview screen. "Say 'thank you'!" Yurt instructed.

"What for?" asked Chelsea.

"The answer to clue number one! We never figured out what a Yurt alert was. Maybe it's me!"

Avery smiled. "Hey . . . it's worth a try!"

Ben agreed. "We'll improvise! *Barnacle* style."

The team cheered, and Kiki shifted the motor into high gear.

🖋 Superstars and Superheroes

The Cods tumbled on top of one another to get a get a closer look at the clearing. "They're all there!" Dillon gasped. "Maeve, Betsy, Danny, and . . . hey, isn't that guy spinning Fabiana around super famous?"

Suddenly, Fabiana landed right in the dirt and screamed!

Nick's eyes looked like they were about to bug out of his head. "What is Ontario Plume doing to my sister?" he growled, turning to march into the middle of the set. Charlotte and Katani pulled him back.

"She's fine, Nick," Katani assured. "Listen! I could be

wrong, but I think that director guy with the red pants . . . he's praising her like she's the star!"

"What?" Nick gulped and leaned forward.

"Such emotion!" The director shouted as he strode toward the Cranberry Boggers. "Perfecto, Ontario! Bravo, Princess Polly!" He helped Fabiana up and the whole group started applauding.

All of a sudden, out in the field looking in on the Boggers' celebration, Charlotte started to cry. "Nobody's even *trying*. Our great adventure is a flop."

Patrice reached over and gave Charlotte a supportive hug. "Charlotte, if I know your friend Avery *and* Ben Briggs, there is no way that they aren't trying to finish this race. I say—"

"We go for it," a determined Katani reached for Charlotte's hand and gave it a squeeze. There was nothing she hated more than seeing one of her BFFs with hurt feelings.

"Me too," Nick grabbed her other hand.

"Group hug," Dillon shouted as he tried to wrap his arms around the team.

Feeling completely foolish and completely blown away by her team's support, Charlotte snuffed back her tears while Patrice punched the air. "Winning this thing was our *destiny*." She smiled at her group and added, "And also saving the kitties. We're kind of like superheroes. And superheroes always win."

The Race Is On

As the determined Salty Cods pedaled furiously away from the clearing, something buzzed in Betsy's pocket.

"The walkie-talkie!" Maeve yelped.

"The scavenger hunt!" Fabiana hefted her canvas bag off the ground and turned to Ontario Plume and Ozmond, suddenly calm and composed. "It was a pleasure acting with you, sirs, but we have a very important scavenger hunt to take care of. BOGGERS, FOLLOW ME!"

From behind boxes and barrels, piles of feathered hats and rows of trailers, the entire team materialized.

"I got two more bonus items," Isabel shared.

"That's six total," Fabiana counted on her fingers. "If we ride as fast as possible, there's a chance—"

"—we could win those ten points for getting back first!" Riley finished.

"Well, what are we waiting for?" Maeve cheered. "The race is on!"

Barnacle Style

Kiki's parents met the boat at the dock.

"Did you get your clue?" her excited mom wanted to know.

"How'd the boat run today? Great conditions! Flat as a pancake out there," said her dad.

Kiki just shook her head and tossed a rope to her father.

"Tie it off, Dad!" she instructed. "We're on a tight schedule, and when an Underwood intends to win . . ."

". . . she wins!" her mother finished. "Good luck, darling." Mrs. Underwood blew kisses to her daughter and for good luck blew ones to the rest of the Barnacles too.

Kiki was already halfway to the shed where the kids had left their bikes. "Thanks, Underwood parents!" Ben Briggs shouted back.

"Your parents are pretty cool," Chelsea pointed out to Kiki as she flung off her life jacket and strapped on her bike helmet.

"Yeah, they're all right," she admitted with a shrug. But then she suddenly seemed to remember her special Empress of Mean status. "Oh, and we're not slowing down for anyone today, got it? So keep up."

Chelsea took a deep breath and shook her head. *The Empress of Mean gene is still intact!* she thought as she hopped on her bike.

With a bunch of whoops and hollers from Yurt and Avery, the team was off, pedaling so fast the trees whipped by in a blur. Chelsea was surprised to find that despite her slightly sore leg muscles, she *was* keeping up much better than yesterday. *Take that, Kiki!* she thought with a smile as she passed by a surprised Empress.

When Chelsea managed to pull up even with Henry Yurt, she shouted, "Barnacle style!"

He honked his bike horn. "Two more miles!"

Soon, everyone was chanting the rhyme.

"One and a half miles!" Kiki interrupted them. "I know a shortcut."

Pump It Up

The Salty Cods whooped with joy as they sped down a hill, feeling the crisp breeze against their faces. Charlotte raced ahead, wondering how fast she'd have to go to break the space-time continuum, like in *Back to the Future*. The trees and objects whizzed by so quickly, she wasn't sure he could trust her eyes when she saw a park ranger turn down a side path toward the beach.

"BONUS POINT!" Dillon shouted. The park ranger was so startled he dropped the armload of guidebooks he was carrying.

"Sorry, dude." Dillon got off his bike to help with the guidebooks while the rest of the Cods joined them. "But can we take your picture? We're, like, on this scavenger hunt, and, hey—don't you spell check these things?" He held up a guidebook. "It's *macaroni*, not Marconi!"

"Dillon!" Charlotte slapped her forehead. "This is a guide to Marconi Station! Hand me that clue you read!"

Dillon sheepishly extracted a crumpled piece of paper from his pocket.

"Just what I thought." Charlotte's face looked grim for a second.

"Are we going the wrong way?" Katani asked, worried.

"What's going on?" Patrice demanded.

"Marconi Station!" Charlotte's face broke into a grin. "The answer to clue number six! It had nothing to do with macaroni!"

The park ranger chuckled. "Guglielmo Marconi invented transatlantic telegraphing. Sent the very first message across the ocean from this spot in—"

"1903!" Dillon finished. "And there's the flag!" Dillon pointed down the path to a telltale red flag planted in the middle of some old stone ruins. The Salty Cods began to clap and cheer.

"We did it!" Katani squeaked. "I feel so . . . so . . . *alive!*"

"Sorry, guys . . . about the noodle thing," Dillon said.

"Forget it, man." Nick slapped him on the back.

"Could you get in the picture with us?" Patrice asked the ranger. "It'll give us an extra point!"

"Sure thing."

As the finder of "Macaroni" Station, Dillon insisted on being right smack in the middle of the photo, and wedged himself between a rather cozy Charlotte and Nick. "Best group ever!" Dillon declared.

Patrice looked at her watch. "Come on, you guys. We only have fifteen minutes before this hunt is officially over. I say we pump it and try to get those ten points by coming in first at Drummer's Cove."

"Sounds like a plan!" Charlotte agreed. They raced to their bikes and poured every ounce of energy into speeding through the mile-long homestretch. Katani felt a bolt of energy surge through her and found herself cycling ahead of Patrice!

"Hey, slow down, Sis!" Patrice laughed.

"I can't!" Katani sang. "I have no control over the speed of my legs!"

"It's called *adrenaline*," Charlotte explained, flying by both the Summers sisters. The boys, both horrified at the thought of being outdone by all *three* girls on their team, also began going faster and soon enough the five members of the Salty Cods found themselves in an unofficial race to the finish line.

20

Onward to the Finish Line

*A*re you *sure* we're going the right way?" Betsy demanded of Fabiana for the millionth time. "Look. There's a four-way intersection up there!"

"Bethany showed me the set location," Fabiana patiently reassured the panicky Bogger, "and it was a straight shot to get to Drummer's Cove."

"Hey!" Danny shouted. "Check out that bike group up ahead!"

"It's Katani and Patrice!" Isabel remembered the Summers sisters' matching orange bikes.

"And that must be Charlotte . . . and Nick . . . and Dillon!" Maeve shouted. "They just turned right on that street up there!"

"Come on, we can catch up!" Fabiana urged her team.

"But do we go *straight* or *right*?" Betsy wailed.

Just then, another group of bikers came into view in the distance, zipping toward the intersection down a battered dirt path that wasn't even a street.

"Hey! That's Avery!" Maeve said, more quietly this time.

"And Chelsea, Ben, Yurt, and Kiki," Riley finished.

"They're going . . . left?" Betsy let her bike fall to the ground and plopped down in the dirt at the side of the road. "What are we going to do?"

"How is this even possible?" Fabiana muttered. "Drummer's Cove is straight ahead, isn't it?"

"We did already get lost once," Isabel said softly.

"And those teams probably know where they're going!" Maeve agreed.

"They're going in *opposite directions*, if you didn't notice," Betsy said.

Danny sat down beside her and patted her back awkwardly. "It'll be okay. Hand over the map, Fabiana! It's in the pack!"

The Cranberry Boggers' leader giggled a little, and found the map on the first try.

"Okay," Danny said. He turned the map sideways. Then upside down. Then he flipped it over and peered at the other side.

"I'll do it!" Betsy grabbed the map, and struggled to get the thing to lay flat on the grass. "What does it matter?" she yelled. "We're in last place anyway."

Danny nodded. "We've already lost!"

"What?" Maeve folded her arms and tapped one foot.

"We'll definitely lose if you two just sit here on the side of the road moaning! Get up!"

Startled, Betsy and Danny obeyed.

"Now let's get moving!" Maeve sped off toward the intersection.

"Which way?" Fabiana asked.

"No idea!" Maeve answered. "We'll figure it out!"

Three Cheers for the Great Scavenger Hunt

The Cods charged into the parking lot at Drummer's Cove in full force to the sound of applause and cheering. "Congratulations!" Mr. Moore exclaimed in delight from behind his video camera. "You are the first team back! Well done, Salty Cods."

Ms. O'Reilly and Mrs. Moore joined them with a cooler full of chilled juice boxes and ice-cream sandwiches—in cow-patterned paper, of course. "This was the bonus reward for the lighthouse clue," Mrs. Moore shared.

The Cods hadn't realized how famished they were. "These taste so *délicieux*!" Charlotte exclaimed, smacking the ice cream off her lips. "Especially now that we can relax and appreciate the creamy goodness!"

"Do you always talk like that?" asked Dillon.

Charlotte was puzzled. "Like what?"

"You know . . . like a writer?"

Nick put his arm over Charlotte's shoulders, making her cheeks turn a deep cherry. "She *is* a writer. Can't help talking like what she is."

Charlotte reminded herself to chronicle this moment in her journal as one of the more romantic instances in her life, when suddenly a chorus of rowdy whooping burst into the parking lot . . . led by (big shocker) Avery Madden.

"BARNACLES! BARNACLES! WHOOOO-HOOO!" Avery hollered. She ran around her teammates, high-fiving everyone, so absorbed in her victory dance that she didn't even notice that the Cods beat her to the punch.

"Aw, man!" Yurt exclaimed, seeing the other group at the far end of the lot. He jogged over, stopped before his classmates, and bowed dramatically. "You may have won the battle, but we shall see who wins the war . . . when Mr. Moore tallies the points. *Wah hah hah!*" he bellowed, in a fake, evil laugh.

"You're nuts, man. We're gonna cream you!" Dillon assured him and, winking at his teammates, added, "fair and square."

The rest of the Beach Barnacles joined them. Charlotte, using her incredible observation skills, immediately knew that something was off. "Hey, why does it look like you were out in the rain?" she asked.

"You get splashed riding in a boat," Kiki replied. "We took my Boston Whaler over to the Wildlife Sanctuary. It's an awesome shortcut."

"You can't do that! Using a boat is against the rules." Katani looked at the teachers. "Isn't it?"

Mr. Moore pondered this for a moment and finally pronounced, "Well, technically there was no rule against alternate modes of transportation. I'll allow it."

The Beach Barnacles cheered and the Salty Cods

groaned. "Well, there *should* be a rule against not working on the scavenger hunt at all!" Katani fumed. "We know what you guys did."

Mr. Moore looked at the kids. "What's this all about?"

When no one answered, Katani—who had become good and heated—continued, "They spent all of yesterday playing on the beach, and didn't even start working on the scavenger hunt until today!"

Ms. Reilly looked the Beach Barnacles in the eye. "Is this true?" she gravely confronted them.

Kiki, Avery, Chelsea, and Yurt hung their heads in shame as Ben Briggs stepped forward. "I admit . . . it's true. We were all having so much fun at the beach . . . well, we made a mistake."

"But we spent all day today working really hard on the scavenger hunt!" Kiki defended. "It's true, I swear."

Mr. Moore sighed. "Ben, kids, I must say, I am disappointed in you."

Charlotte, who had been dreading this moment all day, found she had no idea what to say. There was only one person on the team who she was really disappointed with. Charlotte turned to Chelsea and in a soft voice asked, "After how hard we worked to make this weekend perfect . . . how could you . . . sell out like that?"

Chelsea opened her mouth to explain, but before she even had a chance to get a word out, her big brother intervened, "Now, hold on just one minute! This was *not* Chelsea's idea. She didn't want to hang out on the beach, and was the only one who spent all day yesterday looking for clues on that bonus-list thingy. In fact, if it wasn't for Chelsea, I think this team would have just given up all together. She's the reason we tried to win."

Chelsea blushed and looked up adoringly at her brother. "Thanks," she whispered.

Ben shook his head. "Whatever. It's true. I'm just sorry I didn't listen to you yesterday." The rest of the Beach Barnacles nodded in agreement.

Charlotte felt terrible. "Yikes. I'm sorry, Chels. I had no idea."

Chelsea waved her hand. "Forget about it." She beamed at her brother, relishing the sensation of being recognized for doing the right thing.

"We worked really hard today," Avery offered. Charlotte gave her a disappointed look. "And I'm really, really sorry. . . ."

"Fine," Charlotte sighed. "It's not just you, though. It's—"

At that moment the group was interrupted by an uproar of heaving and guffawing as the Cranberry Boggers shakily rolled into the lot. "Oh . . . my . . . *goodness!*" Maeve groaned. "I have never been so tired in my life!"

"Water! Somebody, quick! I'm dying of thirst," Danny proclaimed, panting like a hungry Labrador.

"You can cut the act," Katani informed them. "Or should I say . . . continue it?"

"Whatever do you mean?" Fabiana feigned innocence.

"We saw you at the movie set today," Patrice declared.

"Um, uh . . ." Betsy stuttered. "There's a really great explanation for that. . . . See, we, uh . . ." The crowd was shocked—they had never seen Betsy Fitzgerald speechless before in their lives.

Mr. Moore folded his arms and tapped his foot. Fabiana took a deep breath and stepped forward. "Okay, here's the story. Yesterday on the scavenger hunt we got lost, and accidentally found ourselves on the set of the Black Sam Bellamy movie. . . . You know," she said, glancing at Ms. O'Reilly, "the one with Simon Blackwell?"

"*You met Simon Blackwell?*" asked Ms. O'Reilly in a squeaky voice. She coughed and revised, "I mean, go on, Fabiana."

"They asked us to be movie extras," she confessed.

"And consultants," Danny added proudly.

Fabiana nodded. "It all happened so fast. We had copies of our photo release forms and the next thing we knew we were in costumes and makeup and Riley even had a couple of lines."

Fabiana, completely enraptured in the story, became more animated. "Lola Lindstrom—she was playing the female lead—quit right in the middle of the last scene. And guess who they filmed to replace her . . . *ME!* Oh, we knew we should have been working on the scavenger hunt and everything, but this seemed like a real once-in-a-lifetime opportunity and . . . well, it was . . . like a dream."

"It was. It really was," Maeve seconded. She got down on her hands and knees before Katani, Charlotte, and Avery, and in a cracking voice implored, "Please, you guys are my bestest friends in the whole world. You have to forgive me. Say you will! Please!"

"Would you get up?" Katani said gruffly, but pointed at the Beach Barnacles. "They kind of blew off the scavenger hunt too."

Avery bit her lip guiltily.

"If it's any consolation, the scavenger hunt seemed totally awesome," Isabel assured Nick and Charlotte. "I would have loved to do it."

Charlotte sighed. "I just feel like everyone has been lying for two days. . . ."

"Well, technically speaking, we weren't lying," Avery explained. "We just weren't telling the complete truth."

"Have you ever heard the concept of lying by omission?" asked Mr. Moore.

Maeve was puzzled. "What do you mean?" she asked nervously.

"Omission. It's when you purposely leave out a part of the truth to trick people into thinking something untrue," Mr. Moore said and glancing at Avery added, "It's *technically* the same thing as a lie."

Avery shrugged and admitted quietly, "Yeah, my inside voice kind of already knew that. But I was so busy surfing and telling that voice to be quiet . . . I'm sorry, guys."

Fabiana looked at her little brother. "I'm really sorry, too, Nick. I got caught up in the moment and I wasn't a good team leader. An awesome movie extra, maybe, but a bad team leader. Please forgive me?"

Nick shrugged. "Yeah . . . you are my big sis, after all." He kicked the dirt with his sneaker and added, "But when you become a mega famous Hollywood star, you owe me a Porsche."

"Deal!" Fabiana extended her hand and they shook on it.

"I'm sorry too, Chels," Ben said. "For all the things that she said"—he pointed a thumb at Fabiana—"and also for being a big jerk on the beach yesterday. You were right, and we were the lame ones."

Chelsea whipped out her camera and took a picture of her big brother looking like a big, sorry goofball. "I wish I had that on videotape!" She giggled, giving Ben a giant hug.

"Want to film it?" Mr. Moore joked, offering his camera.

"I think some of us have had enough of filming for one weekend!" Fabiana said, looking around at her team, who all nodded in agreement.

"Are we cool?" Avery meekly asked Charlotte.

"I'm not mad," Charlotte acknowledged. "We just worked so hard to make the Outdoor Adventure Club's first field trip exciting for all you guys. And no one had a good time doing what we planned."

Isabel tilted her head and said thoughtfully, "You know, the point of the Outdoor Adventure Club is to have amazing adventures, right? And I think we can all agree that everyone had amazing adventures this weekend. So I think the trip was a smashing success, Char."

Charlotte contemplated her friend's positive outlook. "You know, Izzy, I like thinking of it that way." She grinned. "Now that I think about it, we had a blast too. So if everyone had fun . . ."

Katani, who had been talking to Mr. Moore, suddenly bounded over and clasped Charlotte's hands. "WE WON!" she shouted. The Salty Cods stopped what they were doing and starting jumping up and down and hugging each other. (Charlotte was secretly thrilled that Nick hugged her first.) "Mr. Moore just tallied the points. Five clues, six bonus pictures, and first place finish gives us thirty-one points!"

Patrice shrugged and smiled. "What did I tell you?"

Katani looked up at her sister with newfound admiration. Yesterday, she would have expected Patrice to be the most obnoxious winner of all, but as it turned out, her sister was rather gracious about the whole thing. Not only that, but Ben and Fabiana had both let their teams go astray, and Patrice had stayed true to the mission the whole time. As a team leader, she pretty much rocked it . . . and led the Cods to victory.

"Who came in second?" Avery demanded.

Mr. Moore looked at his sheet and shared, "The Beach Barnacles. Three items, including Yurt—I liked your creative thinking; ten bonus pictures—thanks to Miss Chelsea; and second place finish is a whopping twenty-four points. Well done."

Avery glanced at her teammates and, her eyes glimmering with mischief, asked, "Can you imagine if we'd actually *tried* both days?"

"But you didn't!" Dillon sang joyfully.

"What about the Cranberry Boggers?" Isabel bleakly asked.

"Six bonus pictures . . . six points," Mr. Moore said. "Might I ask how you all thought you were going to get away with this?"

The Cranberry Boggers sheepishly looked at each other. "We hadn't exactly gotten that far," Maeve confessed.

The futility of the Cranberry Boggers' non-plan was so completely ridiculous that pretty soon the entire group was in stitches. Betsy Fitzgerald tried to explain. "Technically, we did manage to learn the pirate history. . . ." but she was shouted down. Fabiana laughed good-naturedly and shouted, "Three cheers for the Great Scavenger Hunt!"

When the noise died down, Mr. Moore presented the Salty Cods with their prize: a whole month of free treats from Montoya's Bakery and two free tickets each to the Movie House. Charlotte and Katani rejoiced, as Montoya's was far and away the most delicious bakery in all of Massachusetts.

"Oh, now I'm kind of jealous," moaned Maeve. She might have loved movies more than anything in the world, but hot chocolate from Montoya's was a close second.

Katani leaned over to Charlotte and whispered something in her ear. "Well . . . if you say so!" Charlotte agreed. She turned to Avery, Isabel, and Maeve. "We've decided to share the prize with everyone. After all . . . what's the point of winning if you can't use your powers for good, right?" She looked at Patrice and winked.

	Salty Cods	Beach Barnacles	Cranberry Boggers
Clues **3 pts each**	Camping Yurts Rock Harbor Eastham Windmill Nauset Lighthouse Marconi Station	Henry Yurt Nauset Lighthouse Wellfleet Wildlife Sanctuary	
Bonus Items **1 pt each**	Coyote Street scallop shell pirate ship tide pool sand dune park ranger	fox towel surfboard sandpiper Deer Path scallop shell pirate ship sailboat tide pool sand dune park ranger	prop fox Squirrel Lane pirate hat sailboat tide pool sand dune
Crossing finish line	First - 10 pts	Second - 5 pts	Third - 0 pts
DAY 1 POINTS	31 points	24 points	6 points

How to Make an Entrance

Though looking fashion-savvy movie-star perfect certainly didn't come as naturally to Charlotte as it did to Katani or Maeve, she felt that she'd done a rather splendid job of pulling an outfit together. She'd picked out a silky, plum-colored dress (Katani's advice) to complement the lavender shades in her eyes, and borrowed Maeve's heating curlers. "They work on curly and straight hair," Maeve had assured her after an hour-long Hair Care 101 session in the Tower. All the BSG had to look their best for the big occasion!

Charlotte strapped on her new black dress shoes with the tiny heels and examined her reflection in her closet mirror. *Okay—I'm ready to walk the red carpet. . . . I think.* She had a sudden vision of herself lying in a big klutzy purple heap while cameras flashed all around.

Thankfully, a loud *BEEP-BEEP* from the driveway interrupted those thoughts. Of course that was followed by the overexcited yodeling of Marty and then her father shouting, "Charlotte! They're here!"

Excited, Charlotte quickly smeared on some light pink lip gloss and dashed down the stairs. "I'm off!" she declared while Marty eagerly danced and yipped around her.

"You look absolutely perfect!" Mr. Ramsey proclaimed, "Except . . ."

Charlotte frowned. "Except what?"

"Well, I don't think you want to bring this little accessory to the movie with you." Mr. Ramsey extracted a solitary heating curler from the back of his daughter's head.

Charlotte laughed. "Thanks, Dad! Bye, Marty!" she called, slipping out the front door. But when she saw what was in her driveway she gasped—a white stretch limousine that looked big enough to tote around a blue whale! The tinted window in the back rolled down, and Maeve Kaplan-Taylor, shielded by oversize black plastic diamond-studded sunglasses, leaned out. "I told you we were going to show up in style! Hop in."

Charlotte had been in a limousine before only once in her life for her aunt's wedding. And that limo had been black and—well—ordinary. Nothing like this lavish oversize white one.

Quicker than Charlotte could say "fabulicious," to borrow Maeve's favorite word, a uniformed driver had the door open and she was greeted with a chorus of "Awesome"s and "Can you believe this?" from Isabel, Katani, Avery,

Maeve, and to her surprise, Chelsea, Ben, Patrice, Fabiana, Nick, and Riley!

"It was a surprise for most of us, too," confessed Katani.

Isabel smiled, "After the way that weekend went, giving everyone a ride was the least we Cranberry Boggers could do to apologize for not doing the scavenger hunt."

"You didn't have to do all this!" Charlotte pronounced as she snuggled in the only open seat, between Nick and Maeve.

"Ozmond did it, actually," said a voice from up front. The glass slid open, and sitting next to the driver were Betsy and Danny! She almost didn't recognize them in their matching costumes circa 1717, the year of the movie.

"Well, it was Maeve's idea to get a limo," Fabiana shared. "So she talked to Betsy, who called Ozmond, and he was 'delighted' to arrange everything!" she explained, mimicking the director's crazy accent.

"I volunteered to sit up front," Danny said. "Just in case we need to give directions."

"And I got the costumes together," Betsy informed Charlotte. "Maeve taught me how to make an entrance: arrive fashionably late, and wear something totally unforgettable!"

"I did say that!" Maeve held her hand to her heart and pretended to dab tears from her eyes. "My, my, they grow up so fast!"

Ever since their weekend in Cape Cod, Betsy and Danny had been practically glued together. The whole thing was very weird—Danny would try to outsmart her, she would try to outsmart him . . . so on and so forth all day long. It was the strangest display of flirting that the BSG had ever witnessed, but for Danny and Betsy, it worked.

"Special guests and VIPs!" Maeve announced as she dramatically passed around cups of sparkling apple cider. "A toast! To one of my best friends in the world, and a brilliant writer, that great adventurer Charlotte Ramsey!" Maeve somehow managed to pour the cider into glasses while the limo pulled out of the driveway without spilling any on her lacy pink gown. "And to Nick Montoya, wilderness boy himself, and Chelsea Briggs, the world-renowned photographer! If it weren't for this amazing trio, none of us would be going to the East Coast premiere of my first big-budget film, *The Pirates of the Cape*! Thank you, Charlotte, Nick, and Chelsea!"

As the kids clinked their plastic cups, Maeve leaned forward on the divider between the driver and the back. "Yes, miss?" asked the driver.

"Mr. Limo Driver, when you go down Beacon Street . . . can you please drive as slowly as possible?" Maeve requested. "I want everyone to see our *unforgettable* entourage!" She smiled at Betsy, who beamed with pride.

Avery folded her arms. "Maeve, do you know how environmentally terrible this car is? Honestly when I think of the fossil fuels—"

Katani pulled off the handmade scarf that she had crafted for the occasion and wrapped it twice around Avery's mouth. "Avery . . . be quiet. We promise to reduce our carbon footprint to make up for this five-minute ride!" The BSG shared a good-natured laugh, both proud of and amused by Avery's die-hard devotion to saving the world from global warming.

"We'll make it up by planting some trees in the park in honor of the movie, okay, Ave?" Isabel offered, and Avery nodded enthusiastically.

When the limo pulled up to the Movie House, Charlotte wasn't sure at first that they'd come to the right place. *Is this really the same tiny theater Maeve's dad owns and operates?* Charlotte wondered. *It looks like a slice of Hollywood!*

A red carpet, velvet ropes, and even potted palm trees re-created a glamorous, old-Hollywood feel. As the limo pulled to a stop by the start of the red carpet, a swarm of local news teams flooded their doors.

"You guys, I think they think we're some kind of stars!" Charlotte remarked to her friends.

Maeve smiled at her and drawled, "Darling, *we are* some kind of stars." With that, she popped open the door and stepped onto the carpet, blowing kisses to the throngs of people looking on from the other side of the velvet ropes.

"You gotta give Maeve credit," commented a smiling Katani, as she watched Maeve making her way down the red carpet, signing autographs and posing for pictures. "She's really got her thing down."

The rest of the kids piled out of the limo and followed Maeve as she sauntered past autographed, life-size, foam-core statues of Ontario Plume beside *The Whydah*, Lola

Lindstrom as the black-haired beauty Princess Polly, and Simon Blackstone dressed as his fierce pirate character.

Suddenly, someone in the crowd mistook Fabiana for Lola Lindstrom, who had just appeared on the cover of *Teen Beat* magazine in full costume with her black Princess Polly wig covering her red hair. Hundreds of girls followed along and shrieked at the top of their lungs when Fabiana exited the limo.

"Lola! Lola! I love you!" a weeping young fan proclaimed.

"Lola, I want to be you!" cried another young girl.

"I'm not Lola," Fabiana sputtered, but no one could hear her over the chanting crowd. She dodged a hand thrusting pencil and paper in her face and grimaced at Maeve. "Maybe I'm not cut out to be a movie star. I can't handle the paparazzi!" Then she picked up the hem of her dress, waved politely, and ran as fast as she could into the theater.

"Should we explain that Lola *couldn't make it* to the premiere?" Isabel giggled to Maeve. They were sure Lola could have found a way in the midst of her busy career to fly out for the East Coast premiere, but the picky actress was still miffed that Ozmond cut all her lines at the last second, so she was a no show.

"They'll forget all about Lola when the special guests get here!" Maeve promised.

And she was right.

As the BSG and their friends joined Fabiana in the theater lobby, the crowd outside suddenly erupted in such an uproar Maeve was sure a thousand pirates had just sailed down the street and attacked the Movie House. But then, out of the chaos, Maeve heard two names repeated over and over: "Simon! Ontario!"

Maeve strode back up the red carpet to the door of the Movie House and opened her arms wide. "Welcome!" she announced, "to Brookline."

"It's my honor, milady," Simon Blackwell said in his odd accent, and bowed.

"No, sir, 'tis *my* honor!" Ontario argued playfully, and lifted Maeve's left hand with his fingers, *just* as she'd seen him do in *Princess Daisy*. Of course, Lola Lindstrom played Princess Daisy, but Maeve brushed that aside to revel in the shining wonderfulness of Ontario's attention.

Simon and Ontario together escorted Maeve back into the lobby, and then the two Hollywood heartthrobs took turns walking every single girl to her seat in a special roped-off balcony in the theater!

"That color is smashing on you," Simon complimented Katani's yellow dress. Then he turned to Betsy. "Love the costume."

"You have the most lovely eyes," Ontario told Chelsea. She nearly fainted right off the balcony!

Even Avery looked a little starstruck and let out an unusually girly giggle as she thanked the two polite pirates, who had their own private balcony across the theater.

"That . . . was the best moment . . . of my entire life," Fabiana gushed, draping herself across her seat with one hand on her forehead.

"Just wait!" Maeve said, eyes glittering. "I think the best moment will come when you see Princess Polly up on that screen!"

Maeve looked around at the expectant faces of the entire crew of the AAJH scavenger hunt. Ben and the boys had managed to make their way through the crowd and were seated in the balcony. Even Kiki was down in front with her parents. The theater was so completely packed, Maeve could almost feel everyone breathing as the lights dimmed and the opening music began.

I'm hanging out with pirates, yo ahoy ahoy what up?
You better look out, mates, ahoy, or yo, I'll steal your cup!
My mates are kinda raggy, hey, but that's just how we row.
The captain's all 'What up, homies? The landlubbers lie down below!'

Maeve glanced over at Riley in the seat beside her. "That's your song!" she practically screamed, so proud and excited at once she thought she might start crying for real.

Riley, embarrassed, looked at his lap then at her. "Yup," he said with a shrug. "Turns out Michele with one L wasn't lying. Her dad really is a music producer. Dude owns his own record label. I've been working on this song for the last few months, and Kiki's dad actually let me use his recording studio . . . so I guess the song actually made it into the movie, thanks to those crazy girls."

Maeve swallowed, less enthused. "Oh, yeah?" she huffed.

Riley grinned. "Yeah. But they weren't the song's inspiration. . . ."

Maeve listened to the next verse, which put a smile on her face that literally stretched from ear to ear. "Riley Lee, that is the most romantic thing I have ever heard in my life." She boldly reached across the armrest and gave Riley's hand a little squeeze.

The first half of the movie passed in a whir of sword fights, village scenes, and close-ups of treasure troves.

"Those are the coins I told them to use!" Danny chirped excitedly.

"And I recommended that jacket the captain's wearing," Betsy sang.

But Maeve wasn't even fazed by the constant chatter. She could hardly pay attention to anything except that verse of Riley's song playing over and over in her head:

I'm a powder monkey and I'm monkeying around,
You don't even know the crazy treasure that I found,
A gold doubloon, a string of pearls, a sword or ship I'll trade,
But, yo ho, I'll never tell you 'bout my red-headed mermaid. . . .

Finally, the wedding scene opened with a shot of Riley the powder monkey whistling for his friend—Maeve the scullery maid turned flower girl—to come help him scrub the deck where they would dance a splendid jig!

Suddenly, Maeve's eyes were glued to the screen as Black Sam—a snarling pirate version of Simon Blackwell—burst through the wall and captured Princess Polly! In that scene, Polly was Lola Lindstrom, but in the next—when she emerged from the cabin after the plot flipped around and everyone found out Sir Eric Bonewagon was *really* the brute, and Polly was in love with Yardley Howe, the young deck hand played by Ontario Plume—well, it was Fabiana's eyes that gazed up into Ontario's as the couple made their vows.

Maeve never would have known the difference if she weren't sitting next to the actress herself.

"Oh," Fabiana said. Maeve put a hand on one of her shoulders and Nick took the other. "That's . . . that's . . . *me*?" Fabiana managed to stammer.

"You look beautiful!" Maeve assured her. "You'll get used to the stardom."

Then the camera switched to Maeve, crying beneath the willow tree after Black Sam's tragic death when Sir Eric Bonewagon returned seeking vengeance. Thankfully, everyone's spirits were uplifted in the final, moving speech where Yardley Howe proclaimed that from now on, pirates and locals would live together in peace, and everyone took a vow to never betray the location of the sunken *Whydah*.

Before the credits even started rolling—with their special thanks to historical consultants Betsy Fitzgerald and Danny Pellegrino, and junior set designer Isabel Martinez—frantic clapping broke out from somewhere near the back of the theater. A few sheets of notebook paper fluttered up into the air, and Maeve knew there'd been *another* special guest tonight!

Ozmond stood up in his seat and shouted, "Fantastic! Terrific! Smashing, I say! Just smashing, people! I say! Bravo!"

"Bravo!" Maeve stood up too . . . and soon the entire theater was cheering.

Maeve turned to her BSG. "Okay, I lied. . . . I'll *never* get used to this!"

The Great Scavenger Hunt

BOOK EXTRAS

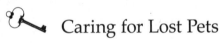 Caring for Lost Pets

 Match the Clues

Trivialicious Trivia

Book Club Buzz

Charlotte's Word Nerd Dictionary

Caring for Lost Pets

Charlotte and Katani's team found an abandoned litter of kittens! Baby kittens weren't on the scavenger-hunt list, but the team decided to do the right thing and call the Animal Rescue League. A league worker came to pick up the kittens, and the Salty Cods got their tale written up in the paper! Keep in mind that every state and animal shelter has different policies concerning lost or abandoned pets. Some places will send a team to pick up the pet, like in *The Great Scavenger Hunt*, but others will ask you to bring the animal to a shelter yourself. Here are some important tips if you ever happen upon a stray pet!

1. Be Very Careful!

Not all dogs and cats are nice, and the pet is probably unhappy, hungry, and scared. It may try to bite or scratch. Also, you don't know if the pet has all its shots, so it could have fleas, infections, or even rabies!

2. Tell an Adult

Get a parent, teacher, or other trusted adult to help you approach the animal and take the next steps toward finding its home.

3. Look for Identification

The pet may have a collar, tags, or even microchips with its owners' information! Microchips are implanted in the animal, and contain a special ID number. Animal shelters, vets, and animal control officers all can scan to check for microchips. Also, write down the date, time, and location where you found the pet, along with important characteristics like its breed, color, size, and approximate age.

4. Make the Call

If the pet has tags, call its owners. If there is a rabies tag with a vet's number, call the vet. Otherwise, look up your local Animal Rescue League online for more info on their policies. They may come pick up the pet for you, or they might ask you to bring it in to the shelter. Make sure you find out how the shelter takes care of strays, and if you'll be able to visit or get updates on the pet you found.

5. Raining Cats and Dogs

Sometimes shelters are overwhelmed with animals and can't promise to find a good home, or you might have to pay a fee to drop off the stray. If you and your parents choose to take the lost pet home, be sure you protect any other pets in your house from the newcomer—especially if you don't know the stray's medical history. It's best to take a stray to the vet before you take it home!

6. Find a Home

You can post Found Pet announcements on sites like Homeagain.com, Pets911.com, or Petfinder.com, but be careful not to post every detail about the pet, so you can check to make sure anyone who responds is the real owner. You can also take the old-fashioned route, posting flyers and notices around town, or taking out an ad in the newspaper. Hopefully, the pet will be happily reunited with its loving family!

MATCH THE CLUES!

1. One is big, the other small, and neither a precipice at all. Near these places, in the dirt, get ready for a yurt alert.

a. Marconi Station

2. From the Orleans circle round, toward a coastal town you're bound. There is much for you in store at the harbor's rocky shore.

b. Eastham Windmill, near Salt Pond

3. Beside a pool all full of brine stands a structure stuck in time. Search among the ponds with care and you will find this wheel of air.

c. Nauset Lighthouse

4. Directly north of where you slept is where this landmark thing is kept. Alone it stands all red and

d. Camping yurts near Big Cliff Pond and Little Cliff Pond

white, known for miles by
its strong light.

5. Where the birds fly free and
high, the water meets the
open sky. Nature here is
on display to show the
world Cape Cod's array.

e. Wellfleet Wildlife
Sanctuary

6. In fourteen hundred and
ninety-two, Columbus
sailed the ocean blue. But
from this spot in nineteen-
oh-three, Marconi signaled
across the sea.

f. Rock Harbor

The Great Scavenger hunt trivialicious trivia

1. What is a yurt?
   A. Henry's last name, nothing more
   B. A fence around sand dunes
   C. A sea bird that lives on Cape Cod
   D. A round tent home used by Mongolian nomads

2. Who led the team Cranberry Boggers?
   A. Patrice Summers
   B. Ben Briggs
   C. Fabiana Montoya
   D. Scott Madden

3. Who rode in the Cowmobile?
   A. The Beach Barnacles
   B. The Salty Cods
   C. The Cranberry Boggers
   D. The Queens of Mean

4. Which of these fictional stars is NOT in the pirate movie?
   A. Ontario Plume
   B. Simon Blackwell
   C. The Royal Brothers
   D. Lola Lindstrom

5. What part does Maeve play in the movie on day one?
   A. Cabin Boy
   B. Girl in Crowd 2
   C. Dancer
   D. Bridesmaid

6. Which of the following is a historical flaw that Betsy and Danny noticed on the movie set?
   A. Tepees instead of wetus
   B. Pirates wearing sunglasses
   C. A motor on the pirate ship
   D. Costumes with zippers

7. What are the names of Avery's new surfing buddies?
    A. Luke and April
    B. Chip and May
    C. Splash and August
    D. Chewie and September

8. What do the Salty Cods find in a box by the side of the trail?
    A. A rabbit
    B. A sandpiper
    C. Baby fox kits
    D. Baby kittens

9. How do the Beach Barnacles get to the Wellfleet Animal Sanctuary?
    A. They ride their bikes
    B. Kiki takes them in her boat
    C. They call a taxi
    D. They walk there

10. Which team won the scavenger hunt?
    A. The Salty Cods
    B. The Beach Barnacles
    C. The Cranberry Boggers
    D. Everyone tied

Book Club Buzz

10 QUESTIONS FOR YOU AND YOUR FRIENDS TO CHAT ABOUT

1. Charlotte, Chelsea, and Nick lead the Outdoor Adventure Club and organize the scavenger hunt for their class. What club do you
   wish you could start at your school? What is
   one activity you would plan?

2. Maeve and the Cranberry Boggers get lost
   in the woods! Have you ever been lost before? How did it feel? What should you do if
   you're lost? Did Maeve and her team do the
   right thing?

3. Katani gets upset with Patrice for boss-
   ing the team around and pushing everyone
   too hard, while Patrice thinks Katani isn't
   trying to win. How do the sisters make up?
   What do you when you're upset with a sister,
   brother, or other relative?

4. On the first day of the hunt, the Beach
   Barnacles spend the day on the beach. Only
   Chelsea worries about finding clues. Have
   you ever been the only one in a group who
   wanted to do the right thing? Did you manage
   to change people's minds, or not?

5. Being in the pirate movie with Ontario Plume
   and Simon Blackwell is Maeve's dream come
   true! If you could be in a movie with any
   famous person, who would it be? What would
   the movie be about?

6. Do you know anyone who always likes to be
   right, like Betsy Fitzgerald and Danny Pellegrino? Think of three really good future
   professions for someone with a head for
   facts like these two characters.

7. Mr. Moore tells a silly ghost story, and the
   boys play a ghostly trick on the girls during the night in the NEED building. What is
   the scariest ghost story you've ever heard?
   The funniest?

8. Kiki Underwood is the Empress of Mean at
   school, but the BSG see another side of her
   at home with her parents and when she takes
   the Beach Barnacles on her boat. Why do you

think Kiki acts the way she does in school? Do you think she deserves the title Empress of Mean?

9. Which team leader do you think did the best job? Patrice, Ben, or Fabiana? What was difficult for each of them? Who do you think would win each of these titles: Most Competitive, Most Fun, and Most Understanding?

10. Have you ever participated in a scavenger hunt? Did you win? Do you think winning is the best part of such activities, or is the adventure worth it either way?

Charlotte Ramsey

Charlotte's
Word Nerd Dictionary

BSG Word

fabbity fab fabulous (p. 16)—*extra fabulous*
rollicking (p. 18)—*exciting*
mooo-arvelous (p. 38)—*marvelous, in a cow voice*
wordage (p. 73)—*a way of saying "I agree"*
crankmonster (p. 141)—*someone acting grouchy*
crack-a-lackin' (p. 239)—*hurrying*
fabulicious (p. 262)—*fabulous and delicious*

Other Cool Words . . .

compelling (p. 3) adjective—*convincing*
exemplary (p. 4) adjective—*excellent*
acquiesced (p. 16) verb—*finally agreed*

feigned (p. 22) verb—*pretended or faked*

chivalrous (p. 36) adjective—*being polite, like a knight would*

precipice (p. 40) noun—*a cliff*

yurt (p. 40) noun—*a round, movable tentlike house used by Central Asian people*

sarcophagus (p. 41) noun—*a mummy's coffin*

nonchalant (p. 45) adjective—*acting like something is no big deal*

nomadic (p. 55) adjective—*having a lifestyle of moving from place to place*

anachronisms (p. 92) noun—*something out of place in time*

effervescent (p. 112) adjective—*bubbly*

brine (p. 117) noun—*salty water*

regaled (p. 134) verb—*entertained*

predicament (p. 135) noun—*a difficult situation*

purged (p. 139) verb—*removed, cleaned*

preposterous (p. 155) adjective—*ridiculous and impossible*

magnum opus (p. 157) noun—*the greatest work of someone's life*

timorously (p. 171) adverb—*with a shy or timid manner*

vehemently (p. 171) adverb—*with great force and energy*

chagrined (p. 175) adjective—*feeling disappointed and sorry*

cartographer (p. 182) noun—*someone who studies or makes maps*

etiquette (p. 191) noun—*polite manners*

affronted (p. 194) adjective—*insulted*

entourage (p. 217) noun—*group*

indignance (p. 219) noun—*upset pride*

protégé (p. 223) noun—*a young person who is very successful in a particular area*

decried (p. 227) verb—*openly criticized*

omission (p. 256) noun—*something left out*

Maeve shook her head in disbelief. "I think this is the movie set level."

The Atrium was an enormous, sprawling space, decorated in shades of gold and green. Floral print couches surrounded small tables carved out of wood, and people were everywhere, checking in with cruise ship staff, wheeling their luggage, or relaxing on one of the sofas and listening to Hawaiian music piped in over the ship's PA system. Elevators with gold doors emblazoned with the ship's logo were tucked away in back, ready to take the passengers to the different decks on the ship.

The BSG squeezed into the elevator with their luggage. "She said we were on the Verandah," Isabel reminded Charlotte. Charlotte pressed the button for their deck and everyone watched the elevator doors slide shut.

"I hope this elevator doesn't break down with the weight of Maeve's luggage," Avery joked.

"Hey, Katani brought more bags than I did!" Maeve retorted.

"Yeah, but yours are a thousand times bigger and heavier," Isabel noted, trying to budge one to make more room for her shoulder bag.

The elevator chimed and the gold doors slid open. "Verandah Deck, Beacon Street Girls Level!" Mr. Ramsey announced.

Past the elevator doors was a long hallway carpeted in the same green and gold pattern of the Atrium.

Charlotte opened her map. "Carla said to take a right—"

Avery let out a whoop and dropped her backpack, running off down the hallway. She stopped about twenty yards ahead. "I found it!"

Charlotte smiled at Maeve, Katani, and Isabel. "Or we can use the Avery method."

The girls dropped their bags and ran off down the hallway, leaving Mr. Ramsey behind. Avery waved at them from the doorway. "You guys aren't going to believe this!"

Their room was perfect! Life jackets, towels, and extra linens were tucked neatly in their places. Two sets of bunk beds lined either wall, each made up with green blankets with gold stitching. There were two closets, two cube dressers, and a desk made out of dark wood. A small fold-out couch covered in floral fabric rested against the far end of the room, right under a large porthole that looked out onto the water.

Mr. Ramsey poked his head through the open door. "I think you girls forgot something." He nodded in the direction of their luggage.

"Sorry, Dad!" Charlotte apologized, and the girls helped Mr. Ramsey bring their bags into their room.

"You girls settle in and unpack. I'm just through that door."

He pointed to a door that was next to the closet near the entryway. He opened it to reveal a similarly appointed stateroom, although instead of bunk beds it had a queen-size bed with a green and gold comforter and a gold foil chocolate on the pillow.

"I call top bunk!" Avery shouted, tossing her backpack up onto one of the beds.

"I'll take the one under you, Avery," Maeve decided. "I'm afraid I'll wake up in the middle of the night, forget where I am, and fall off!"

"Does anyone mind if I take the couch?" Charlotte asked. "It reminds me of my writing nook in the tower."

"Then Isabel and I will take the other bunk bed," Katani said. "Top or bottom?"

"Top?" Isabel asked. She thought it would give her a better view out the porthole. She could already see gulls diving outside the window.

"Fine. I'll take the bottom." Katani began to unpack methodically, removing her clothes from her customized bags, shaking out the wrinkles, and either folding them neatly and placing them in the oak dresser or hanging them on hangers. There was no point in packing nice things for a trip if you ended up looking like a human wrinkle when you got there!

The rest of the girls looked on, impressed. "I gotta look sharp. It's part of the job of a fashion designer," she reminded them.

"Katani, unpack for me too?" Maeve begged. "I thought as a VIP I would have someone take care of that stuff for me." She batted her eyelashes at Katani, who laughed and swatted her with a red and gold scarf.

"I'm not going near those suitcases! They'll probably explode when you unzip them!" Katani and Maeve had gone to a fashion show in New York City together, so Katani knew all about Maeve's packing problems.

Maeve sighed, dumped a wadded-up ball of clothes out of her first suitcase, and set it on her bed. She tried to mimic Katani's folding technique and regarded her work.

"It still looks like a wadded-up ball," she complained.

"*This* is how you pack, girls!" Charlotte, the global traveler, opened her one suitcase and took out a few books to reveal lined-up rolls of clothing. All her toiletries were in a special pouch, and other compartments held things like a compass, binoculars, and a camera. "Each roll is one day's outfit," Charlotte explained. "So I don't even need to unpack! This suitcase is all the dresser I need."

"Charlotte, you're totally amazing!" Isabel said, awed by her worldly friend's packing talent.

"You guys are all crazy! *This* is how to unpack!" Avery called out from her top bunk. She unzipped her backpack and dumped her belongings on the floor. "An unpacking world record! The crowd goes wild!"

Isabel giggled. "Impressive. But I think I'm going to try the Katani method since it's too late to pack like Charlotte."

The doorknob on their cabin started to jiggle.

"Is it your dad?" Isabel asked.

"Wouldn't he come through *that* door?" Charlotte replied, pointing to the one next to the closet.

The doorknob stopped jiggling, and everyone breathed a sigh of relief. Until the door began to shake like someone was pulling on it!

Collect all the BSG books today!

#1 Worst Enemies/Best Friends ☐ **READ IT!**
Yikes! As if being the new girl isn't bad enough . . . Charlotte just made the biggest cafeteria blunder in the history of Abigail Adams Junior High.

#2 Bad News/Good News ☐ **READ IT!**
Charlotte can't believe it. Her father wants to move away again, and the timing couldn't be worse for the Beacon Street Girls.

#3 Letters from the Heart ☐ **READ IT!**
Life seems perfect for Maeve and Avery . . . until they find out that in seventh grade, the world can turn upside down just like that.

#4 Out of Bounds ☐ **READ IT!**
Can the Beacon Street Girls bring the house down at Abigail Adams Junior High's Talent Show? Or will the Queens of Mean steal the show?

#5 Promises, Promises ☐ **READ IT!**
Tensions rise when two BSG find themselves in a tight race for seventh-grade president at Abigail Adams Junior High.

#6 Lake Rescue ☐ **READ IT!**
The seventh grade outdoor trip promises lots o' fun for the BSG—but will the adventure prove too much for one sensitive classmate?

#7 Freaked Out ☐ **READ IT!**
The party of the year is just around the corner. What happens when the party invitations are given out . . . but not to everyone?

#8 Lucky Charm ☐ **READ IT!**
Marty is missing! The BSG's frantic search for their beloved pup leads them to a very famous person and the game of a lifetime.

#9 Fashion Frenzy ☐ **READ IT!**
Katani and Maeve are off to the Big Apple for a supercool teen fashion show. Will tempers fray in close quarters?

#10 Just Kidding ☐ **READ IT!**
The BSG are looking forward to Spirit Week at Abigail Adams Junior High, until some mean—and untrue—gossip about Isabel dampens everyone's spirits.

#11 Ghost Town
The BSG's fun-filled week at a Montana dude ranch includes skiing, snow boarding, cowboys, and celebrity twins—plus a ghost town full of secrets.

☐ **READ IT!**

#12 Time's Up
Katani knows she can win the business contest. But with school and friends and family taking up all her time, has she gotten in over her head?

☐ **READ IT!**

#13 Green Algae and Bubble Gum Wars
Inspired by the Sally Ride Science Fair, the BSG go green, but getting stuck slimed by some gooey supergum proves to be a major annoyance!

☐ **READ IT!**

#14 Crush Alert
Romantic triangles and confusion abound as the BSG look forward to the Abigail Adams Junior High Valentine's Day dance.

☐ **READ IT!**

Also ... Our Special Adventure Series:

Charlotte in Paris
Something mysterious happens when Charlotte returns to Paris to search for her long-lost cat and to visit her best Parisian friend, Sophie.

☐ **READ IT!**

Maeve on the Red Carpet
A cool film camp at the Movie House is a chance for Maeve to become a star, but newfound fame has a downside for the perky redhead.

☐ **READ IT!**

Freestyle with Avery
Avery Madden can't wait to go to Telluride, Colorado, to visit her dad! But there's one surprise that Avery's definitely not expecting.

☐ **READ IT!**

Katani's Jamaican Holiday
A lost necklace and a plot to sabotage her family's business threaten to turn Katani's dream beach vacation in Jamaica into stormy weather.

☐ **READ IT!**

Isabel's Texas Two-Step
A disastrous accident with a valuable work of art and a sister with a diva attitude give Isabel a bad case of the ups and downs on a special family trip.

☐ **READ IT!**

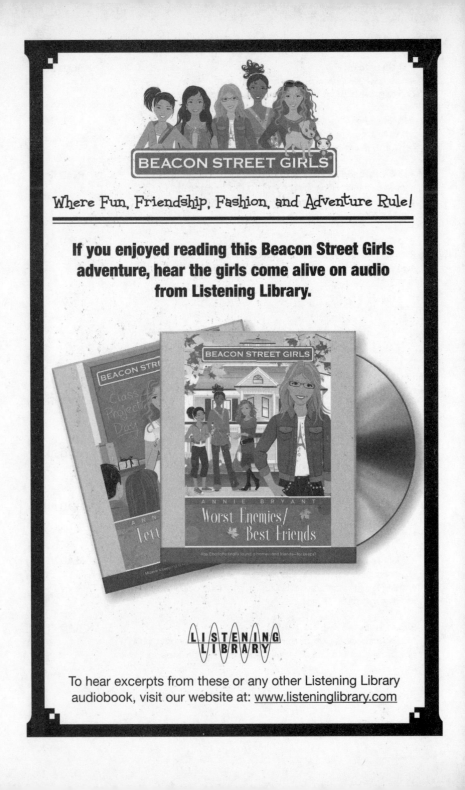